More cheers for Jess L[...]
Murder-By-Month Myst[...]

D1203922

MAY DAY

"All the ingredients for a successful small town cozy series are here . . ."
—*Publishers Weekly*

"Lourey's debut has a likeable heroine and a surfeit of sass . . ."
—*Kirkus Reviews*

"*May Day* is fresh, the characters quirky. Minnesota has many fine crime writers, and Jess Lourey has just entered their ranks!"
—Ellen Hart, author of the Sophie Greenway and Jane Lawless Mystery series

JUNE BUG

"The funny, earthy heroine of *June Bug* is sure to stumble her way into the hearts of readers everywhere. Don't miss this one—it's a hoot!"
—William Kent Krueger, Anthony Award-winning author of the Cork O'Connor series

"Jess Lourey offers up a funny, well-written, engaging story . . . readers will thoroughly enjoy the well-paced ride."
—Carl Brookins, author of *The Case of the Greedy Lawyers*

"Jess Lourey is a talented, witty, and clever writer."
—Monica Ferris, author of the bestselling Needlecraft Mysteries

KNEE HIGH BY THE FOURTH OF JULY

Shortlisted for a 2008 Lefty Award from Left Coast Crime

Chosen as a September 2007 Killer Book by the Independent Mystery Book-sellers Association (KillerBooks.org)

"Mira . . . is an amusing heroine in a town full of quirky characters."
—*Kirkus Reviews*

"Lourey's rollicking good cozy planted me in the heat of a Minnesota summer for a laugh-out-loud mystery ride."
—Leann Sweeney, author of the
Yellow Rose Mystery series

AUGUST MOON

"Hilarious, fast paced, and madcap."
—*Booklist* (starred review)

"Another amusing tale set in the town full of over-the-top zanies who've en-deared themselves to the engaging Mira."
—*Kirkus Reviews*

"[A] hilarious, wonderfully funny cozy."
—*Crimespree Magazine*

SEPTEMBER FAIR

"Once again, the very funny Lourey serves up a delicious dish of murder, may-hem, and merriment."
—*Booklist* (starred review)

"Lively."
—*Publishers Weekly*

"[A]n entirely engaging novel with pathos, plot twists and quirky characters galore . . . Beautifully written and wickedly funny."
—Harley Jane Kozak, Agatha, Anthony, and
Macavity-award winning author of *A Date You Can't Refuse*

MAY
DAY

ALSO BY JESS LOUREY

June Bug
Knee High by the 4th of July
August Moon
September Fair
October Fest
November Hunt

MAY DAY

A Murder-By-Month Mystery

jess lourey

MIDNIGHT INK
WOODBURY, MINNESOTA

First Edition
Third Printing, 2011

Book design by Donna Burch
Cover design by Ellen Dahl Lawson
Cover illustration © 2010 Carl Mazer

Midnight Ink, an imprint of Llewellyn Publications

Library of Congress Cataloging-in-Publication Data
Lourey, Jess, 1970-
    May Day : murder by month mystery / Jess Lourey.-- 1st ed.
       p. cm.
    ISBN-13: 978-0-7387-0838-6
    ISBN-10: 0-7387-0838-0
    I. Title.

PS3612.O833M39 2006
813'.6--dc22   2005056179

Midnight Ink
Llewellyn Publications
2143 Wooddale Drive
Woodbury, MN 55125-2989
www.midnightinkbooks.com

Printed in the United States of America

For Diane and Ray, two good friends of mine

ONE

TUESDAY MARKED MY TENTH official day alone at the library, but the heady draw of being my own boss had worn off. I didn't even like the smell of the lilac bushes outside the open windows anymore. The old black circle-dial phone was taunting me. I wrestled the urge to call the number to the Battle Lake Motel, where Jeff was staying. He knew we were supposed to meet last night, and he hadn't come. I needed to find a good space with my emotions where I could be cool, not shrill, inviting but not needy, before I called him.

I tried not to dwell on the fact that the only decent man in town had stood me up. Actually, he may have been the only literate, single man in a seventy-mile radius who was attracted to me *and* attractive. The warm buzz that was still between my legs tried to convince the dull murmur in my head that it was just a misunderstanding. To distract myself from thoughts of Jeff's laugh, mouth, and hands, I downed a couple aspirin for my potato chip hangover and began the one job I truly enjoyed at the library: putting away the books.

I glanced at the spines of the hardcovers in my hands and strolled over to the Pl–Sca aisle, thinking the only thing I really didn't like so far about the job was picking magazine inserts off the floor. Certainly the reader saw them fall, but without fail, gravity was too intense to allow retrieval except by a trained library staff member. I bet I found three a day. But as I teetered down the carpeted aisle in my friend Sunny's flowered prom heels, I discovered a new thing not to like: there was a guy lying on the tight-weave Berber with his legs lockstep straight, his arms crossed over his chest, and a reference book opened on his face. He was wearing a familiar blue-checked shirt, and if he was who I thought he was, I knew him intimately. A sour citrus taste rose at the back of my throat. Alone, the library aisle wasn't strange; alone, the man wasn't strange. Together, they made my heart slam through my knees. I prodded his crossed legs with my ridiculously shod foot and felt no warmth and no give.

My eyes scoured the library in a calm panic, and I was aware of my neck creaking on its hinges. I could smell only books and stillness, tinged with a faint coppery odor. Everything was in order except the probably dead man laid out neatly on the carpeting, wearing the same flannel I had seen him in two days earlier. I wondered chaotically if dead people could lie, if they still got to use verbs after they were gone, and if maybe this was the best excuse ever for missing a date. Then I had a full-body ice wash, five years old all over again, a nightmare pinning me to my bed as I silently mouthed the word "Mom."

Had proximity to me killed him? My mind flashed grainy, film-reel clips of my father pushing me on the swings before his brutal death. I veered to thoughts of another dead body, one I'd stumbled across twenty years ago. It was a newborn kitten squashed on a gravel road, so little that its eyes never had a chance to open. I wanted to bury the kitten in a shoebox, but my seven-year-old brain was too easily distracted to dig a hole that big. I settled for wrapping it in a pink sock, hiding it

2

in the woods, and saying a solemn, loving goodbye. I was never again able to find the spot where I had deposited it. Now it was kitty bones in the dirt, and Jeff was going to be man bones in the dirt, and some waxy part of me realized that I was losing my grip.

I shook my head once, like a dog, and pinched my ear, yanking myself back from crazy. The horror let up a little, and I found myself bizarrely wondering what Jeff's face looked like now. His body was neatly laid to rest in a grotesque homage to those of us who fall asleep while reading, and the open encyclopedia shielded his face. I noticed it was the twelfth volume, containing all of the noteworthy *L* words, and then I was surprised to observe my hand pulling the reference book off him.

His face didn't have that slack-mouthed look of the processed dead. Rather, he appeared to be in an irritated sleep, his lips unyielding, his beautiful straight nose still, and his eyes tightly shut. Except for the clean circle of a hole in the center of his forehead, I would have thought he was napping. I knelt down, careful not to touch his body, and leaned in. The symmetry of the hole surprised me, as did the complete lack of blood around him. It was like someone took a hole punch to a mannequin's head, except for the angry, reddish black contents I could see inside. I was perched inches from his body and could smell his cedarwood bath soap mixed with something sweet-rotten. Solid coldness radiated from him.

I wanted to touch him. I needed to gather him in my arms and shake him awake and kiss the soft spot under his earlobe until he tingled. Then a buzzing fly landed on his body and danced over the cold earth of his face toward the hole in his forehead. My stomach churned, and I turned away. It was from that precise angle that I spotted the small, darker shape in the shadow of the newest Anne Rice book butting out from the bottom shelf a few feet away. At first I thought it was a magazine insert because of its size and shape, but then I realized it was too thick. I gently rested the encyclopedia back on Jeff's head, careful to keep it on the same page. I pushed myself off the floor and reached toward the shape in the shadow. It was a fancy envelope, thick with something, on which was printed "For Your Eyes Only" in ornate type. I grabbed it just as the front door of the library opened with a somber dong, making me realize my heart was still in my chest, because it stopped beating. I was pretty sure my urethra relaxed a little, too, but I was out the door in such a flash of speed and light that the underwear I hadn't worn would have dried too quickly to notice. The prom shoes made me realize exactly what was meant by the phrase "running like a girl." It wasn't pretty.

I zipped past my first live patron of the day, Mrs. Berns. She was one of those elderly ladies who shaves her eyebrows and then pencils them in, giving her a permanently shocked look completely appropriate for this occasion. Once in the parking lot, I shook myself from head to toe. Mrs. Berns followed behind.

"What's wrong, Mira? See a spider, dear?" she asked.

"Bigger, Mrs. Berns. Can you get the police? I think we need some help here." The calmness of my voice amazed me. Living life at a distance has some benefits in crisis times. I smiled ruefully at her as I stuffed the envelope into the back of my jeans and covered it with my shirt.

Mrs. Berns squinted her eyes suspiciously and looked reluctant to leave. Needing the police for something other than underage drinking or toilet-papering a house was big news in a small town, and it was currency at the Battle Lake Senior Sunset, where Mrs. Berns lived. Something cop-related could get her a week's worth of lemon bars.

"I'll wait right here and not let anyone in until you get back, Mrs. Berns. If you hurry, you can beat the police." This was a small lie, maybe. The police station was one block over, and Mrs. Berns was closer in build to a stewing chicken than a spring chicken, but I wanted to at least give her a chance. I suppose I could have gone myself, but I was feeling a little proprietary about the body now that I was distanced from the horror of it. After all, I had found him, in more ways than one. Once Mrs. Berns was gone, I went over to the bushes and heaved until my stomach was as empty as my heart.

TWO

It all started with a cockroach.

Don't get me wrong. I'd had bad days before in Minneapolis, but this one was the mutha of all bad days. I had moved to the Twin Cities straight from high school, on the run from Paynesville, the small Minnesota town where I'd first played hide-and-seek in a cornfield that stretched for miles, and where I later learned the guilty pleasure of drinking stolen sweet wine in an abandoned farmhouse and the delight of wearing Guess jeans with a rainbow shirt while I curled my bangs into the perfect tube. Then I grew up but quick and headed east to Minneapolis the minute it was legal, high school diploma in hand. I was tired of the small-town gossip and people referring to me as "Manslaughter Mark's daughter."

In Minneapolis, I quickly learned two things: anonymity is lonely, and being able to make the perfect curlicue on a Dairy Queen cone didn't cut one many breaks in the big city. I was more than a little fish in a big pond—I was Bananarama in the land of Hüsker Dü. I grew out my perm and let my dark hair flow long and natural, I stopped wearing mascara and eye shadow to bring out my deep-set gray eyes, and I started smoking clove cigarettes before switching to the real ones. I even relaxed enough to cease being a walking foot watcher when I realized nobody within a hundred miles had heard of my dad or cared that I had gone to the prom with Linda Dooley, the girl who always smelled like farm, because no guy would touch me with a ten-foot fishing pole. I blended in and earned my BA in English in under six years.

Somehow, though, I morphed into one of those slack-eyed West Bankers who waited tables during the day so they could afford to drink at the music clubs at night. I squeezed in a few graduate classes so there seemed to be a point to it all, but I started to feel like I was back in Paynesville, only with more places to drink. My dad had been a heavy boozer for as long as I could remember, and I knew I would have to make some changes soon, before my denial card expired.

Enter the cockroach, who set in motion a sequence of key events that slapped me on the ass and sent me to Battle Lake, the land of no return. I had been discussing my day-to-day existence with Alison, my supervisor and friend at Perfume River, the Vietnamese restaurant where I'd waited tables for six years.

"It just seems like I'm not where I'm supposed to be, you know?" We were wrapping silverware in paper napkins for easy grabbing during the lunch rush. It was a sunny March day, and the fresh-mopped floor was soon to be a salty, slushy gray.

"What about Brad? I thought you two were doing great."

"I don't know. He always seems distracted when he comes over, which now he only does after bar close." Brad and I had been dating for five months. He was cute, in a blonde-Jim-Morrison sort of way, and he was in a band. That had been enough.

"Maybe you should get a tattoo." Alison put the last silverware package on top of the pyramid as the first customers walked in. "I got 'em," she said, heading toward the man and woman at the door.

She seated them in my section, and I grabbed a couple glasses of ice water and strolled out.

"How are you two doing?" I could tell from her immaculate makeup and his manicured fingernails that they weren't the regular college crowd we drew.

By way of an answer, he sneered at me. "What are your specials?"

"All our meals are $4.95 or less. We think everything is special." I capped this off with my best perky smile.

The woman gave a slight eye roll and turned her page. "How many shrimp come with the shrimp and bamboo shoots?"

"Six."

"Well, isn't that special." She flipped the page again. "I'll take your vegetarian spring rolls, no carrots in them, around them, or in the area they are prepared in. Do you understand?"

I could feel the skin at the base of my neck crawl. "Sure."

"Then why aren't you writing it down?"

I wrote down "VN1," the code for spring rolls, and made a mental note to rub a whole carrot up and down both rolls like it was their wedding night. "Got it."

"Can I see it? What you wrote. I need to make sure you got it right."

I glared over at Alison, who was wiping out ashtrays. She raised her eyebrows and gave me a better-you-than-me look.

"Sure." I handed the woman my pad. As I did so, a black cockroach peeked at me from behind the Kikkoman soy sauce bottle. Its shivering antennae felt the air, possibly sensing the tension and wondering if it should come back at a better time. I had seen cockroaches at the dingy Mexican restaurant I worked at when I first moved to the Cities, but never at Perfume River. Ba, the owner, was meticulous about order and sanitation in his kitchen. I shook my head at the little guy.

The woman grabbed the pen out of my hand, scribbled "no carrots" next to the "VN1," underlined the words three times, and handed the pad back to me, a smug look on her face. "You must not work for tips."

I think I may have actually been leaning forward to spit in her hair when the cockroach darted to the middle of the table and stood stock-still, basking in its public premiere. The no-carrots woman screamed and jumped up, knocking the table over. The soy sauce crashed to the ground just as a table of ten walked in.

"You horrible, dirty people! Dirty people! I'll call the health department. I'll have you shut down!" The woman's shrieking reached a glass-shattering pitch.

The man with her handed me a card out of his wallet and said, "Expect to hear from me," and like that they were out the door.

I looked down at the card. "David Jones, Jones and Jones Law Offices. Somebody's Gonna Pay."

It was at that point that Ba rushed out of the kitchen. When I explained what had happened, he was so upset that he made me go home. Forever. It didn't do any good to tell him that it wasn't my fault. I was now and everlastingly associated with cockroaches in his mind.

I walked home with my hands thrust in my pockets, my face down against the biting wind. I was so intent on not thinking that I almost ran down a man in a street-length sheepskin coat.

"Sorry. I didn't see you."

His close-set eyes lit up when I addressed him. "Wanna buy a guitar pedal? I have reverb. Fifty bucks."

"What?"

He opened his coat and showed me a bag of colorful electric guitar pedals. His breath smelled medicinal up close.

"I don't play guitar."

"Maybe you could learn. Or what about your boyfriend? You gotta have a boyfriend."

"No thanks."

I tried to walk around him, but he put himself back in front of me and dropped his pants, quick like a wink. "How about some of that?"

His cold weenie stared sadly at the ground, looking for all the world like an overcooked green bean on a big, white plate. Before I could think of a suitable response, someone brushed past the Bean Flasher. He packed up his treats, gave me the peace sign, and ran off in the other direction.

"Thanks for making a shitty day a little bit shittier!" I yelled at his back. I stomped the two blocks back to my Seven Corners apartment, where I had lived since moving out of the dorms. A gray cloud with a black lining lumbered over my head until I saw Brad's bicycle parked by the back door. My doubts about dating a man who biked in the winter gave way to relief that there was someone at home for me.

Brad didn't have a key and he wasn't out front, so I figured he must have gone to the store. I entertained thoughts of him right now buying flowers to surprise me with or fixings to make dinner for us both. He wasn't normally the romantic type, but after my day so far, I deserved to dream.

I went inside to wait for him, passing the two other apartments on the second floor on the way. My three neighbors and I all lived above an art supplies store, and our apartments were actually refurbished offices. They had fifteen-foot ceilings, hardwood floors, and cheap rent. One neighbor was a law student, and the other was a professional saxophone player in his sixties. His name was Ted, and we had had many great hall conversations in passing. His niece had been watching his apartment for the last month while Ted was on tour, and I was surprised to hear from the music wafting from 1B that she was home in the middle of a weekday.

As I turned the key in my door, I realized it wasn't just any music I heard coming from Ted's apartment. It was the very hard-to-find music of Portuguese flute players that I had special-ordered for Brad's birthday last month.

"Oh no you dih-unt," I whispered to myself as I tiptoed over to the door kitty-corner from mine and slapped my ear to it. I couldn't hear anything inside except the music and some rustling. I kneeled down to peek through the old-fashioned keyhole on the leftover office door that served as Ted's front entrance but could only see prisms of light glinting through the houseplants.

The quiet part of my brain that some people might call my common sense told me that Ted's niece could also like Portuguese flutists and that I should just go in my apartment and wait for Brad to show up. I rarely listened to that part of my brain.

Instead, I tiptoed back down the hall and tried the door handle to Ted's outdoor garden space. I had seen his patio area from mine and knew that it was directly in front of his apartment's skylights, a feature my apartment didn't share. His patio door was locked. I considered breaking it down, or just knocking on Ted's front door, but both ideas lacked the stealth I was after. I was feeling crazy, but not crazy enough not to know it.

I thumbed through my keys and found the tiny one that unlocked my patio door. I hadn't been out there since I had cleaned my herb and tomato pots in October. The area was small, maybe ten feet by five, and it was covered with brittle March snow accented by a chute of gutter ice. There was also a rusty ladder leading to the roof. Before the quiet part of my brain could organize its arguments, I climbed up the ladder, hauled myself onto the roof, and crawled over to Ted's side of the building.

The March wind hit me like needles up this high, but the rush I always got from acting instead of waiting kept me moving forward. When I was by Ted's skylights, I army-crawled over and peered down. Staring back at me was my second penis of the day, and here it wasn't even noon. Brad was tied up to Ted's loft, about four feet from my face, and if his eyes hadn't been closed in ecstasy, he would have seen me staring down at him.

Ted's niece, whose name I was really going to have to find out, was swaying toward him like a naked snake charmer, only she was on her knees because there wasn't enough headroom in the loft to stand. When she got to him, she put her mouth near the top of his penis, and from my angle, I swear it looked like she was blowing and tickling him at the same time. For an absurd moment, I wondered if she was one of those poor women who had taken the term "blowjob" too literally, but then I realized what she was doing. She was playing Brad's flute, accompanied by the nice Portuguese musicians I had bought for his listening pleasure. I had seen enough.

I crawled carefully back down the ladder, the March wind no match for the fumes coming from my head. I considered storming into the apartment and demanding an explanation, but Brad wasn't clever enough to juggle shame and an erection at the same time. Besides, I hated confrontations. The shitter was I had been thinking of breaking up with him, and now he would get the last word. Or the last note, in this case.

No, clearly there was only one way this could end well for me. I let myself out the back door, removed the nuts holding the front tire onto Brad's bike, and went for a walk. When I returned home that night, having decided nothing except that my life sucked and today would forever be known as Cocks 'n' Roach Day, I was grateful to get a call from my good friend Sunshine Waters. Sunny and I had met when my college roommate freshman year, Cecilia, took me to her hometown of

Battle Lake, Minnesota, over Christmas break. Battle Lake was a town of 798 people three hours west of the Twin Cities and two hours north of Paynesville. Sunny had stayed around there after high school because she had emotional ties. Her parents had died when she was young, and the land she'd inherited from them provided her comfort. It was 103 acres of rolling hills, hardwoods, and lakeshore with a doublewide trailer—gray with maroon trim—in the center and various outbuildings sprinkled around it. That's where I had first met Sunny, at a Christmas party at her place, and we had hit it off instantly. Sunny was smart, funny, and not afraid of chocolate.

"Hello?"

"Hey, Mira! It's me. Sunny. What's up? You sound funny. You OK?"

I wiped my eyes. "Sure, if you consider losing your job, getting flashed by an out-of-work guitarist with a penis like a microwaved legume, and finding your boyfriend cheating on you OK."

"You caught Brad cheating on you, huh?"

"Yeah. The good part is he doesn't know I know, so I technically get to break up with him."

"He was a weasel anyhow."

"I know."

"Hmm. You want to hear my good news?"

"Will it make me feel like even more of a loser?"

"Probably."

"I'm all ears."

"I'm in love. You remember Rodney Johnson?"

I riffled through the list of Battle Lake names I knew from visiting Sunny so often, and I finally pulled up a picture of a short, dark-haired guy who was always smiling. "The guy who took a girl to her prom when he was thirty-one?"

"That was a few years ago. He's changed. He's a real sweetheart."

I sighed and switched the phone from my right to my left ear. Sunny picked up boyfriends like old ladies picked up cats. "Well, good. If you're happy, I'm happy."

"I am happy. Gotta favor to ask, too."

"Yeah?" I was at the window, and I made a fist, pressing the side of my hand into the frost edging the glass and then dotting five little toes over the top of it. A baby snow-foot.

"I'm moving to Alaska for a few months. I decided. It's for sure. Rodney has a job lined up on a fishing boat, and we can make a thousand dollars a week."

"When?" As far as I knew, she knew no one in Alaska and hadn't lived anywhere but Battle Lake her whole twenty-eight years. She must really like this one.

"The first week of April. Here's the favor. I need someone to housesit when I leave."

She paused, and I didn't fill the empty air. Lord help me, if I had known what I was in store for, I would have screamed "No!" with my last breath.

"You can garden, you can hike, you can do all that stuff you used to like to do. C'mon, Mira. If it doesn't work out, you can always leave. You've got nothing to lose." Her voice was rushed but cocky. "You got to get back to the dirt, Mira."

"I don't know. Battle Lake is so small. What would I do there?"

"The library is hiring, and you can always waitress." Sunny's voice changed to a more serious tone. "I need you, Mira. I can't bring Luna with, and nobody else will watch her." Luna was the goofy-smart mixed breed Sunny had found at the side of the road a few years ago. "And I need someone to make sure the pipes don't freeze. I think Rodney is the one, Mira. I don't want to blow it."

Sunny always thought whichever guy she was with was the one, but she very rarely asked for help. I looked around. Ricki Lake was making over spandex-clad large chicks on my TV, my stove was hissing out dry heat in my kitchen, I no longer had a job or a boyfriend, and I was sitting in my all-purpose room waiting for my life to start. Still, I hesitated. What sort of person just gets up and moves, and to Battle Lake of all places? I cradled the phone in the crook of my shoulder and put my hand to the graffittied window just as a pigeon crashed into it. I jumped back. The bird fluttered to the roof across the street, dazed and confused.

I sighed. "If you need me, Sunny, I'll be there."

It only took a couple weeks to sever, or at least put on hold, my Minneapolis ties. Alison, Shannon, and Maruta from Perfume River had a going-away party for me, and I left with an armload of cockroach memorabilia and even a pair of penis earrings. There were a couple women in my grad classes who made me laugh, and I left messages on their answering machines saying I was withdrawing this semester. I did the same with Professor Bundy, the journalism teacher whose class I was haphazardly attending. He told me I had a real talent for writing and should be sure to come back. I considered calling the financial aid office at the U, but they were pathologically unhelpful, and I would have to repay my loan whether or not I was in class. I had a month-to-month lease that I ended with a phone call.

My books and my clothes I tossed into tall kitchen garbage bags with yellow cinch ties at the top and stuffed in my brown two-door 1985 Toyota Corolla's trunk. I put the same type of bags, only more gently, around my plants to protect them from the cold and transported them to the back seat and floor. My cat, Tiger Pop, named after my second-favorite candy and his mottled, white-splashed fur, was brought down last and unwillingly. I set his litter box and water dish on the floor of the passenger seat, knowing full well he would be attached to my shoulder and howling the whole two-and-a-half-hour trip.

I looked around my first apartment for the last time. The living room that was also my dining room and bedroom looked beige and lonely. Even the blue, green, and yellow watercolor willow trees I had painted my first summer in the apartment didn't add life. I realized they would be painted over within the month. My secondhand orange-flowered couch and mismatched chairs would be brought to the dump, my three pots, five bowls, and twelve plastic cups would be recycled or trashed, and all traces of my existence would vanish. Ten years in Minneapolis, and I had nothing but an English degree and a budding drinking problem to show for it. Now I knew how people ended up in small towns. Battle Lake, here I come.

THREE

Sunny's doublewide was small, a cozy nine hundred square feet. The front space was a permanently wallpapered living room with woodsy furniture, and behind it was the kitchen, with a white and brown speckled vinyl floor, particleboard cupboards, and green-topped counters. To the left was the master bedroom, with its own bath, and to the right was a spare bedroom, an office, and another bathroom. By the time I arrived, Sunny had moved all her personal stuff into the office, and she was waiting outside with Rodney, both of them playing with her beloved dog, Luna. After a too-quick exchange of information and hugs, they were out and I was in.

The first order of business was finding a job, and I took Sunny up on her suggestion to try the library. It was rare for a town this size to have its own stationary book collection, but a wealthy benefactor had provided the money to get it running, and city funds kept it going. I slipped into an assistant librarian position pretty easily after I lied about my knowledge of the Dewey decimal system. I was working on my master's in English, sort of, so they didn't ask many questions. At just over minimum wage, they were happy to have a warm body. They probably wouldn't have been so quick to hire me if they had known about the murder following just one step behind me, ready to pounce once everyone settled in.

I learned my job and settled into the town—hooked up with my one local friend, Gina, filled the fridge with fresh foods from Larry's, and read a lot of books I'd been meaning to get to. Meanwhile, the snow melted, the gray receded, the air started to smell fresh like cucumbers, and the buds on the trees and seeds in the dirt trembled and hummed until they exploded in splashes of color so bright green they were almost yellow. Spring in Minnesota happens scary fast. When Sunny called to check up on Luna and me, I told her confidently that things were going to happen for me in Battle Lake. I could feel the buzz in the air like the hum of bees.

Once the head librarian, Lartel McManus, saw I had a knack for the library job, he flew to Mexico on a three-week vacation he said he had planned for months. Friday, May 1, was to be my first official day alone at the Battle Lake Public Library. May Day had always been one of my favorite holidays. When I was ten, my dad sneaked into my room and left a foam cup decorated with pastel ribbons and filled with waxy Tootsie Rolls and cherry-flavored Dubble Bubble gum. I pretended I was asleep until I heard his footsteps on the creaky stairs. The note read "Happy May Day! You know I love you."

I wondered about the power of small gestures as I woke up without an alarm clock on May Day, and I actually whistled as I slipped out of bed. The night before, I had ceremoniously dumped out all the bottles of liquor in Sunny's house, and I arose reborn. I decided to go to town early to open a savings account with my sixty dollars cash. Call me an optimist. The seven-minute ride to town was beautiful, with young morning fog webbing the low spots by the sloughs. The air had that waiting-for-the-school-bus smell, and through some cosmic wrinkle, I could actually tune in the good radio station out of Fargo. Sheryl Crow commiserated melodically with me as I pulled toward town.

There were short stretches of road where I couldn't see any houses, just oak and sumac pressing against the air. It brought to mind the research I had just finished for the second part-time job I had landed as an on-call reporter for the *Battle Lake Recall*, the local newspaper. The library job alone didn't pay enough to cover my student loan payments and buy gas and groceries, and besides, I needed to keep my English muscle in shape for when I went back to grad school.

For my first article, I wrote a retrospective piece for the Battle Lake Lady of the Lakes celebration, the first festival of the year. It marked the end of winter and the beginning of the farming season and involved an all-town garage sale, a parade, and a dance at Stub's. The celebration wasn't until Memorial Day, but the chamber of commerce wanted to get the word out so they could sign up people for the parade. On the surface, Battle Lake was your average Minnesota town with a population under a thousand—most of the residents were farmers or blue-collar workers, most radios were tuned to the country music station, everybody ate their lunch at the Turtle Stew Café, and the whole area bloated with tourists in search of the perfect fish every summer. My piece delved below the surface, however. It was a full-page article, complete with photos, on the official founding of Battle Lake on Halloween Eve 1881.

As I drove into town, I cracked my window and sucked in some fresh air, thinking how similar it may have smelled a hundred years ago. I stopped near the curb in front of First National Bank, which was tucked on a corner of Main Street. The Battle Lake Public Library, Lakes Area Dental, and a temporarily abandoned building that used to be Kathy's Klassy Klothes occupied the other three corners. Laid out alongside each of these cornerstones were little knickknack and antique stores, a bakery, a couple hardware stores, a drugstore, a post office, a church, and various service offices—chiropractor, accountant, Realtor. Standard small-town fare. I saw that the bank was still closed, so I pulled into the library parking lot.

The yellow brick structure was a relatively new addition to the town, built twenty years ago, when William T. Everts had bequeathed his entire estate to create it. The library's inside smelled like slick magazine paper and recycled air, as it had every morning since I had started working there over a month ago. I walked past the rack of new arrivals, sniffing at *Deer Hunter's Digest*, *Good Housekeeping*, and *Bow and Arrow World*. The irony, I thought, of magazines created for hunters. It was like having a stadium for agoraphobics.

I peeled off my favorite suede jacket on my way to the library's front desk, the spring air of lilacs and green melting away from me. After a little fumbling in all of my pockets, I found a damp piece of cinnamon gum, hidden under a glow-in-the-dark fish from a twenty-five-cent machine, a crushed Jägermeister cap, and a tattered fortune cookie strip that said, "You enjoy the fun" above my guaranteed winning lottery numbers. I draped my coat on the back of the swivel chair behind the desk and chewed tentatively on the gravelly Trident.

I flicked my dark, disheveled hair over my shoulder, settled in the captain's chair, and clicked on the front desk computer. I was now the mistress of this domain. I considered creating a new printing sign. The "NO COLOR PRINTING!!!!! BLACK AND WHITE 10¢ A PAGE!!!!" had way too many exclamation marks and seemed rude with all the caps. I made a mental note to get to that later. Pushing back from the desk with a little whirring sound that propelled me the fifteen feet to the front entrance, I flipped the sign to Open, unlocked the single glass door with my keys-on-a-spiral unit, grabbed the four books resting askew in the overnight dropoff bin and the newspapers off the ground, and scooted back.

For a small-town library, it was pretty well stocked. The new fiction section was kitty-corner from the front desk, next to the newspaper and magazine racks. On the other side of the reading carrels were the metal turning displays stuffed with paperback romance and mystery books, so popular with the tourists and the elderly. Twelve tall wooden bookshelves were filled with the more scholarly works: the Dickens, the Hemingway, the *I'm Not Crazy, I'm Angry: How to Cope with a Bad Temper.*

The reference section was tucked into a dark spot near the storage room. The children's area, with its Lilliputian blue and yellow chairs, ratty stuffed animals, and big-lettered books, was parked in a cozy corner under the windows. This was my favorite spot, because of the sunlight and because the kids always got so excited about the books. It was comforting in my current situation—single, barely employed, and mildly superior with no one to appreciate it. You see, I now considered myself a cosmopolitan gal. It was easier to pretend that I was biding my time and finding my wings in a small town rather than to face that I had failed in the big city.

I finished the setup routine as Lartel had taught me—put away the books, make sure sufficient pencils are lined up on the counter, dust the tables—and then settled in behind the counter. The cheery chime of the door opening revved my heart up a little, I'm ashamed to say. Here I was, a city girl excited about dealing solo with my first library patron. I turned to see who the eager reader was but also reached for a magazine so we could both pretend I wasn't snooping. The library can be like a doctor's office. Patrons reveal deeply personal information about themselves by what they choose to read, and discretion is a must, especially in a small Minnesota town. The married mother of four who checks out *The Joy of Sex* paces nervously, paging through the new fiction section until the gas station owner has left, himself shoving *Prozac*

Nation between a book on fly-fishing lures and Chilton's latest. I loved looking inside people's windows, so to speak.

And speaking of love, it just so happened I was wondering if I was going to get any in this town I was tied to, at least for the summer. My only hope was the massive tourist population bringing in some dark-haired male who knew that the word "seen" couldn't be used without a helping verb, as in "I seen the biggest buck in the woods today!" Maybe I was shooting too high.

I studied today's first solo library patron out of the corner of my eye and corrected myself. Here was a stranger with brown hair that curled around his ears, late thirties, and I swear his green eyes reflected intelligence. I crossed my legs to keep a whistle from escaping between my thighs. If practice makes perfect, I'm pretty good at judging people, and I judged him to be worth further examination. Of course, desperation does lend a certain graciousness to my opinion.

"Good morning." His voice was mellow, cheerful. "I need information on the history of Battle Lake. Where do you suggest I start?"

I smiled. It was serendipity, baby. I filled him in on the pieces I knew from my recent *Recall* article, focusing on the details that I thought would impress him. I explained that the village of Battle Lake was platted Halloween 1881 for Torger O. and Bertie O. Holdt. By 1885, there were 182 residents of the village, but newspaper references allude to unusual amounts of bad luck being visited on the inhabitants—mysterious plagues, crop rot, and intense weather were only the beginning. The first white settlers found Ojibwe burial mounds scattered in the region, forty-two near the lake's inlet alone. Local legend had it that whoever took over the land that had once belonged to the Indians would be cursed.

Ninety-some years later, the settlers' descendants, filled with church-supper-type guilt, used city funds to erect a twenty-three-foot fiberglass Indian warrior, complete with faux-leather beaded pants and brown moccasins molded onto him. They called him Chief Wenonga, after the Ojibwe chief who originally named the town, and planted him in Halverson Park on the north side, where he forever looks northeasterly across the lake at his old battle site.

His statue looked exactly like one of those little plastic Indians that came with the cowboys in a bag of a hundred in the 1970s, but in full garish color. That, in fact, is when the Chief was built—1979. A fiberglass monstrosity popular with tourists and the trophy mentality of central Minnesota. I had splashed a photo of him—full headdress, six-pack abs on a half-naked body, tomahawk in one hand, other hand raised in a perpetual "How"—in my Lady of the Lakes article. The stereotyping killed me, but I had to admit as I snapped the photo that if I were a single, twenty-one-foot-tall fiberglass female, I'd be cutting my eyes at the Chief.

"Fergus Falls will have even more information," I told the patron, wrapping up my story. "It's the county seat. Or try the East Otter Tail Museum in Perham. We pretty much just carry brain candy."

He smiled at me. I could tell by the way his eyes crinkled at the corners that my first estimate of his age had been correct—about a decade older than my soon-to-be twenty-nine, give or take a year. His teeth were strong and white, and I chose to ignore the fact that he was short, only a couple inches taller than my five foot six. He was also stocky, with a broad chest and ample arms extending from his white polo shirt. He had on the Teva-type sandals that suggest activity, and his khaki shorts revealed strong and evenly haired legs. I hate patchy leg hair on guys. You wonder what's rubbing what. Around his waist he had tied a blue-checked flannel shirt.

I held out my hand. "My name is Mira James. Can I ask why you're interested in the town's history?"

He took my hand with his warm, hammy fist and shook it firmly. I'd lay money that he held it a little longer than necessary. "My name is Jeff Wilson, and I'm working for a company that wants to bring some business this way. I need to get the lay of the land, so to speak."

"So you're like a surveyor?" I asked, disappointed. I was hoping he was something cool, like an independently wealthy explorer or a psychiatrist who didn't mind house calls.

"Something like that," he said, chuckling. "I'm an archaeologist."

Ooh. I quickly added that to my list of cool things a guy could be. "Well, this town could use some more business. And I'm sure you won't have any trouble finding whatever you need about the town's history. It's pretty straightforward Minnesota stuff."

"The paper history search is the least exciting part of my job," he said, leaning on my counter. "The fun stuff is hiking around the area and surveying the land."

"I bet that's fun," I said enthusiastically. I loved being outside in the green. "There's some great hiking around here. What area are you going to check out?"

"A mile and a half southeast of town."

"Over by the old Jorgensen farm? It's beautiful over there. I just hiked in those woods," I lied. I wanted to connect with him.

"Actually, it *is* the Jorgensen farm. I understand there are no heirs, and the estate can't afford to pay the mortgage, so it's due to go up for sale."

"Mortgage? From the way people tell it, the Jorgensens have owned that land for years." I hadn't been in town long, but I had visited Sunny enough to be current on local gossip.

He shrugged. "Things happen, people need to borrow money against their property. It's pretty common in farming communities." He looked around the small library and back at me. "You're welcome to come out there with me, Mira," he said, trying out my name. "I'm doing a preliminary exam this afternoon. We could get some grub afterwards."

Some part of me knew better than to go out with a guy who used the word "grub" when asking someone on a first date, but I gave him the benefit of the doubt because he wasn't from around here. How little I knew.

FOUR

"HAVE YOU EVER EATEN an Indian onion?" Jeff pulled the lone purple flower out of the ground. A baby bulb, white and covered with dirt, dangled off the end.

"Nope," I said, "and if that's your idea of 'grub,' this date's over."

He laughed. "I was just thinking that if you ever got trapped on the Minnesota prairie, you'd be able to survive if you knew how to forage."

"Thanks, Pa, but me and Mary always carry pemmican in our bonnets just in case," I said dryly. "So what exactly are you looking for out here?" I made a sweeping gesture toward the Jorgensen acreage.

"Evidence of artifacts, burial grounds, ceremonial sites, that kind of thing. We have to make sure we don't disturb anything where we dig and build."

"But wouldn't that be in the town records?"

"Not necessarily. A lot of official records involving Native Americans are spotty at best. The government did quite a bit of shady dealing back then."

"So what if you did find evidence of sacred ground?" I tried to stand lightly while glancing around surreptitiously for any bony, angry fingers pointing out of the ground at me.

"It would depend how much area the artifacts covered."

"What if they were wall to wall?" I asked.

"Then likely the theme park would need to be built elsewhere."

"Theme park?" I asked, amazed. I put my full weight back on my feet. "You're going to build a theme park out here?"

"Not me. The company I work for. Trillings Limited." He grimaced slightly as he said the name.

I was too self-involved to be much of an activist, but the rolling hills, arching oaks, and dancing bugs really were beautiful, and the air moved a soft breeze laced with the smell of apple blossoms and spring wildflowers. I wiped the sticky white sap from the milk flower I was twirling onto my pants. "But you come off as Mr. Granola. You're going to destroy all this to build some plastic carnival?"

He tensed slightly. "Not a carnival. A heritage museum with outdoor attractions. It will glorify the original culture of this region. It'll be an outdoor museum with various distractions for kids."

I furrowed my eyebrows. "You mean like the Paul Bunyan Land Amusement Center, glorifying big blue oxen and enormous pancakes? Or like the statue of Chief Wenonga, glorifying the twenty-three-foot Indian warrior? Sounds pretty cheap to me."

I thought briefly about cleaning my social filter. These bursts of metallic honesty hadn't won me any long-term relationships to date. Nope, I decided a full second later. I meant what I said. I softened my forehead wrinkles as a compromise.

He looked hurt but laughed softly. "This land is important to me, too, Mira. That's why I'm here. I need to make sure it's regular land. And if it is, they'll build the heritage museum and you'll see that it's very tasteful. People will see authentic Dakota and Ojibwe homes, artifacts. They'll get to see and respect how the original people lived. Sure, there'll be a couple rides, maybe a Ferris wheel, but you need that to draw people out here." He touched my cheek and pretended to brush something off. "I'm working for a very responsible company, Mira. Or they never would have sent me out here."

His warm hand softened me a little. "Well, the locals will never go for it," I said grumpily. "They're all garage sales, jelly jars with quilted, ruffled covers, and mailboxes shaped like fish. They like it slow and clear, and a Native American theme park isn't that."

"You'll see, Mira," he said, laughing ruefully. "It'll bring jobs, and as far as progress goes, it's pretty harmless." His hand was still on my cheek, and he looked at me with a peculiar light in his eyes, like he'd just remembered something that had been nagging at him. He leaned in closer. "You know, you're very attractive when you're righteous."

"Mmm. You should see me when I'm drunk," I said, immediately wondering why I said it. I tried to smile, but my lip caught on my tooth. I looked away and pushed some imaginary hair from my face to distract him from my double-crossing mouth. The cosmopolitan me was supposed to be much cooler than this.

He pulled back and grabbed my hand impulsively with a half-smile on his face and then towed me off into a slow hike, and we both quietly contemplated our surroundings.

The green in Minnesota springtime is so intense it becomes a smell and taste along with a color. It is a vital, almost desperate green. The trees and grass and shrubs and plants seem to know that they only have four months or so every year to stretch, so like a painter with only one canvas, they throw out everything they have in a wild flourish. This turns a simple oak into an exotic rainforest masterpiece and a white ash into a monument that feeds the eyes. The yellows and whites of the spring prairie wildflowers contrast and deepen the nearly audible activity of life in the outdoors.

I ran my fingers through my hair and was surprised by thoughts of my father forcing themselves into my head like angry bees. I missed him the most when I was outside in the spring, and I didn't know why. It certainly wasn't because we ever spent much time outdoors together. Most of my memories are of him sitting in front of the television, in his hand a glass of vodka that he would claim was water. It was funny how much more I was thinking of him now that I had returned to the backwoods.

Jeff stretched his fingers around my hand and pulled me back into the moment, making me realize that I had been squeezing his right hand tightly. I flashed a lips-only smile at him and looked away. We walked for a long time in silence, each of us studying the land for different reasons. It took us over an hour to circumnavigate the hundred-plus acres that made up the Jorgensen estate.

"I need to head toward the middle of the property now," Jeff said. "You tired yet?"

"Not at all." I reached down and plucked a buttery dandelion and held it to my face. The warm, hairy smell tickled my nose and made me smile. I recognized wild honeysuckle as we passed the edge of the woods, but when I pointed it out to Jeff, he corrected me.

"That's actually columbine," he said, leaning down to break off a blossom and bite the sweet nectar balls on the end of the watermelon-colored flower. He handed me another blossom, and I did the same. "I'm actually surprised at the number of wildflowers already in bloom. It must be this warm early spring." He pointed out the patches of white dotting the field in front of us. "Those are bladder campion all around there." The bright petals looked like a simple oat flower, but underneath every one was a large swelling. I was familiar with them. As a child, I used to pull open reams of them, always looking for what caused the swelling. I think I expected to find baby worms, or pearls.

"And of course these are wild strawberries." He pulled me into the woods and pointed out the miniature, jagged, three-leaved plants, some of them looking ready to sprout tiny blooms. "Nothing like eating wild strawberries. My mouth waters just thinking about that tartness . . ." His voice trailed off, and he let go of my hand as he stepped off the trail. "Well, I'll be," he said softly, and leaned down. In the rich undergrowth of the forest edge, there was a stalk, eight inches or so, protected by a large, showy leaf. On the end was a simple white flower with a yellow pistil.

"Do you know what this is?" he asked, to no one in general. "It's a bloodroot. Come here, Mira."

I knelt beside him and heard the crisp snap of a juicy green. He held the severed flower in front of me, red-orange sap dripping from the bottom. "See that?" he asked me. "The bloodroot bleeds."

"Maybe we should become blood brothers," I joked.

The sunlight dappled his hair and eyes as I looked at his excited face. I was surprised at how comfortable I felt with him, considering I had only met him that afternoon. In my experience, it takes an hour or two for some major flaws to surface in a potential partner, flaws that usually only intensify the closer I let him get. Jeff was skating by pretty well so far, but I was sure something would float up. The strange thing was, I found myself hoping I was wrong. I held out my hand, palm up, and smiled weakly.

"It's a deal," he said, laughing. He rubbed some of the sticky orange sap on my palm, some on his, and then we clasped hands, my right to his left, and he kissed me softly on the lips. It reminded me of what I always wanted to happen when I was an adolescent girl and would run off into the woods to play with my friends. We would make up games, like "Run from the Prince," or "Look Stricken under the Tree Waiting for the Prince," or "Where's My Prince?" The basic plot was waiting for a boy, preferably a prince, to come and whisk us away. Sickening, to be sure, but I guess all that practice was paying off now.

The warm stickiness melting on our joined palms was pleasant, but it made further intimacy difficult. We both stood and walked back out into the warm sun. He shivered.

"Cold?" I asked.

"It is only May in Minnesota," he said. "That sun can be a little deceiving. So anyhow, Mira, what brings you to this part of the world? You seem a little incongruous out here."

I hope he didn't mean out in nature, because I was really trying to fit in. "Oh, I grew up in a small town a lot like this one."

"What was that like?"

I immediately felt the familiar defensiveness, the need to distance myself from my past. "Nothing much."

Jeff looked at me quizzically, then turned away. "We all have stuff we'd like to get away from. How about we make a deal? I don't ask you about your past, you don't ask me about mine, and we'll take this as it comes."

It was too good to be true. "Deal, blood brother."

"It is beautiful here," he said vaguely, rubbing my back. "And it's a good place to spend a summer, or longer. It's always good to refocus before forging ahead. And speaking of which, I need to take some field notes as we walk. You mind?"

I shook my head as he pulled out a worn leather notebook and an exquisite pen. I'm a sucker for good pens. As he scratched out his notes, I followed alongside, feeling the warm sun coax out my freckles. The world felt a lot more right for me than it had in a long time. We walked, almost touching, exchanging body heat and stories in hushed voices, giggling like old friends, and smiling at the sky.

When we ended up at my place early that evening, it seemed like the most natural thing in the world. And when he kissed me, it itched like new love.

I felt overwhelmed and like I was in the right place at the right time. "I could make us some supper," I suggested.

His face was inches from mine, and he was looking at me with warm, predatory eyes. I felt fireworks in my pants. I think I may have even smelled sulfur. He leaned in purposefully to finish the kiss, and either my legs buckled or we both decided to drop to the floor and make love like forest creatures.

"Morning," he said sleepily as I shifted in the bed.

"So that's what you meant by 'grub,'-" I said, laughing. I looked at the cool early-morning sun spotting his hairy chest. We never had gotten anything to eat the night before. "I thought you meant supper." I tried to feel guilty about being easy, but I just couldn't muster it. I felt too safe and cozy, in a way I hadn't with Bad Brad or my two boyfriends before him.

Jeff pulled me toward him and kissed me, and either he was getting even better at it or we were starting to meld. "So how long did you say you plan to stay in this town? You're definitely not cut from librarian cloth."

I looked across the room at the full-length mirror on the closet door. My hair was tousled with a fair-sized screw knot making shadows in back, my gray eyes a little puffy but otherwise acceptable. I had never liked my pointy nose, but sometimes I convinced myself my lips made up for it. They were perfectly curved and plump, at least when I wasn't smirking. My boobs, on the other hand, were doing that awkward, lying-down-in-different-directions, every-nipple-for-herself thing that *Playboy* boobs never did. I pulled the sheet up and leaned into the crook of Jeff's arm. "I'm taking a break from life," I reminded him. "I'll know when it's over."

"So you don't mind working at the library?"

"And the newspaper," I said. "Nope, I don't. I've been going to school for almost six years in a row, and it's time for a break. I can finish my master's when Sunny gets back."

I was happy to hear a conviction in my voice that hadn't been there yesterday. I had never been certain about school. Growing up, I had always planned to be a psychologist or a lawyer, but somehow English fit. A master's seemed like the next natural step after I earned my BA. Plus, there's not much to do with a four-year degree in English, short of opening an English store.

"I miss college." He played with my hair and looked at the ceiling. "Pennsylvania is a beautiful state, and the U of P in Greensburg has an amazing archaeology lab. I felt like we were discovering everything for the first time. Digs were like Christmas."

"You still have the option of discovering new stuff now, right?"

"Yeah, but now they don't always want me to," he said. His voice seemed a little deeper than usual.

Intrigued, I asked, "You mean Trillings doesn't want you to find anything on the Jorgensen land because then they couldn't build there? Isn't there plenty of lucrative theme park land elsewhere?"

"Yes, but not with the built-in tourist flow of this area. The lakes bring in a lot of people. Plus, this is the site of one of the most famous Indian battles in Minnesota, and it was a precursor to the Dakota uprising. This area has the history, the layout, and the clientele. It's perfect."

"You know," I said, chewing my thumbnail, "I should write a piece on you and the potential heritage museum for the paper. If I got it into the *Recall* office before Friday afternoon, it would make it into next Monday's paper. Would you be OK with that?"

He thought for a moment. "I don't see why not. It would be some good advertising, and we're not doing anything illegal. Ask me some questions."

"How about over breakfast? I'm hungry, and I believe you still owe me a meal. Whaddya say?"

He rolled over on top of me and pushed the hair back from my face, his eyes inches from mine. The pressure between my legs told me we weren't going to be eating anytime soon. "Don't you have to work today?" I asked him.

"Don't you?"

I smiled. "The library doesn't open until ten o'clock on Saturdays. And except for an article on a hot archaeologist, I don't have anything on my plate. Speaking of which, aren't you a little worried we're gonna starve?"

"Oh, we won't starve," he said, lowering his mouth to my stomach. Sure enough, it stopped growling as he kissed it. I closed my eyes and enjoyed the ride. For an aspiring loner, I can get used to people pretty quick under the right circumstances.

The next few days sped by exactly like the falling-in-love sequences in the movies in which two destined lovers meet. There might have even been a soundtrack. Jeff did as little work as possible, and we snuck time together in the corner of the library, at the base of Chief Wenonga, in his bed in Room 6 at the Battle Lake Motel, and in mine in the doublewide. We were even starting to finish each other's sentences. When he trotted out the "I think I'm falling for you" line, I rode it all the way home.

We had been together only a week, and already I felt a stability that I never had with my family, even when my father was there. My mom was always kind, but she was aimless, bopping from one secretarial job to another so she could support my dad's twisted lifestyle, which consisted of waking up and drinking, going to the mailbox to see if his disability check was in yet, and then strolling back to the couch to drink some more. My dad, well, he was my dad. With Jeff, though, I felt like I finally had someone on my side.

On Friday night, a week after we met, we were at the movies, my head on his right shoulder, and we both went for the popcorn at the same time. Our hands bumped, and he grabbed my left with his right and kissed my ring finger. "You're the kind of woman a man could grow old with, Mira," he whispered in my ear.

I snuggled in closer to keep from floating away. Looking back, I wonder if I could see the shadow of death hanging over Jeff even then, waiting to rip yet another man from my life.

FIVE

"MORNING," JEFF SAID GRUFFLY, kissing my neck. "Today, I actually have to work."

I was going to spoon him, but I was suddenly too crabby. "But it's Saturday!"

"And if I had been working all week, missy, like I'm being paid to, I wouldn't have to work today. I've got to go back out to the Jorgenson land and take soil samples, do more surveying, and issue a preliminary report to my bosses. There was that odd roll in the land out there that I wouldn't mind peeking into either. Then I'm going to the Cities tonight and tomorrow to do some more research and meet up with some contacts."

"Ooh, archaeological contacts," I said. "Sounds scintillating."

He ignored my sarcasm. "But I'll be back Monday, just in time to read your full-page article on me. The town'll love that." He chuckled tensely at some private joke. "Want to have dinner when I get back Monday night?"

"Yes. But Monday seems like an awful long ways away."

Jeff brushed my hair away from my face and behind my ear, then kissed my forehead. "It does, doesn't it. How did I get so attached to you?"

"Well, I am cute."

Jeff laughed and pulled me to him. After some productive messing around, I slapped him on the butt and sent him on his way. One trucker's shower later and I was at the library, doodling little hearts on scratch paper and making happy moon eyes at the handful of preseason tourists trickling in.

When Gina meandered in at lunchtime, it was all I could do not to tell her she'd better get used to calling me Mrs. Wilson. I had known Gina through Sunny for a number of years, and when Sunny skipped town, it made sense for me to take up the friendship. Gina worked as an RN, and like most nurses in the area, she was built like a brick shithouse. She had short blonde hair, so pale I was never sure if she had eyelashes, mischievous green eyes, and a white smile that showed all her teeth. She was simple and genuine and a great listener. An exactly perfect friend, except for her sick sense of humor.

She grinned when she saw me. "If it isn't the town whore!"

My grin melted off my face. "You heard?"

She caught my embarrassed look and howled. "It's a figure of speech, Mira. Why, you gettin' some that I don't know about?"

Suddenly, the last thing I wanted to do was tell her about Jeff. "Not so you'd know." I planted the smile back on my face. "Are ya here to treat me to lunch, big spender?"

"Even better." She pulled a wrinkled computer printout from her denim purse and slid it across the counter. "I'm here to treat you to love."

There were four thumbnails of men's heads with titles and descriptions next to them. "What is this?" I asked. "Are we shopping online for men now?"

"Not we. You. I want you to be able to double with me and Leif so I can see more of you. I signed you up with an online dating service. It's free to post your ad. You just pay if you want to respond to a guy's ad."

The dots were not connecting. "You wrote an online ad for me? People can shop for me?"

Gina touched her pointer finger to her nose. "Bingo! I'm tired of hearing you bitch about how there are no smart men around here to date. Welcome to the twentieth century."

I shook my head. "It's the twenty-first century, Gina. And I don't want to do this." I firmly believed that men, like leather pants, shouldn't be bought online. Besides, I had Jeff.

"You don't have to do a thing. I'll screen them for you and forward the good ones to your e-mail account. Be on the alert for love, crazy love." She winked at me and waltzed out.

"Cripes," I said to the photos of the four men I was still holding. They were all cute, in a tiny, black-and-white sort of way. There was even one, a Moorhead State professor according to his ad, whom I wouldn't mind meeting in a dark alley. But not online. And not when I had Jeff. I balled up the paper, tossed it in the trash, and went back to my moony eyes for the entire day.

I spent most of Sunday morning prepping my gardens and playing with Luna and Tiger Pop. By the time Sunday night rolled around, my yearning was at a fever pitch. Monday at the library, it was all I could do not to rush to the windows and search for Jeff's car driving past. He was smart, funny, kind, and not from around here. Almost too good to be true.

I wondered if this was the same love bug that had bitten Sunny before she up and moved to Alaska. I picked up the picture she had just sent me of her and Rodney, each holding one end of a ginormous salmon. Rodney looked short and hairy in the picture, decked out in a Vikings sweatshirt, his impressive monobrow dominating the scene. Sunny was grinning widely, her cheeks flushed with pride or sun. It looked like they were enjoying themselves, but I was sure it was nothing like the love I was feeling.

On Saturday, before he left, Jeff had brushed my lips with his and told me he would meet me at six at the Turtle Stew, one of Battle Lake's three diners, when he got back to town Monday night. After I locked up the library, I went into the bathroom and actually curled the ends of my hair and put on eyeliner and lipstick. Jeff was obviously a natural type of guy, so I was careful to add just enough makeup so I looked extra-me but in a wash-and-wear kind of way.

I got to the diner at quarter to and walked up and down the streets a few times. I actually initiated some of the traditional hellos and head nods as I passed people on the street I knew by sight, or didn't know at all. I spent about four minutes looking through the window of the bead store before I couldn't stand it any longer. I went into the Stew.

And I waited there, alone, until almost seven-thirty. I'm normally one of those people who gets pissed instead of worried when others are late, but after an hour and a half, I started to wonder how much of the past week I had made up. The chicken sandwich I had eaten sat like an acid rock in my stomach. I had wanted a burger, really, but had given up beef in deference to mad cow disease. I could read the writing on the wall as well as anyone. I hate sitting alone in restaurants anyhow, and I could only pretend to look at the car and house ads in the *Otter Tail Midweek* for so long. When I found myself actually reading the auction page, I knew it was time to put the newspaper down.

People-watching was my personal favorite time killer, but there hadn't been much going on tonight. The usual group of grizzly farmers was sitting at the round common table in the corner. When I waitressed in the Cities, the big table was reserved for big parties. Around here, an unspoken rule transformed this table and most like it into a social club, and one needed to have the right stories and age for membership. I was always curious what the men at the table talked about as they sipped their coffee and buttered their sweet rolls. Watching them was like watching a private dance where every one of them innately knew the steps. There was easy laughter, but their stiff spines and leathery worry lines pointed to hard lives, or at least a life of hard work.

I was sucking on an ice cube and imagining myself between Harold Schmidt and Ethan Wardrip, talking about the first time I changed a spark plug by myself, when a gaggle of silver fingernails with red, white, and blue stick-ons clacked onto my table.

"Hello, Mira," drawled a voice from above. I knew it was Kennie Rogers without looking. Somehow, maybe as an homage to her country name, Kennie was the only person born and raised in Battle Lake, man or woman, who had a southern accent. I guess she made it work for her. She was the town mayor, through a combination of might and fright, and she had her clackety nails in everyone's business. Officially, Kennie oversaw town meetings and was in charge of the beautification of the city, but in reality, she was merely a force of nature that no one wanted to move.

She was in her late thirties, divorced, with no children that I knew of. She looked like a large, overly made-up doll, most notably in her hair, which had probably been naturally blonde at one time but was now bleached to a crispy platinum, curled, and beaten around her ears and face. When I was first introduced to her at the newspaper, she had smiled a wide politician's grin at me. I cut her some slack, though, because with a name like that and a face like Makeover Magic Barbie in a microwave, I figured she had taken a lot of teasing in school. We're all a product of our environment.

"Hello, Kennie," I said with mock cheerfulness. "How are you?"

"Better than you, I think, dining alone," she said, and then laughed as if we shared a private joke. "Please don't tell me a cute thing like y'all is gettin' stood up?"

I clenched and pursed my lips. "OK," I said, "I won't."

"Well, who're y'all supposed to be meeting?" Her eyes glittered beneath the weight of powder-blue mascara. I thought they had discontinued that shade out of respect to the Cure disbanding.

"Nobody you know," I said, growing angrier with Jeff.

Kennie crossed her arms and leaned back on her ample hip, her arms crinkling the puff-paint whitetail deer etched across her blue sweatshirt. "You'd be surprised who I know, and y'all best remember that." The tight, lipstick-shrapnel smile she gave me did little to alleviate the sudden tension. She leaned forward and I flinched involuntarily. With one straight finger, she pushed some loose hair off my face, her fingernail scraping my skull. "Y'all should comb that pretty hair a yours, you know? If I had pretty hair like that, I'd be combing it all the time." She laughed loudly, breaking through some of the pressure.

I wondered if Kennie had had the mad cow hamburger for supper. "Sure," I said blankly, racing to figure out if she was acting weird or if I was just being paranoid. She'd always seemed a little eccentric, but she had never focused this much of her odd brand of attention on me before.

She winked and pointed her talons at me one last time, then sashayed out the front door. I swear the little balls on her booties waved goodbye like malicious bunny tails. I had never even seen her coming.

The pang of fear she inspired in me belatedly turned to anger, as is my pattern. I slapped down a three-dollar tip for the waitress, and at exactly 7:31, I walked out the door of the Turtle Stew. The brief but intense encounter with Kennie made me even madder at Jeff, but not so mad that I didn't hold out hope he would meet me on the way to my car with some dramatic archaeological emergency story.

I almost ran down Karl Syverson, a local banker, on my way out. We'd become friendly since I'd arrived, through his frequent library visits. He was about five foot eleven and had a slight build for a Minnesota farm boy, nondescript sandy hair, plain blue eyes, and a face like Norwegian food: white, bland, and comforting. A very married gentleman in his mid-thirties, he was born, raised, and rooted in Battle Lake and embodied all the good qualities of Minnesota—true care backed up by time for others, otherworldly patience, and a dry, subtle sense of humor. He had made me feel welcome in the town right away and thawed some of my natural itchiness.

"Whoa! Following up on another hot lead?" He held me at arm's length to keep me from barreling into him.

"Another?" I asked, my ticked-offedness clouding my memory.

"The whole town is buzzing about that Jeff Wilson article in the back of today's paper," he said, looking at me curiously. "You didn't know who you were interviewing?"

I returned his puzzled look. "Jeff Wilson, archaeologist," I said. "Did I miss something?"

Karl smiled and shook his head, shoving his hands into his pockets and looking down the street in an uncharacteristically boyish gesture. "Jeff Wilson is a legend in this town. He took the high school football team to state three years in a row, then left to attend college out East on a full ride some twenty years back. He was a star quarterback, destined for pro. Battle Lake's prodigal son."

"Well, why didn't he tell me any of that?" I asked, more to myself than to Karl. The Jeff altar I had built started cracking.

Karl clucked his tongue. "Maybe he moved past that. Not all of us live for our high school years."

There was more to it than that. Moving past high school is not the same thing as forgetting it ever existed, and Jeff had given me every indication during our time together that he was a stranger in Battle Lake. I was suddenly deeply uncomfortable with how little I knew about this man I had slept with.

"Well, thanks for the info, Karl. If you happen to see this prodigal son, tell him to give me a call so I can get the rest of the story." I was going to walk away but couldn't shake the twitch in my shoulder. "Say, maybe you could explain something weird to me. I just saw Kennie Rogers in the Stew, and she was Mary Kay nice and then just turned on me. You think she's mad because I didn't interview her as mayor for that article on Jeff?"

Karl laughed out loud for the first time since we had met. "Could be."

I glared at him, my meager patience allotment for the evening long used up.

He grinned. "Kennie Jensen, Miss Teen Minnesota 1981, homecoming queen in 1982, and high school girlfriend to the all-time Battle Lake football star, Jeff Wilson."

I didn't know where to go first. "So her *married* name is Rogers? She didn't *have* to do that to herself?"

Karl shrugged and pulled out a crisp white handkerchief. He began polishing his fingernails. "Her and Jeff were quite the pair back in high school. You know the spiel—high school sweethearts, he a football star, she a cheerleader, both attractive and popular with the world at their feet. And then he just up and left for college. I guess Kennie wanted him to stay here and raise a family."

I pushed down a surge of Kennie-flavored jealousy with both hands. Jeff, like me, had obviously had past relationships. Duh. "So why's she pissed at me?"

43

"Oh, it could be anything, but I'm sure it's mostly nothing. Maybe Jeff didn't let her know he was back in town. She's probably just jealous because you spent time with him and she didn't. It'll blow over," he said. "It always does."

I thought of Mrs. Pavechnik, a local legend thanks to her husband. From the way I heard it, Mrs. Pavechnik was still marked from the scandal created because Mr. Pavechnik had had relations with the livestock, and he had been dead for over seventeen years. "Well, nothing I can do about it now," I said doubtfully. "Remember to tell Jeff I'm looking for him, if you see him." I couldn't tell if it was desperation or anger shading my voice.

"I'll do that." He nodded his head firmly, a smile still in his eyes. "Good night!"

I drove back to Sunny's house in my puddle-jumper Corolla, listening to the oldies station, my mind wandering. Heart came on singing about a magic man, and I turned it off. I had been sleeping alone for two nights now and had been looking forward to Jeff's company. It sure didn't help to know he was a high school football star. I'm not as cynical as I pretend, and I could get as soupy over a real jock as the next person. I suppose I was lucky to find a real man at all, but it was too early in our fling for him to blur his past and stand me up without a phone call. I shoved a sharp but persistent panicky feeling toward the back of my head. Jeff was old enough to take care of himself, and it was just rude that he hadn't shown up.

I glanced over at the copy of the *Recall* I had saved for him, folded over on the passenger seat. The article had come in too late to fit anywhere but the second to last page. That was lucky, because otherwise the mug shot I had taken of him Friday morning by a tree would be staring back at me.

It had turned out to be a fairly short article because there was a lot I didn't know, more than I thought. It mentioned his name, his profession, and that he worked as an archaeologist for Trillings Limited. I wrote that Trillings employed Jeff to investigate the Jorgensen property, which had been rented out or rested under the government's CRP plan since Ella Jorgensen passed away seven years earlier. I referred vaguely to Trillings's "development plans" for the area. Out of fairness to Jeff, I had mentioned the number of jobs it would bring to the community and how it would offer more family-oriented activities.

Ron had been happy to run my article because the bowling alley had pulled its full-corner ad at the last minute, the reason being that Liza Klohn, the owner of Bowl Me Over, had heard that the newspaper was going to start charging the Lutheran church for its bingo advertising. It was Battle Lake's version of an economic embargo. My article fit perfectly in the hole.

As I watched the night-clouded trees whisk past, I thought about being back in a small town, and I was a little disturbed by how quickly I had fit back in. The nearest town to the hobby farm I had grown up on with my mom and sometimes dad was one of those two-bars-one-church-and-a-post-office settlements that make up the Minnesota landscape. Everyone knew each other, at least enough to gossip, and most of the boys worked at the turkey farm, and the girls worked at the Dairy Queen. We'd all converge on summer Saturday nights to pour our pilfered liquor into a big garbage can with some ice and Kool-Aid. We called them "wop" parties, and we'd get drunk, dance to Top 40 tunes, and end up making out with someone. When I was in high school, we picked up dates like you pick up cockleburs. If they stuck, they were yours for a while. At least, that's how it was until I became Manslaughter Mark's daughter, a social pariah at sixteen. After that, no boy dared get close to me, even under the cover of night. I told myself that I didn't go to the parties anymore because I was in track and it would blow my chance at placing in regionals.

I met my friend C.C. the fall I started at the U, and we had been drinking friends ever since. She was the roommate who introduced me to Sunny, who had gotten me to Battle Lake. I felt some pull toward this slow life, as much as I mocked it. Besides, in my pre-life crisis there was something comfortable and soothing about returning to a small town for a while—it was like visiting the people I used to be.

And Sunny's farm was beautiful. It was a house in a box—just add water—but it was new and clean and it looked out over Whiskey Lake. The hundred-plus acres were covered with hardwood forests, rolling hills, and wildflowers. A person can get used to waking up with hummingbirds outside her window and apples trees blooming on her lawn.

I was still only slightly above tourist class to locals, but the more they saw me, the more they got used to me, especially since I was a friend of Sunny's, whose open smile and relaxed attitude had made her a town favorite. It was all starting to feel pretty comfortable, and having Jeff in the picture only helped.

But now, I discovered he had lied to me by omission *and* he had stood me up. I wondered if it was because I had slept with him on the first date. Popular culture holds that this is a turnoff to men, the thrill of the chase being over and all that. However, in a farming community where bars and churches are the main entertainment, sex becomes more of a welcome distraction than a taboo, accepted but not acknowledged. Of course, Jeff likely was not recently familiar with the customs of the region, archaeologist or no. I sighed as I pulled into the long, rutted driveway.

Oh well, I thought, I was no worse off than before he had arrived. I was pretty sure I loved him, though. He was funny and well read and laid back, and he noticed the little things that made me happy. He was an exceptional lay, too, in a way that only men in their late thirties can be. Maybe he would show up and have an explanation for everything, I told myself as I parked the car. He could have gotten in a car accident, banged his head terribly, and forgotten about our week together until he found the picture of me I had snuck in his wallet and then realized I was the one, for example. Could be he was shopping for a ring right now. I got out and stretched in the temperate night air and decided to do some gardening to clear my mood.

The house was unlocked, as usual, and I traded my white tank top and Levi's for gardening clothes. This unusually warm spring had goaded me to plant early despite the warnings of locals. I planted vegetables to have an excuse to pull weeds, anyhow. Weeding always relaxes me. Something about the quiet ripping sound makes me feel in control. And when I'm done, and I inspect my clean, straight rows of hairy little carrot sprouts, store-bought tomatoes, and zucchini leaves peeking out of the ground, I believe there must be some sort of order in the universe. Tonight was no exception.

After the weeding was done, I pruned any third sprouts at the forks of my tomato plants and built up the mulch at their bases. I used newspapers covered with grass clippings to keep the weeds out and the moisture in, and as I straightened them, I scared up the unique smell of rotting newspaper—musty, fertile, and brown. Next, I arranged the seeking baby arms of my hardy new squash plants so they would have room to spread. I was careful not to disturb them where their tendrils had grasped the ground.

I gardened in the moon-colored dark, a contented Luna at my side, until the cool air made my fingers stiff and the toothless bugs of spring became annoying. I went inside to shower and took the edge off by mowing through an economy-sized bag of dill pickle potato chips and watching *Fried Green Tomatoes*. I was trying not to take my date's disappearance personally. I was a nice person. At least Tiger Pop and Luna thought so, when they weren't too busy harassing one another. I headed to bed early, wondering what sort of day it was going to be at the library tomorrow.

SIX

THE FIRST DISASTER OF Tuesday morning involved urine and high-heeled, timelessly tasteless prom shoes. I was showered, dressed, and ready for work. All I had to do was slip on my black leather sandals and I'd be ready to face the day. When I reached for the sandals, however, I discovered that both shoes were glistening with liquid that smelled an awful lot like ammonia. Luna and Tiger Pop had been vying for my attention ever since I had moved in, and apparently they had stopped pussy-footing around. There really is nothing like peeing on someone's apparel to make them notice you.

"Tiger Pop, did you pee on my shoes?"

His ear twitched, but otherwise there was no motion from the calico ball on my bed. I sighed and reached back for my tennis shoes, which I quickly discovered were hosting their own urine pool party. Now I was worried, as these were the only two pairs of shoes I owned. First Jeff stood me up, and now animals were peeing on my stuff. My morning deflated further as I realized that I wouldn't have time to buy shoes before I opened the library, as all the stores opened the same time I did.

I scoured Sunny's office, piled high with boxes, and could only come up with one pair of shoes: the dreaded prom/wedding/funeral pair that every Minnesota woman owned and wore in that order. They were ridiculously pointy, dyed a soft pink (goes great with taffeta!), and at least three inches high. Christ. I went back and sniffed the sandals, which were starting to go white in spots. I looked from the heels in my hand to the spotted sandals. I bet I wouldn't even be able to smell the pee when I walked. My hoofers were at least five feet from my nose. I got my toe halfway in one before I thought better of it. I chucked the sandals in the garbage, the tennies in the wash, and snatched up the scary feminine footwear. I slipped on the heels, thinking clown shoes would have been more fitting, and stumbled toward my car.

I could walk in heels about as well as I could swim in boots, so the short trip to my car was peppered with foot-sinking, ankle-twisting hitches. I soon realized that the trick was to not move in the hips at all and keep my toes pointed forward and my legs goose-step straight. At least that way, I didn't fall over. And, if I pulled my jeans extra low, you could hardly even see the crusty flowers on the toes.

I was actually feeling a little OK about the shoes by the time I pulled into town, all Laura Ingalls Wilder meets Carrie Bradshaw. That's about when I discovered the second disaster of the day, this one at least as bad as having to wear someone else's prom shoes to work: Tuesday was Dead Body Day at the library. When I literally stumbled across Jeff's body in the Pl–Sca aisle, my new life broke apart and rained around my head like glass shards.

It didn't take Mrs. Berns long to roust up the local police, and I didn't want to open the envelope scratching at my back until I was alone.

When law enforcement arrived, they placed the requisite yellow tape around the scene, snapped photos from every angle, and after what seemed like years but was actually a few hours, wheeled the body away on a gurney into a waiting ambulance.

I posted myself outside the library doors during the worst of the commotion and hated my conspicuousness. When I was nineteen, I had sneaked into a bar with a friend and gotten drunk on lime vodka sours. I started sassing a greasy biker, childishly thinking that I was six foot tall and bulletproof, and he had slapped me across the face. That's how I felt now as I tried to assimilate Jeff's death. I was horrified, embarrassed, angry, shocked—all these intense emotions racing through me at such a high speed that they all got stuck in a clot right behind my eyes, not one able to squeeze past and organize a reaction.

I realized I was using my pointer finger to trace infinity shapes on my thumbnail, a nervous habit I had when I was just a kid who wore long socks with her skirts because she liked how it looked. The police had told me I couldn't go home, though, so I spent the time checking out the people who were checking me out, hoping my eyes looked defiant. I wasn't going to be a victim twice in my life.

I didn't see anyone who had directly impacted me since I moved to Battle Lake, though I thought I caught a glimpse of platinum-blonde hair toward the back of the crowd of twenty or so that had gathered. I dismissed the possibility that it was Kennie. There was no way she could walk by an audience like this without making a statement.

Most of the gawkers left shortly after the ambulance, leaving Chief Wohnt, the local enforcer of the law, and me. He was a large, muscular man who had become head of the police force not long before I came to town, and people talked with pride about how many speeders he regularly caught racing past Chief Wenonga on the north side of town. It had been enough for him to justify buying a new Jeep to police this one-horse burg. Word on the street, though, was that Gary Wohnt was more interested in Kennie Rogers than in catching criminals.

The police chief had a hard time suppressing an officious smile, or maybe it was a smirk, as he got my story while we sat on the stone benches behind the library. I might not have noticed the set to his mouth except for the lip balm he applied thickly when he first sat down across from me. He pulled the white and yellow pot out of his back pocket like some men pulled out chew, and tapped it once on the table. The black lettering across the top reminded me of the Carmex-induced cancer legends that had gone around my high school. Chief Wohnt screwed off the top and spread the yellow cream on deep. When he unlocked his mouth to talk, I could see slick feathered edges where it overlapped in the corners of his tight lips like a poorly frosted cake. I wondered about his self-satisfied manner as I tried not to look directly at the greased pink mouth asking me questions. I focused instead on his deep-set brown eyes, like burn holes in his tanned, pock-marked face. His hair was thick, black, and waxy, comb lines separating one strand from the next like a perfectly plowed field.

He wanted to know what I knew about Jeff and his body, and I was desperately trying to shove my independent social filter into place so I didn't accidentally tell him too much. A murder was enough to turn this town on its ear. If I added sex to the mix, people would do something wild like turn off their TVs. I thought about Mrs. Pavechnik and her bispecies husband for the second time in a week.

I told Gary Wohnt what I knew, minus the sex. I imagine Mrs. Berns, who was pretending to tend the rock garden next to the sidewalk, would add that in later. But Gary Wohnt got the just-friends version of how I had met Jeff, and he scribbled it down faster than I could talk. At the end of the interview, he reapplied Carmex with a breadth and zest usually reserved for a smoker's last cigarette, and I started to wonder, not for the first time in my life, if it was possible to kill someone with bad thoughts. If I could mentally do away with a father for neglecting me and a lover for standing me up, what would happen to the person who cut me off in traffic? I needed to do something, and quick.

SEVEN

THE LIBRARY WAS OFFICIALLY closed for the rest of the day while the state police investigated and then the local janitorial service sanitized the building. Actually, the local service was just Mr. Bethel, who cleaned cabins and businesses during the summer, and I wondered if he had the proper dead-removal products. He wouldn't need much. There was very little blood on the scene, including Jeff's clothes. Before Chief Wohnt left, I asked him what he thought of that.

"I think he was shot somewhere other than the library, his clothes changed, and then his body brought here."

That Gary Wohnt was going to make detective yet. After he drove away and I was convinced I was alone, I went to my car and yanked the envelope out of my waistband. "For Your Eyes Only," embossed in an elaborate green script, were the only words on the creamy envelope. I pulled out the silver card inside and flipped it open, surprised to find that it was an invitation. A smaller version of the ornate script scrawled out this message:

You are invited to a Class of '82 party to be held on Friday, 15 May. Come masked. You cannot enter without this invitation. One invitation per person. Go south of Battle Lake on 78, east on Eagle Lake Road 2.7 miles. On left, blue house, white mailbox. C U there!

I did a little math and had a tickling at the back of my brain. This card was telling me something, and I wasn't going to let the English major in me be distracted by the annoying, vanity-plate-cute "CU there!" on an otherwise elegant invitation to a masquerade being held in three days. Try as I might, though, I couldn't make sense of it, so I stuck it in my glove compartment for later study.

Suddenly, I felt lost but couldn't think where I wanted to be. I craved a huge drunken bender, but I'd been doing so well curbing my drinking. I settled for a chocolate binge, and I knew just what kind I needed.

To the uninitiated, the Nut Goodie isn't much to look at. The frenetic pine-green and clown-red wrapper yells of old-fashioned candy stores where you could dig your hand into a jar and pull out ten waxy pop bottles for a dime. The Nut Goodie itself looks like a rubber gag toy, the kind you wouldn't want to find next to your cat. The whole bar is as big as the palm of a grown woman's hand and consists of a domed sugar-maple center with peanut halves sprinkled on thick. Then, there is brown, waxy chocolate spilled over it all and hardened in a free shape around the outside. It looks like the unfortunate result of a bad meal, but it tastes like heaven.

If you're a Nut Goodie newbie, I suggest you start with one of the chocolate lips that has spilled off of the whole. It's just chocolate-covered peanuts, and it's a good way to get your feet wet before biting into the so-sweet-it-makes-you-cry maple center. The maple concoction is the magic in a Nut Goodie. It's not gooey like caramel. It's a nice, staid, Minnesota middle, the texture of thick buttercream frosting—one bite would kill a diabetic. The Pearson's Company first started creating them in St. Paul in 1907 and hasn't looked back.

I'm addicted to the Nut Goodie, but I'm a controlled addict. I only allow myself one in times of stress or joy, and then I always let the chocolate and maple bites melt in my mouth until the peanuts are the only solid before I chew. I savor them, feeling the maple center get under my fillings and into my brain, enjoying the tingling sugar rush that follows, the clarity of vision and purpose that can only be induced by a Nut Goodie high. Thank you, Mr. and Mrs. Pearson. Of course, there's a price to pay. The Nut Goodie come-down is rough, with an accompanying pain similar to an ice cream headache. I needed a Nut Goodie now, God help me maybe even two. I barged into the gas station, fisted them, paid for both at the counter without making eye contact, and returned to my car. I ate the first like a starving rat, and it calmed me enough to suck on the second slowly. As I felt the soothing buzz hit, I had an idea of what to do with myself.

I needed some physical action to offset the heavy feelings that were threatening to smother me. Returning to Sunny's trailer seemed too confining, and the stares I was already feeling around town told me I didn't want to hang out here. I decided to to buy some shoes and go for a drive. Twenty minutes and a pair of cowboy boots later, I found myself at the old Jorgensen farm, the Nut Goodie magic maple center still corroding my teeth. I parked and walked out toward the spot Jeff and I had visited the Friday before.

Strange how death gives a person ownership over the life of the deceased. I had spent a week with Jeff, but now that he was dead, we had a permanent relationship. What could have been if we had had more time? We were obviously compatible. He was the most interesting person I had met in a long time. I felt cheated and was starting to feel a little scared. I was a murder victim, once removed.

I sat down heavily and ripped at the grass, the backs of my eyes growing hot. This was just shitty. I suppose the shock was wearing off and I was beginning to feel the stress of traumatic death, but what I was feeling seemed pretty self-centered to be called grief. A man had lost his life, and I couldn't think beyond what I had lost—a new friend and lover, if not a potential partner. My thoughts strayed to my dad and wondered if this was what grief really was, a sort of inner reckoning where you faced what was no longer possible, followed by self-pity and an eventual reassignment of resources. I'd always hoped when I grew up that my grief would finally have more meaning, or at least less selfishness. I needed to work on this grief thing.

Out of the corner of a damp eye, I spotted movement near the grove where Jeff and I had become blood brothers. I turned my head slowly, expecting to find a deer pacing the woods. Instead I saw Karl Syverson. I watched him step out of the woods and walk toward the road. Could he not see me?

"Karl!" I yelled, wiping my eyes. I was happy not to be alone.

He startled his head toward me, waved, and began walking in my direction. When he drew close enough to hear me without raising my voice, I said, "Did you hear? The star football player died."

"What?" he said, looking over my shoulder, his lips tight. "Jeff Wilson is dead?"

I nodded, feeling sorry for myself. "What're you doing out here?"

He cocked his head, patting me on the shoulder a little roughly. "The bank asked me to come out. They manage this land and wanted to know how the museum plans are coming. I was actually hoping to run into Jeff. I got a phone call that led me to believe he would be out here finishing up."

My logical mind latched onto this tidbit, grateful to avoid emotions for the moment. "When was the phone call? Was it Jeff? What did you talk about?"

Karl's bland face looked sad. "I don't know, Mira." He looked into the distance where the old Jorgenson homestead was located. "Yesterday sometime. I talked to a representative from Trillings who said Jeff's report was in and the property looked good and that I should get the papers ready. It was a short conversation, all business."

"What do you mean the bank manages the land?" I was unwilling to let go of the facts I had the power to understand.

He shrugged, sighed, and looked back off to the landscape. "We're responsible for handling the mortgage and dispensing the land. No biggie."

"So what are you doing here?" I asked again. I just didn't want him to leave me alone.

He chuckled softly. "Well, Ms. Lois Lane, the Jorgensen estate is in arrears, and it would be in the bank's best interest to sell the property pronto. Trillings seems like our best bet, and the rep I talked to made it sound like a done deal. We want to have a satisfied customer, if that is the case. You know how I like to have everything neat and orderly when it comes to business." He said it again. "Bank stuff, you know."

Actually, I didn't know. It didn't seem right, Karl out here in his suit. But my thinker felt broken, full of Novocain and cotton. "I don't think he found anything," I said. "I came out here with him, and he seemed to think this spot was ideal. The only thing he needed to check out was that rise over there." I pointed toward the mound Jeff had spoken about.

Karl looked at me with new interest. "Rises everywhere around here. You were out here when he was surveying?"

"Yup," I said, suddenly defensive. "I had to interview him, remember."

"Mmm-hmm." Karl was back in thoughtful mode, a distant, teasing smile on his lips. "I'll just bet. Jeff was always very personable. Well, let me know if I can do anything for you." He patted me on the shoulder, this time softly, before walking back to the road. He must have parked up and around the bend from where I was, because I hadn't seen his car.

When he left, I shook my head in wonder. Too much was happening too quickly, and I had too many questions. Was this land related to Jeff's death? And why had Jeff's dead body been brought to the library? What sort of weirdo killer would change their victim's shirt? What had Karl meant when he said Jeff was "personable"? And why couldn't I maintain any sort of lasting, adult relationship with a man?

From where I was sitting, detective work seemed a better fit than feeling sorry for myself. I needed to make things stop happening to me. I had to find out what was going on, and I was going to start by looking at that rise that had interested Jeff. It was the only material thing I had to focus on at the moment. I had seen the Indiana Jones movie and the necessary sequels. I knew the basics of archaeology. This should be a piece of cake.

I walked the half mile to the mound and knelt down by it. The sense of purpose felt good. I smelled the same fresh-dirt smell I associated with gardening and poked methodically at the sod. A slithering in the grass made me jump back.

"It's just a snake. A little snake sunning itself," I said out loud. Suddenly, it was all I could do not to run, and I wondered about the legend of haunted Battle Lake. Maybe Jeff had disturbed some spirits and paid the price?

Foolish, I told myself, and I even half-believed it. This side of the mound was unremarkable, so I walked over to the other side. The wind picked up, and I heard a soft moaning in the trees that I didn't remember from when Jeff and I hiked out here. The palm of my hand tickled where Jeff had squeezed the bloodroot sap. My skin felt prickly suddenly, and I couldn't stand still any longer. I turned to walk back to my car at a calm, I-don't-believe-in-ghosts pace, caught my heel on a rock, and fell flat on my face.

My fingers sunk deep into the earth when I hit, deeper than they should have. I felt around and was surprised to find a loose piece of sod about two square feet, representing maybe a seventh of the size of the mound. Somebody, probably Jeff, had already scalped this spot. I pulled back a corner of the grass, and what I saw underneath made me sit back. I would have whistled through my teeth if I knew how. Instead, I just said, "Whooeeeh."

At my knees was smooth gray rock that had been carefully brushed clean, with only sprinkles of dirt freckling it from where I had pulled the sod off. What was amazing were the images etched on the stone. They looked like sections of the crude but vivid stick figures I had seen on a History Channel story about the Pueblo Indians in the southwestern United States. On this section of rock, I could see the bottom of a primitive man holding what looked like a spear, and an arrow shooting toward a four-legged creature. I rocked back on my heels and ran my eyes over the entire length of the mound, thinking, "If I pulled off all the grass, I bet I could piece together the whole story." I leaned forward and rubbed my fingers over the rough design, fascinated to feel that it wasn't a painting but a carving in the stone.

The Lady of the Lakes article I had written about Battle Lake's origins again puttered through my head. For me, the interesting part of the article came before the official founding. The Ojibwe had originally named the town Battle Lake in honor of a fierce 1795 battle between their tribe and the Dakota. A party of Ojibwe hunters had left their community at Leech Lake for their annual beaver hunt. When they neared Leaf Lake, they discovered fresh signs of their Dakota enemies. A beaten path led them to the lake, where they were surprised to find long rows of three hundred Dakota lodges on an open prairie.

The first Ojibwe gun brought down the Dakota leader, but the Ojibwe were terribly outnumbered. They fought on until more than thirty Ojibwe were killed. Less than a third of the original hunting party returned home. The Ojibwe and Dakota had many skirmishes in that area until Indian ownership of the land was "legitimized" with the federal government's Prairie du Chien peace treaty in the early 1800s. But settlers and more treaties pushed the Indians back until the area was almost totally Norwegian—white people who ate white food.

Jeff had referred to the battle the town was named after as one of the most famous in Minnesota history. Now I wondered if these carvings were tied into that. Jeff must have found them after he came back on Saturday to do one more visual survey. That explained why it had taken him longer than he expected in the Twin Cities and why he couldn't make our date last night, but why had he died? It occurred to me then that I had assumed Jeff had been killed recently, either late last night or early this morning. But he may have never reached the Cities, instead decomposing somewhere, his killer waiting to position his body in the back of the library at just the right time. Meanwhile, I had been going about my life thinking he was still alive.

I felt sick in my blood. It's an unsettling feeling, the idea of waiting for the dead, believing that they're alive and thinking of you. It's mental grave robbery. I needed to find out exactly how long Jeff had been dead before I freaked myself out any more.

I walked back to my car, my head buzzing with new thoughts. I searched for the roughed-up digital camera the *Recall* had issued me and returned to snap photographs of the rock carvings from every angle. Then I gently replaced the sod and used a gardener's touch to blend it back with the other prairie grass.

I returned to my car again, this time to begin some research. I had enough questions. Now I needed some answers, like what Jeff had found out in this field that was worth killing for. On a hunch, I decided to drive by Kennie's house. She had the evil eye on me last night in the Stew, and with Jeff dead, I wanted to know why.

I swerved off the main road and onto the back streets to get to Kennie's faster. Her house was in the residential area of Battle Lake, close to the base of the water tower. If Tammy Faye Baker made $27,000 a year, she would have a house just like Kennie's. At some point it had been the standard fifties square, one-story house, but when Kennie moved in, her personality infected the entire quarter-acre lot. Her lawn was immaculately mowed and weed-whacked. The one pine tree in her yard was Christmas-hearth perfect and strung with pink flamingo and chili pepper lights. The bright plastic flowers in her window boxes and tracing her front walk would never die, but they could also never hope to outshine the acid-pink-with-lemon-yellow-trim electric box that was Kennie's home. If that house had a smell, it would be strawberry soda mixed with Aqua Net. I had never been inside, and the Hallmark ceramic collectibles lining her windows told me that was just fine.

I spied the new police Jeep out front of Kennie's house. Gary Wohnt had come a-calling. It occurred to me that there should be a better place for the law to be the night after a murder, and that further cemented my suspicions of Wohnt. Growing up in a small town where the only regular crime is being a teenager—breaking curfew, smoking, vandalizing—I had an inherent distrust of the law that was deepened by Wohnt's greasy appearance and authoritative demeanor.

I parked my car at the water tower and strolled down the hill to Kennie's, searching for a suitable lie should I get caught snooping. I wanted to peek in her windows, but it was barely dusk, and it was too likely that I'd be caught.

At the end of her walkway, I decided that people do talk to the law, especially if they found a dead body that day. I would sit on Kennie's stoop, and if she or Wohnt came out, I would ask them something. What I would ask, well, that would have to come to me.

I scrunched into myself, looked left and right, and then floated down Kennie's walk and parked my ass on her stoop. Voices drifted out at me, a man's and a woman's, but I couldn't decipher their words. I stood up and leaned my back against Kennie's door. That wasn't much better, so I tipped my ear against the wood, cultivating a look of bored disinterest should a neighbor notice me. I was just a polite gal waiting for the Chief to come out. Ho hum.

"He didn't come over here. Y'all know me better than that."

My ears perked up, and I leaned toward the open window closest to the front step.

"Remember, I knew you back then, too." The Chief.

Kennie giggled flirtatiously. "Better than most, and that and a buck'll buy y'all a cup of coffee."

There was a shuffling of furniture and clinking of glasses that obscured the next few exchanges. I pictured Kennie and the Chief inside, he in his uniform, she in a sheer chiffon robe and wearing those high-heeled shoes with bursts of feather over the toes, stirring their martinis and admiring one another. My throat tightened queasily, and the background noise inside quieted down.

". . . told you this town isn't ready for gambling. You know that."

"If I knew that, y'all think I woulda ever brought it up? People don't know what they're ready for until I tell 'em. This town is full of sheep and hens."

I wondered what sort of animal that made Kennie, being that she was the mayor of said sheep and hens. January of this year had marked the beginning of her third term as the town leader. She usually ran unopposed, but last year the local militia started a movement to unseat her. Their candidate was named Les Pastner, and his campaign slogan was "Les Government Is More." His campaign team, made up of four guys who spent most of their productive life in a fishing shack, went so far as to craft homemade buttons with Les's picture over an eagle and two crisscrossed rifles. At the final count, Les received 97 votes to Kennie's 392. Battle Lake clearly believed that the devil you knew was better than the one you didn't, even if she was nosy and had big hair.

I leaned farther toward the window, pressing my hands into the vinyl siding to keep my body at the correct height. My calves creaked with the extension.

"You know that's not why I came. I'm here about the murder. I'm wondering what I need to know."

The Chief's stern words made my stomach twist. They were talking about Jeff. I stretched my body out as far as it would reach and swiveled my ears forward, until I was all but sitting in the window.

"The only thing you needed to know I already told you. Jeff was in my . . ."

"Harumph." The faux cough from directly over my shoulder startled me right off the wall, and I fell over into the bushes. I glanced up hurriedly to see one of Kennie's neighbors, broom in hand, giving me the "should you really be doing that?" eyebrow lift. A chair screeched inside the house, and I darted away like an antelope.

What sort of person sweeps outside anyhow? How did he know when he was done? Damn neighbor. All the good reasons I had for lurking outside Kennie's door whipped behind me with my hair. It was just as well. Lies only worked if I was caught spying, not spying and running. Running implied a certain level of guilt. That's why I didn't stop at my car and kept cruising through people's yards and down the quiet streets. Logic told me the Chief would have no problem catching me if I was in my car. He had a radio, after all. If he caught me walking the streets, well then, I was just a citizen out on a nice night. I slowed to a stroll and regulated my breathing.

The school park seemed like a good place to stop, so I pulled up on a swing and studied the brick of the Battle Lake Public School, grades K–8. The rumors in town were that Kennie and the Chief were an item, but small-town rumors were notoriously noxious and exaggerated. Their conversation, at least what I had heard of it, had been official: police chief talking to mayor in the wake of a murder. But why had he thought Kennie would know something about the murder? And what was the talk of gambling? And why couldn't I shake the feeling that jealousy had colored the Chief's voice when he asked Kennie about Jeff? And what had Kennie been about to say about Jeff when I had fallen off her stoop? "Jeff was in my past"? "Jeff was in my spinning class"? "Jeff was in my closet right up until I put his mutilated body in the Pl–Sca aisle of the library and isn't that good rich fun"?

Half an hour passed before I ambled back to my car. By the time I returned to the water tower, the Chief's Jeep was gone and Kennie's lights were extinguished. I would get no more information here tonight, but I knew where to go for the real dirt.

EIGHT

ANYONE WHO IS ANYONE knows the best small-town information can be found in a local bar, and the best local bar in the county was Bonnie & Clyde's. Ruby, the bartender and owner, used the four-finger rule when mixing her drinks—four fingers of alcohol with a soda spray for garnish. The pool tables were usually full, the jukebox slammed everything from Joan Jett to Metallica to Shania Twain, and everyone knew not to drink the water or eat the ice. Something about a cistern problem in Clitherall, the tiny town located a bunny jump from Battle Lake.

I had spent quite a few nights at Clyde's, because it was a place where anyone could feel comfortable. People just didn't care here, or they cared too much, but they never ignored you. On a Tuesday night, I didn't expect to see much action. The karaoke machine in the bar across the street had drawn away the big dreamers, which was just fine by me. I was looking for pickled locals, the older the better. I had a hunch baking in my head about the Jorgensen land, and I wanted to knead it a bit.

The bell over the door probably jingled when I walked through, but I couldn't hear it over Patsy Cline lamenting on the jukebox housed in the corner of the massive room. Hal Henricks was swaying next to it, a whiskey Coke more whiskey than pop three-quarters full in his hand and threatening to spill. He had his eyes closed and his mouth open, every other tooth standing proud. "I . . . falllll . . . to pieces!" He was actually doing a pretty good job backing up Patsy. The smell of GPC cigarettes, aged beer, and something that would make good mushroom fodder crept under my pants and stroked my thighs.

My eyes scanned the room, picking up the two epileptic dart machines against the wall, both empty except for plastic bar darts hanging from one. The two pristine pool tables, their surfaces a soft field of white-dotted green, dominated the bar, clearly the ruling gods of this space. In the rear, even more poorly lit section were the tertiary distractions—a foosball table, a Star Trek pinball machine (the genuine Star Trek, with Captain Kirk, Spock, and Dr. Bones lit up in all their campy glory), and a tabletop bowling machine that came with its own sawdust dispenser to make sure the bowling puck didn't get hung up. At intermittent points, the bowling machine would flash the encouraging message "I owe you a pitcher, cowboy!" Tonight, only Captain Kirk, in his tight black Federation pants, paid attention.

The walls were a golden, polished knotty pine, looming around handmade tables and plastic elementary school chairs. The floor had once been high-gloss maple but had since lost its polish, and if you sat in the right spot, you could peek through the floorboards and watch Ruby switching kegs below. The tiny, dimly lit bathrooms in the back had locks that never worked, and those in the know could tell you that Ruby kept the spare toilet paper in the unused wood stove by the foosball table. The majesty of the place was the magnificent bar that ran the length of the left wall. The wood was a soft butter color that the leather bar stools matched.

All in all it was a perfect mix of comfortable and redneck. Tonight the bees on this flower were belly to the bar: Shmitty, Lena, and Ortis. Perfect. They were Bonnie & Clyde's staples. Seeing them outside of the bar in Clitherall would have been like spotting Oscar outside of his garbage can on Sesame Street.

I knew at least Shmitty owned a car, the old blue Chevy Impala out front with the bumper sticker "Charleton Heston Is My President," but I had never actually seen him drive it. Shmitty was one of those grumpy old guys for whom life is terminally unfair, who could have been great if only ever given the opportunity. I suppose if there were a place for career pessimists like him, it would be a bar in a town named Clitherall. He was harmless, though, and always kept the conversation lively.

Lena and Ortis, a married couple who lived in Clitherall, likely walked to and from the bar if they left at all. I had doubts. Rumor had it that they had been champion ballroom dancers back in the day, and they were still in pretty good shape. I would put both of them at around five foot six, 130 pounds, but I hadn't actually seen them off their bar stools, so I couldn't be sure. They wore matching green Clitherall Sportsman's Club jackets and blue jeans with the cuffs rolled up around brown leather work boots. Their short gray hair and round gray eyeglasses made them a matched pair. You could tell them apart because Lena smoked.

I purposely sat five spots down from the three stoolers because I didn't want to seem nosy. I hung out for about four minutes before Ruby acknowledged me. I was pretty sure she liked me as much as anybody, but she was not one to hurry to help.

"Thirsty?" she said without coming to my end of the bar. Ortis looked my direction when Ruby talked and tipped his head when his eyes landed on me.

"I'll take a Diet Coke, no ice." I nodded back at Ortis. He winked.

"How's Mira doing tonight?" he asked.

"I'm fine, Ortis," I said, smiling at Lena. "How're you and Lena doing on this beautiful spring evening?"

"I'd say I can't complain, but you know that'd be a lie, hon," Lena said, chuckling huskily as she tapped her Virginia Slim on the corner of an ashtray the shape and color of a liver. One of Ruby's boys had made it in high school art class a million years ago.

"I hear ya," I said, trading Ruby a dollar for a pop. Her dyed red hair was pulled back in a poufy bun, as always, and I could see a heart embroidered on the hip of her homemade blue jeans. I slid two quarters over the lip of the bar. I knew from experience that the tip would be gone within minutes, but I could never catch Ruby actually taking it. It was a game we played.

"Yah, but dose damn barnstormers are killin' all da good walleye wid der spray, ya bet on it," Shmitty said, apparently picking up the conversation where my entrance had interrupted it.

The more he drank, the more his Norwegian came out. The majority of the older folks in the area had traces of it, left over from their recent Scandinavian ancestors. The accent mostly manifested itself as a sharp, primary "t" where there should be a soft "th," as in "He caught tree fingers in his combine's uptake," or if the "th" was hard or came at the end of a word, it was pronounced as "d," as in "He hadta dial da phone wid his pinkie." Throw in a conversational lilt where random words were drawn out, as in "I shuuurrrhuh know what ya mean," and you had Shmitty after a six-pack. He took a pull on his tap beer and continued.

"Useta be, I put in my boat and get tree, four, five nice fish wid a couple good leeches. Now I sit out der for a day and get nuttin'. It's dose damn barnstormers sprayin' dem potatoes."

"Whaddya think, Mira?" Ortis said, giving me a Lutheran invite to join them. "You think the barnstormers are killin' the fish, or you think old Shmitty forgot where the honey spot is over there on Clitrull Lake?"

I slid over to the empty stool next to Shmitty, smiling at the thick drawl. Even in Ortis's watered-down version, "Clitherall" lost its soft "th" and a syllable. I also smiled at Ortis calling Shmitty "old." None of the people at the bar were under seventy on a good day, Ruby included.

"I think I know just enough about fishing and Shmitty not to get involved in this conversation," I said, enjoying my pop. There were questionable things about Bonnie & Clyde's, but the temperature of the beverages wasn't one of them. They always tasted ice cold and clean.

"What *do* ya know 'bout?" Shmitty asked, obviously not ready to have the subject changed.

"I know there's talk of sacred Indian monuments and burial grounds around here," I said, stabbing into the thick. My heartbeat picked up, and I hoped my question sounded casual.

"Ach. You and da rest of da world know dat," Shmitty said. "I can't hardly turn da plow widout pullin' up a leg bone here, an arm bone der. No herbicide'll take care of dat. You don't farm round here and not know dat."

"Ain't that the truth," Lena said, dragging on her white light. "That curse has hung on this town ever since the battle it was named after."

"You wanna find out about the Indians, you go ask Curtis at the old folks' home in town," Ortis said. "He'll help you."

Ruby, Lena, and Shmitty laughed heartily at that. I smiled, confused. "Curtis?"

"Curtis Poling," Ruby said, not looking at me as she took a draw off her dark drink. "Crazy as a loon, but he's the town memory. He's lived in Battle Lake nearly since it was named, and he knows everyone who's worth knowing. If they don't keep an eye on him at the Sunset, he'll sneak up on the roof with his fishing pole and fish into the sky all livelong day. You want to talk to Curtis, you bring him a fish."

There was another round of laughter at this, and I joined in. I didn't know if they were serious or not, and I didn't want to let on.

Sometime over the course of our conversation, Hal had dismounted the jukebox and sidled up next to me, eyeing the base of my neck with pure blue concentration. "Wanna dance?" he asked, all eighty-plus years of him meaning it.

"No thanks," I said, turning back to Ortis. I wanted to ask what they knew about Jeff, but I had a hard time bringing it up. I couldn't imagine that everyone in the county hadn't heard, but I didn't want their sympathy or questions. "What do you all think of the development on the Jorgensen land?"

Ruby rolled her eyes, and Shmitty set his drink down hard. "I tink dat land was meant to lie fallow, and fallow it should lie!" He picked his drink up again quickly.

Everyone but moon-eyed Hal seemed suddenly off, much like Kennie had at the Turtle Stew last night. Something about my newspaper article or Jeff's return had set this town on its ear. I was starting to wonder what was really under the grass at the Jorgensen land. Maybe it was some sort of mass burial site for a town of serial killers and I was minutes away from being body-snatched for asking too many questions. I quietly clucked my tongue and wiggled my two little toes, my personal defense against evil.

Before I could follow the train any further, the door opened. In walked a group of Battle Lake High graduates from a few years earlier, their acne clearing but their cheeks still pink and tight. They looked around shiftily, too young to be used to getting into bars legally. Ruby shook her head but walked over to the corner of the bar.

"What do you kids want?" she barked. I wasn't sure if she was taking their order or kicking them out. It's hard to tell with Ruby.

"A Coke," one said. Two more nodded in agreement, but the fourth asked for a beer. Ruby got them their order and set it on the corner of the bar. The four paid and set up on the back pool table. Soon the neat click of pool balls meeting created a backbeat, and the jukebox slid out some Kid Rock. The mood in the bar markedly changed, and the older crowd was not going to talk anymore. I slid my empty glass toward Ruby and stood up. Dirt on Kennie and the Chief would have to wait.

"It's been nice talking," I said to no one in particular. Ruby had gone back to studying the muted television mounted on the far wall, and Shmitty was on a new tirade. On my way out the door, I could hear him setting forth on the problems with the metric system as it related to the sizing of Wrangler jeans. Once outside, the cool spring air washed over me but wasn't enough to kick out the bar smell. I could hear laughter and emphatic, off-key singing wafting from the karaoke bar across the street, and I made my lonely way back to my car. I heard the door to Bonnie & Clyde's open and close behind me, and I wondered dimly if Hal was about to officially join my fan club.

"Hey," one of the kids from the bar called over.

I turned and eyed the guy. He was twenty if he was a day, dark hair curling under his Nike cap, brown eyes looking me over foot to head and back again in an involuntary glance, hands shoved into his baggy jeans. I recognized him as Scott Benson, the son of the owner of the local bait shop, Ben's Bait. That made him the closest thing to royalty in this land of fish worship. He was cute, in a little dude sort of way, and he had always been polite when I saw him around.

"Aren't you, um, aren't you the lady who works in the library, the one who wrote the article about that guy that was killed this morning?" he asked.

"I suppose," I said. He called me "lady." That's the kiss of death to any chick nearing thirty. I sucked in my stomach and pushed my shoulders back, trying to look relaxed.

"They know who did it?" he asked.

"Not that I know of," I said brusquely. Since I wasn't really getting any information tonight, I didn't feel like giving any.

He pushed his baseball cap back on his head and then returned it to its starting point. "Me and some guys were partying out at the pit Saturday night," he said. "You know, over on the edge of old lady Jorgensen's land."

I nodded. I didn't know the spot, but I knew the pastime. "Drinking in a Field," one of the favorite sports of high school juniors and seniors and the recently graduated. And creepy older guys looking for young blood.

"We saw that Jeff guy there. He came over and had a beer with us. I recognized him because his picture's all over the football wall at school." He tweaked his cap again. "I got a partial football scholarship to the CC. I pay attention to all the football stuff."

I raised my eyebrows, trying to appear suitably impressed while filing this information. "You sure it was him?"

"Sure. He introduced himself. He was a real nice guy. Said he was meeting somebody and then left when her car pulled up."

"*Her* car?" I spat out before I could catch myself. I could feel my brow wrinkling with tension.

Scott was little more than a boy, but he had grown up in farm country and knew what piles to avoid. "I suppose. Coulda been a sister or something." He shrugged. "It was dark and our tunes were loud. I couldn't hear much of what they were yelling."

I shook my head. "Did he say anything else?" My heart was tripping. Jeff was supposed to be in the Cities Saturday night, and instead he was drinking in a field with boys outside of Battle Lake. And then he was arguing with a woman. I guess there was no question any longer that he was from around here. "What time did all this happen?"

Too late. The smell of my estrogen singeing had turned Scott off this conversation a couple beats back. "Dark, I think. He didn't talk too much. I better go play pool. I bet it's my turn."

Well. Nothing like jealousy to warp the grieving process into something much more manageable.

NINE

I almost had no choice now but to sneak into Jeff's motel room. I had decided to take the long way home from Bonnie & Clyde's, driving past big, strong Chief Wenonga. I was starting to get a thing for him. He was cute, he wouldn't cheat on me, and he couldn't die. I actually considered pulling over to hang out by his feet to clear my head like some sort of groupie for tall, dark, and unattainable men, when I caught the faux-log-cabin Battle Lake Motel out of the corner of my eye. The owners had redone the front in a blonde, Lincoln Log–style siding along all seven rooms. People driving by could see the original green siding on the back and sides of the building, but I wasn't driving by just yet. I knew fate had led me here. The police may already have checked the room, but then again, maybe I was the only one who knew exactly where Jeff had been staying.

I parked my car in the lot for the lake's public access boat landing, just up the road from the motel, and walked back over the crunching gravel. Another car in the motel parking lot probably would not have aroused suspicion, but I knew what I was about to do was illegal, and

I wanted as little evidence of my visit as possible. Some friends and I had snuck into a local church and stole pickles from the basement refrigerator one night once when I was in my early teens, but otherwise I was no criminal.

The motel's seven units were all set out in a strip like a really long trailer. I could hear the lapping of Battle Lake behind me as I neared door number six, and I glanced over at the tall chief, who stood shadowed in the streetlights about a block from the motel. He surveyed the lake impassively. "Watch my back, OK?" I whispered in his direction. I looked back at the door and peered in the window. The cheap canvas shades were drawn, but I could see in the cracks around the edge. The room was dark, of course. I tried the knob. Locked. What had I thought was going to happen? I considered some elaborate lie to get a key from the clerk, but I doubted she would believe that I had left my inhaler under the bed when I stayed in the room last week.

I put my hand on the cool glass and listened to the soft whomping of moths flying into the streetlight. On the right side of my peripheral vision, I thought I saw a hint of a shadow move against the glass of Jeff's room. I jumped back, visions of his zombie body waiting for me pillaging my brain. Why deer stare at the headlights of approaching death was no longer a mystery to me. I couldn't move. I forced myself to take deep breaths and count the passing cars. Safety was close.

A shadow flickered against the glass again, the same time as a soft wind lifted the hair at my neck. It had just been a breeze, and if it had moved the curtains inside, there must be an opening. I slid my fingers across the shiny surface and dug them into the lip of the window, into the hairline crack where it had been left unlocked. The window slid open. Jeff may have moved to the big city, but inside he had still been the boy who grew up in a small town where people left their windows open at night and didn't lock their doors when they went out. I stared at the curtain in front of me, able now to make out the print of flying ducks.

My heart was hammering so loudly it sounded like it was skipping beats. I pushed the curtain aside, the material rough against my fingers, and hauled one leg over the waist-high sill. When no icy hand grabbed my ankle, I did the same with the other leg. I closed the window behind me and made sure the shade was completely shut before I turned on the flashlight I had nabbed from the emergency winter kit in the back of my car.

It didn't look like the police had been here. It didn't look like anyone had been here, actually, including Jeff. The bed was made and the coffee cups on the TV counter were still wrapped in plastic. My heartbeat dropped as I considered the possibility that I had snuck into the wrong room. I flashed my light to the telephone and made out the "Room 6" typed on the calling directions. I was in the right room, but where were Jeff's belongings? I swung my light toward the corner and caught a lumpy shape. I felt the characteristic icy rush of fear. I had found another body. It happened once, it could happen again.

I forced my fear-stiffened legs over and made out a bundle of extra bedding sealed in a plastic bag. The blood moved in my toes again. I unzipped the bag and looked inside, holding the flashlight between my teeth. The television in the room next door came on with a muffle of canned laughter and I squeaked, then felt a wash of relief to be back in the human world. Part of me had expected to find monsters in this room, and nothing dispels monsters more quickly than safe, reassuring television.

I found nothing in the bag of bedding, and nothing in the bathroom, and nothing in the drawers or the cabinets. The room had been completely emptied out, and I wondered again if the police had already visited the room. From my limited knowledge of police business in the case of murders, it seemed to me that if they had been here, they would have put up police tape. Either the police had already been here and found nothing, Jeff had checked out before he died, or whoever killed him had also cleaned out his room. Suddenly, the air felt crackly and I wanted to be anywhere else. I used my shirt to open the door handle, which was foolish considering the amount of time I had already spent in this room with Jeff, and shuffled quickly to my car.

I could hear Jeff's voice, and I was so happy! He really was alive. I went into the next room to tell him about my terrible nightmare, but when I reached the voice, I saw it was my father pretending to be Jeff. As I turned to go, a hand grabbed me. I looked down and saw a bony claw, and I screamed and pulled away. I ran, too afraid to look behind me and see if I was being chased. I ran so fast that I didn't see the dropoff open in front of me, and I slipped over the edge of a cliff and fell, the ground racing to embrace me.

I sat straight up in bed, early morning sun streaming down on me. It had been a while since I had had the chasing dream. Right after the tumult caused by my dad, I had run in my dreams every night. Sometimes I would wake up only to fall asleep and run again. After a while, it didn't happen as much, maybe once a week. The last time I could remember being chased in my sleep was right before I moved to Battle Lake.

I lay in the white wrought iron bed Sunny had left, the blankets tangled around my feet and my hair fuzzy from constant shifting. The house still had the residual odor of all the cigarettes smoked in it in the years Sunny had occupied it. The funny thing about cigarette smoke is that it never goes away, even if the cigarettes do. It transforms itself into a composting, almost fresh question of a smell, but it's always undeniably there.

I had quit smoking myself in the past year, and like all quitters, I couldn't stand the smell of my past mistakes. I had burned incense, sprayed the bizarre magical potion named Febreze, and placed fans in windows, but the smell still hung around like an awkward silence. This morning my mood made the quiet stench a little more aggressive, and it pushed itself up my nose as the "what-cheer, what-cheer, birdie, birdie, birdie" call of the cardinal that I had been feeding knocked at my skull.

For me, birds fell in the same category as snakes—weird, dirty, and to be avoided—yet I fed them obsessively, kind of an offering to the bird kingdom to keep them pacified. If all the birds banded together, humans would be in some kind of trouble, and I wanted to be on the right side of that fight. This respect/disgust relationship I had with birds actually resulted in me being pretty knowledgeable about them. Know thine enemy. I had coaxed some song sparrows, a goldfinch, a couple rose-breasted grosbeaks, and I think maybe even a brilliant orange oriole to the backyard via various birdfeeders, a birdbath, and orange halves nailed to a tree. To the casual observer, be she bird or human, I looked like a supporter.

The bird noises pushed me out of bed well before my alarm went off. I had to go back to work today, I knew, and my stomach was heavy at the thought. I hadn't been back since I found the body yesterday morning. The anger I had felt at the thought of Jeff meeting another woman and the exhilarating fear of breaking into his hotel room had turned to tart depression. Before I learned about his Saturday night rendezvous, his death had been tragic and our love destined. Now, he was just another guy I probably shouldn't have slept with.

But depression, along with most other extreme emotions, spurs me to action, so after a hot shower and a breakfast of vanilla soy milk over 100% Whole Wheat Total, the cereal of the gods, I was ready to figure out what exactly was going on in this town. Where before I was Mira the Stricken Lover in search of answers, I was now Mira the Righteous in search of truth.

The message from Ron Sims, the editor of the *Recall*, that was waiting on my machine when I got home last night had only paved my path. He had asked me to write a full article on Jeff's death for the front page. Now I had a justification to be nosy.

I set out a plan for the day. I would go to work, spray some Lysol to get rid of dead body germs, conduct online searches to find out what it was I had seen on the Jorgensen farm, call Karl at the bank to find out what he knew about the Jorgensen land and consecrated ceremonial grounds, and, at lunch, go fishing with Curtis Poling. Somewhere in there I'd need to track down Gina to find out what she knew about our esteemed mayor and our police chief.

While digging through my disorganized closet, I recognized the need to feel attractive today. There's something about the death of someone you had sex with that makes you feel like you have to prove something. Plus, there was another woman out there I was competing with, even though our prize was dead.

I wasn't much for makeup, because I noticed that women who wear it regularly experience some sort of face drain. This is most obvious when you catch them without their makeup. They look pasty and much like fetal pigs in a way that non-makeup-wearers never look. Makeup is the great body snatcher of our time, some sort of addictive, living substance that preys quietly on the heads of its victims. This is not to say I was above some serious chick-in-an-MTV-video eye work, base, blush, and lipstick on a good night out. But every day? No way.

Since I wasn't changing the face, it had to be all about the clothes. The proper uniform for this battle would involve my faded button-fly size 32 Levi's, which were almost comfortable after a couple hours' wear, a sports bra under a tight white T-shirt to insinuate breasts, and my brown cowboy boots. I was still getting used to the boots. They had looked cool in the store yesterday, but wearing them always seemed like too much of a statement, somewhere between high heels and farm work, and I didn't fit in that spectrum. I topped it off with my raggedy brown suede jacket.

I left my hair as is because I never combed it wet. Tim Veeder, the "new boy" back in my seventh grade, whispered once to me in class that Victoria Principal, star of *Dallas* and the woman he loved, never combed her hair when it was wet. She swore it destroyed the hair's natural state. Since Tim was the boy I was going to marry that month, what with his black Irish good looks and not-from-around-here mysteriousness, I decided it best that I model myself after Victoria Principal to make following fate's plan for us that much easier on him. That single habit was my only carryover from that female-norming period called junior high, thank God.

On the way out the door, I remembered I didn't have any earrings and went into the bedroom to grab my favorite pair of silver Bali hoops. One slid out of my hand and rolled under my bed. I got on my knees and felt around, my fingers quickly running across the cool metal. The hoop caught on something when I pulled it out. Once in the sunlight, I could see it was a notebook. Jeff's field book. I recognized the worn leather cover, and when I held it to my nose, his smell whispered out—laundry soap and cedar. It must have fallen out of his knapsack when he was last here. This was the gold mine I'd been hoping to find in Jeff's motel room the night before.

I paged through the dated notes, stopping at the first mention of Jorgenson. On a page dated April 12, Jeff had written, "abstract, Jorgensens sold the land by U.S. government in 1877, R. B. Hayes, President, and B. L. Lang, Secretary. Land passed through various hands over the years, all of them Jorgensens. It's a gamble." My brain lurched back to Kennie and Gary Wohnt's conversation. "This town isn't ready for gambling," the Chief had said. Had Jeff uncovered a plan by Kennie to bring illegal gambling to Battle Lake? Would that be enough reason for her to murder him?

I paged forward to May Day, the day Jeff and I had met. On the sheet, he had written land measurements and flower names in his chicken scratch, and on the bottom of a page full of scribbles, he wrote "beautiful woman." I smiled in spite of myself, and then stuck my tongue out as I realized maybe I wasn't the woman he was referring to.

The next page had the information I was looking for: "Petroglyphs? Call Trillings v.p." and a phone number. The following page had the words "Interview C. Poling." That was the second time in twenty-four hours I had heard that name. I was more certain than ever that I had to visit the Senior Sunset. The rest of the pages didn't offer up anything beyond doodles and measurements, and a thorough search of the bedroom assured me that Jeff hadn't left anything else. I stashed the important pages in an ornamental tin and then popped the field book into my pocket and the hoops into my ears.

I slid behind the wheel of my Toyota, wet hair stiff from the cool morning air, cheeks baby-naked, and clothes an hour and a half away from being comfortable. When I arrived at the library door, the first thing I noticed was that the police tape was gone. Say what you will, that Gary Wohnt was one efficient cop. I pictured his shiny lips and hair, intimidating bulk stuffed in a uniform, and the overall darkness of his aura. He might have some Native American blood in him by his coloring, but his attitude was all small-town authority. It occurred to me that Wohnt was about the same age as Jeff and had grown up in Battle Lake as well. It might be worth my while to deal with him head on and find out why he thought Jeff had been killed. If nothing else, if he knew it was me spying on Kennie and him last night, I would rather seek him out than have him hunt me down. In my experience, the more aggressive a woman is, the less guilty she seems. Or maybe it's the guiltier an aggressive woman is, the less rational she becomes. That's a hard thing to judge from the inside.

I pulled Jeff's field book out of my back pocket. I opened up the book to the first clean page, pulled out some paper tails stuck in the spiral coil, and wrote "talk to Wohnt" on my to-do list. I was a pretty good multitasker, but the combination of a new relationship and a death had handicapped me. I thought it best to write stuff down. Besides, it made me feel cool, organized, *and* secretive.

The pages I had pulled out verified that Jeff had gone back to look at the carvings. Petroglyphs, he called them. They must have been so important that he contacted a colleague immediately, perhaps a chick like Lara Croft, Tomb Raider, who had met him at the Jorgensen farm that night. That's who Scott the Bait Boy had seen him with.

This colleague corroborated Jeff's findings, probably screwed him in an exotic and mutually satisfying way that a native Minnesotan could only dream about, and then killed him so she would get credit for the find. Or some competing company sent in a female assassin so they could buy the land and its treasure of authentic Indian carvings right out from under Trillings.

Or something like that. I was hoping Curtis Poling could fill in some blanks for me, because I was pretty certain the mound was connected to Jeff's death. I needed to know why it was such a big deal, and the library would provide answers. I just had to figure out how I was going to talk myself into entering the building where I had found Jeff's body twenty-four short hours earlier.

TEN

I HAD MY GHOST-FEELERS out as I approached the front door of the library. Except for the guided tour Mrs. Berns was leading for her fellow old-homies, everything seemed in order for a Wednesday morning.

"And here is where I first heard about the murder," Mrs. Berns creaked as she pointed at the spot on the sidewalk where our paths had crossed about this time yesterday.

"Are milk or rolls included in the cost of the tour, honey?" an old woman in the back of the group asked, her arm raised, revealing dangling, old-lady chicken wings waggling out of her short sleeve. She wore a pink paisley-print dress under a yellowed sweater, an apron, knee socks, and sparkling white tennis shoes.

Mrs. Berns adjusted her sun visor, causing the hand-lettered "Murder Guide" card to fall to the ground. I picked it up and handed it to her. "Good morning, Mrs. Berns."

"When you gonna open the door?" she asked, eyeing the apron-wearer in the back.

"At opening time, Mrs. Berns," I said, tapping my finger on the sign on the other side of the glass. "It shouldn't be more than fifteen minutes."

"Well, I'm going to need you to speed it up," she said, fists on hips. Her liver spots brawled for sun space on the back of each hand.

Normally, I'm a stickler for rules that allow me freedom or control over others, but I was in no hurry to be alone in the library today. "OK, Mrs. Berns, you can all come in now, but you can't check out books until I get the computers up and running, and don't expect to get in early every day."

Mrs. Berns snorted but didn't want to risk losing her in by stating the obvious—crowds weren't a real 911-type problem at the Battle Lake Public Library.

I inserted the key, rolled the lock back on the tumbler, shoved the door open, and paused a moment. I expected there to be a distinct odor fingering my nose, maybe a mausoleum tang, but between the pungent smell of cleaning supplies in front of me and the push of old folks behind me, there wasn't much out of the ordinary I could sense.

I stepped back to let the crowd pass and flicked on the lights. I sucked a deep breath, turned on the computer and printers, and performed assorted library stuff, surprised to find the routine soothing.

Lartel, the head librarian, had hired and trained me in, being the only other employee of the library. He was a tall, thick man with eyes green and busy like bottle flies on the dark meat of his face. In his early forties, Lartel was bald except for one of those weird rings of hair bald men refuse to shave off. It started above one ear and wrapped around his head to directly above his other ear. It was like his head wore a mini mink stole to keep it warm. Despite his build and the constant white noise of his wind pants, he managed to fit into the library environment. He had a strong sense of order and talked only when necessary.

"Unlocked the door?" he asked me on my first day on the job.

"Yup."

"Turned on the computer?"

"Yup."

"Then walk the aisles."

This was his term for "shelf reading"—going up and down the rows, book by book, and making sure no one had defiled the memory of Melvil Dewey by slipping out an H347.23 to glance at the cover and sliding it back into the H347.12 spot. I walked the aisles a lot under Lartel's fleshy gaze, and sometimes, when he wasn't looking, I marched down them like a soldier.

I stumbled through pretty well during my three weeks of training with him. It wasn't that hard to be a librarian's assistant, really. Type an author or title in the computer, and if it comes up, you got it; if it doesn't, you don't. If the book is available, you walk over to the appropriate aisle and hunt till you find it. I had always had a gift for finding things, probably because I was so good at hiding. My favorite part of the job was putting away the books. It had a sensory appeal, the smooth and colorful hardbacks sliding cleanly into place, a little bit of the world falling in order.

I tuned out the chicken chatter of Mrs. Berns's tour as I gathered up the books from the overnight dropoff. The bin had been empty when I left the crime scene yesterday, but it was nearly full today. I suspected the unusual number of returned books was more a product of ambulance chasing than a sudden surge in civic duty. I must have been in a mini-trance, because Mrs. Berns and her group were at the front desk all of a sudden.

"Where's the mess?" Mrs. Berns demanded.

I focused my eyes and grimaced. "It's all cleaned up, Mrs. Berns." Then I paused. "Right?"

"Riiiight," Mrs. Berns said, wagging her head and drawing out the word. "It's all cleaned up and we've wasted our time. I promised a tour, and everyone is terribly disappointed that there is no murder evidence here."

I looked past her blue hair to the group of six waiting behind her. Actually, they all looked pretty pleased just to be in a new building. They also all were starting to look a little birdlike, and I wondered if I was going to have to start putting out old-people feeders to appease them like I was doing with the feathered population. I dismissed the idea as too expensive—bridge mix and date bars didn't come in bulk like thistle seed. So I did the best I could given the circumstances.

"He wasn't shot in the library, Mrs. Berns, so there wasn't really any blood here. But the police did find a bunch of pencils on him, and we're giving them away as souvenirs to our first visitors of the day." I reached below the counter and pulled out the box of omnipresent library mini-pencils. I had always wondered why libraries didn't just buy regular-length pencils that would last longer, but now that I worked at a library, I knew there were some things you didn't question. That's just how it was.

Mrs. Berns eyed the box suspiciously but didn't have any options left if she wanted to keep the crowd happy. She grabbed the container out of my hand, passed it around, and dumped what was left into her purse. "Come on!" she said and marched toward the door.

They were almost all out when a thought occurred to me. "Wait!" I yelled.

The Apron Lady in the back stopped and turned to me, smiling kindly. "Yes, dear, you don't have to yell."

"Sorry," I said, walking over to her. "Do you know Curtis Poling?"

She blushed and looked down at her pristine tennies. "Yes, but you should ask Mrs. Berns about him. They're an item, you know."

87

Super, I thought. Even the octogenarians were getting some around here. "I don't need to know anything personal," I said. "I just wonder if you think he would be around about eleven o'clock today. I wanted to ask him some questions about the town's history. For an article I'm writing."

Apron Lady smiled. "Curtis is always around," she said. "Around lunchtime, he'll be out fishing."

"Thank you," I said. She opened the door and twirled out. I hoped I could still twirl when I was her age. I turned my attention back to the library and realized that I should go check out the place where I had found Jeff's body. I wasn't going to have anything sneak up on me. I strode purposefully toward the aisle and turned to look down it. Nothing but fresh, clean, tight-weave Berber.

Out of curiosity, I went back to the reference section. All the encyclopedias were accounted for and in order, even the *L*. Around the encyclopedias were two unusual displays Lartel had told me were from his own personal collection: on the top shelf, his stuffed fish collection, and on the bottom, his array of Battle Lake High yearbooks, starting in 1953 and going right up to last year. On a hunch, I kneeled down and traced my fingers across the annuals' green faux-leather spines and slipped out the book for 1982, the text of the invitation I had found by Jeff's body imprinted in my mind.

The yearbook's front cover had a red-faced Indian in a headdress, a fighting "whoop" coming out of his mouth. Underneath were etched the words "Battle Lake Battlers Class of 1982." This yearbook was from the self-involved eighties, before racism and violence were recognized as contagious. In recent years, the high school had changed its mascot to the bulldog. It was still mean, but no dogs were going to picket the choice.

I made my way to the seniors' section and marveled at the shiny, feather-haired class of '82. Class song: "Thriller," by Michael Jackson.

Class movie: *Zapped!, Porky's, Gandhi* (three-way tie). Class TV show: *The A-Team*. Sad world deaths: John Belushi, Princess Grace of Monaco, Barney Clark. Class colors: green and silver. Class motto: "Love Lift Us Up Where We Belong."

I flipped past these specs as well as the Best Smile, Best Attitude, Most Likely to Marry a Lawyer, Most Likely to Go to Jail, et cetera, results and went straight to the *W* section, which didn't take long given the meager number of graduates in this small town. Sure enough, Jeff Wilson's picture stared back at me, his hair shaggier and his eyes tighter but his smile still wide and generous. I felt a lurch on my heart and had to sit on my heels. He had been really cute.

I ran my eyes over the picture to Jeff's immediate right and was satisfied to find a replica of Chief Wohnt, then listed as Gary Wohnt, his hair greased back with some sort of shiny, dirt-attracting substance, his acne fierce, and his neck muscles intimidating even in the head shot. I wondered what having a name that is a negative sentence does to a person. Turns one into a cop, apparently.

Kennie Jensen, now Kennie Rogers, was on the preceding page, actually looking beautiful in an early eighties sort of way. She could really pull off that drugstore doll appearance back then, her hair tight and curled, skin firm, blue eyes bright. I could see why Jeff had fallen for her. I glanced at the rest of the senior class, but no one else stuck out.

I closed the book with a muted thump and slid it back in its home, then went out to my car to get the invitation. It must at least be related to Jeff's arrival, if not his death. It was too much of a coincidence that he graduated in the class of 1982 and there was an invitation to a class of '82 party by his dead body. I suppose "class of '82" didn't have to refer to Battle Lake's graduating class of 1982, but there really is a pattern and order to the universe if you look for it. Besides, the invitation was in the class colors, green writing on a silver background.

I traced my fingers over the date: Friday, 15 May. The military format of the date struck me, as did the lack of a year. Of course, since there was a day, it had to be either the day after tomorrow or a Friday, May 15, six years in the past or six years in the future.

I didn't know whether this invitation to a masquerade had fallen out of Jeff's clothes or been intentionally left by his killer, but there was a really good way to narrow the possibilities. I added mask shopping to my notebook list of lunchtime activities.

I returned to the front desk to check my e-mail. The only thing in my inbox was a forwarded e-mail from Gina. Apparently, she had entered her e-mail address when she created my online dating ad, and the cute Moorhead State professor had written to say he enjoyed my ad and would like to meet for coffee, considering he was only a hop, skip, and jump—eighty miles—from Battle Lake. I considered replying to her and telling her to knock it off. Then I considered replying to him and telling him it was a mistake and I wasn't looking to date. In the end, I just deleted it. I had too much on my plate right now.

I spent the next chunk of the morning searching the Internet for "Minnesota Indian carvings." There were 1,470 hits, but through a combination of luck and doggedness I came across one with pictures that matched what I had seen: the Jeffers Petroglyphs. The page was a link off of the Minnesota Historical Society site and informed me that the Jeffers Petroglyphs were over five thousand years old and found among the prairie grasses of southern Minnesota. According to the site, the carvings illustrated holy ceremonies and hunting rituals. The picture on the web page, like the carvings I had seen, was breathtaking in its simplicity and importance. And certainly petroglyphs in west-central Minnesota, hundreds of miles from the Jeffers Petroglyphs, would be something to write about.

It would also be something to immediately call your supervisor about if you were a surveyor for a company interested in building. Jeff had told me that Trillings wouldn't build over Indian artifacts. When he found the petroglyphs, he must have called the company and told them that this spot was a no-go. But then why had Karl told me a rep had called him and said they wanted the land? I wondered how much Jeff really knew about the company he worked for. Apparently they had no compunctions about building on sacred ground or lying to their employees. Maybe they didn't mind murder, either.

I picked up the phone book and dialed First National. "Hello, this is Mira James. Is Karl available?"

"I'll check," came the reply. I waited and was patched through.

"Karl here."

"Karl!" I said, my voice excited at the thought of potentially solving Jeff's murder. I caught myself before I showed my whole hand. "What happens if the Jorgensen land isn't saleable?"

"Why wouldn't it be saleable?" he asked in his typical banker manner.

"I don't know. Say it had historical value and just couldn't be sold."

I could hear him trying to hold back one of his chuckles on the other end. "Mira, all land has historical value, if you look closely enough. You can sell any land you hold the deed to. It's just that whoever buys it may be restricted on what they can do there."

I didn't really feel like being laughed at. I was onto something. "Well, let's say the Jorgensen property doesn't sell for some reason. What happens to it then?"

"First of all, I think it will sell. Like I said, Trillings called the other day and said they want to go ahead with the deal. Second, all land sells, eventually. Since there is no one alive with a claim to it, it's not particularly pressing. However, the bank would like to get the mortgage paid, and soon."

I sighed. "Karl, if there were special Indian things on the land, could Trillings still buy it?"

"Well," he said, and I could hear a squeak as he wheeled his way over to his filing cabinet and a zoom as he opened one of his immaculate drawers and pulled out one of his perpetual files, ". . . yes. But what they could do with it would depend on what those 'things' were. According to . . ." I heard paper flish on the other end. ". . . Minnesota Statute 307.08, if there are human burials, the land can be built on, but the burials cannot be disturbed. Anything short of a burial grounds isn't protected by law and can be treated as the owner or buyer wishes."

The other side of the phone was quiet for a moment. When he spoke, his voice was soft. "What did you find, Mira?"

"I'll tell you when it all makes sense to me, Karl." I still wasn't ready to give up the details. "Just tell, please, if you think Trillings would still buy the land if there was a sacred Indian site on it."

The moment of silence told me he was respectfully considering my question, probably while lining up all his desktop space fillers in perfect soldier rows like he always did when he was thinking hard. "If they're like most big businesses, they'd be delighted to buy it. Wouldn't that be a perfect addition to their Indian theme park? Built on genuine, sacred Indian land."

"I suppose you're right." I was disappointed that I was probably correct about Jeff working for an unethical company, but that didn't mean I was wrong about Jeff being principled. Maybe when he contacted Trillings about the petroglyphs and told them they couldn't build on them, they decided to take him out of the picture. People did crazier things for money, and Jeff had said the Jorgenson land was ideal for what Trillings was after.

I started to put the phone down but pulled it back to my ear quickly. "What was the name of the person you talked to at Trillings?" I asked. "Was it a woman?" If the caller was female, she might be the one Jeff met at the Jorgenson land Saturday night.

"Nope, not a woman. A Tim something or the other. Anything else I can do for you?"

"Just keep being my friend, Karl."

"That I can do."

ELEVEN

THIS DETECTING WASN'T GOING as I had planned. At first, I was certain that Jeff died because someone else wanted credit for the petroglyphs. Next thing I know, Kennie and her gambling ring, which were somehow tied to the class of '82 party, pop up. Then, there seemed to be a good chance Jeff had died because Trillings didn't want the word out about the sacred Indian relics that would keep them from building, but what Karl had said made sense. Why wouldn't they want to buy the land and preserve the parts that were sacred? It fit in perfectly with their theme park idea. And my saner brain convinced me that if Jeff was going to get in the way of the development, it would be easier for Trillings to fire him than kill him. My detecting was currently treading water.

I got out a piece of paper and a pen to map what I knew. My head was just circling things, so I had to pull out those squirming thoughts and nail 'em to the paper. I started three columns. There had to be at least three reasons Jeff had come to Battle Lake, because all things happened in threes. Two I knew. One was the Jorgensen land, and one was probably this class reunion thing. I started flashing lights in dark corners of my head, looking for a third reason. My right hand doodled unsupervised as random thoughts and images flitted through my brain—archaeological tools, peanut butter sandwiches, ice cream, petroglyphs, and buxom, boyfriend-stealing hussies.

I squirreled my eyebrows and looked down at my white sheet of paper with three columns, only two with headings. In the margins I had drawn the soft m shapes of birds flying through puffy clouds over a wavy lake with a broccoli tree on its bank. Same thing I always drew, childlike and soothing. I started to draw wavy bark lines in the tree when I heard a popping flare, the sound of a moist synapse finally firing. Of course. A tree—a family tree. Jeff must have family here if he went to high school here. There was the heading for my third column: "Family Ties."

I looked at the list. One of the three must have killed him, which left me with three leads to follow: a fishing expedition with an old-timer, the velvety invitation crinkling in my back pocket, and a friendly call to some long-lost relatives. I didn't know what I would say to Jeff's family and I couldn't rush to Friday, but I could meet my lunch hour more than halfway. At about ten-thirty, I hung the Out to Lunch sign on the door and headed up the street to the Senior Sunset.

Although my original intent in interviewing Mr. Curtis Poling was to get the scoop on the carvings, I figured I still might learn something by finding out what he knew about the Jorgensen land in general. It felt good to get outside, too. There is so much promise in spring, but you need to be outdoors to taste it.

It was a four-minute walk to the Sunset, but I was in no hurry. I liked my old people free, and I wasn't too psyched to walk into a raisin ranch. I hadn't been in one since eighth grade, when we were required to go as part of our home economics class. We were each assigned a "grandma" or a "grandpa." I lucked out and got a sane one who kept her dentures really clean and could remember my name. Peter Maston was paired with a wrinkled vegetable whose hairs he had to comb, and Carrie Anderson got a genderless person who just whispered "Help" over and over again. For a group of fourteen-year-olds simply trying to figure out our bodies, pass civics class, and not stand out in a crowd, it was scarring.

The Sunset looked OK from the outside, like a one-story apartment building. It had a 1970s feel, low and uninspired, but the grounds were well manicured and there was a small pond to the left of the front door.

As I opened the vacuum-locked door to the Sunset, the thick smell of hospitals, oldness, and cheap pine deodorizer nearly brought me to my knees. The front lobby was the size of large classroom, with a main desk in the center. Various doors and one hallway led off from this central room, all of them painted institutional green and each guarded by a plastic corn plant. I staggered through the odorous sanitation to the front desk and asked if I could see Curtis Poling.

"And your name?" the overweight attendant asked. She opened an appointment book.

"Mira James. I'm here on behalf of the *Battle Lake Recall*," I said, thinking quickly. I'd forgotten that these old people had guards. Who'd want to steal one? "I'm doing an article on the history of the Jorgensen land."

Her penciled eyebrows went up at the mention of the Jorgensen farm (I was still hanging onto the serial-killer/burial-ground theory about the land), but she didn't ask me any more questions. "Sign in here. Curtis's room is 11A, down the main hall on your right."

I shifted the plastic grocery bag I had brought in from my right hand to my left and signed my name and time of arrival. As I walked down the hall, I tried to ignore the moans and yells. This place would make a great haunted house, I thought. My boot heels echoed, and when I peeked in open rooms, they all looked the same: TV set bolted to the ceiling and a hospital bed covered with a thin blanket with a table on one side and the dresser on the other. It was lonely. When I got to 11A, I wasn't surprised to find Curtis's bed empty. If what Apron Lady told me was correct, he would be casting for a big one right about now.

I headed toward the rear and through doors that led to a garden area, grateful to be back in the land of natural warmth and light. Three old ladies were out smoking, one of them Mrs. Berns. They tried to hide their smokes when they heard the door, but nothing happens quickly when you're nearing ninety. I had already passed them by the time they pulled their cigarettes out of their mouths. "Don't worry, I won't tell," I said, floating the words behind me. I actually wished I had some liquor to give them to make it a complete experience. It was too depressing to think of leading a full life only to have all the good stuff taken away when you finally have time to enjoy it.

Once outside, I saw the roof had railings around it and realized there must be a patio area up there. It was a good use of space. I followed the line of the roof and spotted two bare feet dangling over the side, the ankles the only part of the legs visible under blue hospital-issue pants. Between the feet hung a fishing line, bobberless, its hook about twelve inches off the ground. This is what I had come for.

Earlier that morning, acting on Ruby the bartender's tip, I had stopped at the grocery store to check out their fish section. They had a small frozen selection of whole fish, so I picked a meaty-looking one, defrosted it in the microwave in the library's break room, wrapped it in paper towels, and stuck it back in the grocery bag. It smelled ripe when I pulled it out, but it was a welcome offset to the nursing home odor nipping at my ankles.

I wasn't sure about the protocol, if I was supposed to pretend that Curtis had caught the fish himself or let him know I was putting it on. Actually, I wasn't even sure if the crew at Bonnie & Clyde's had been serious about bringing Curtis a fish. I could be unintentionally provoking a mentally unwell man. I opted for subterfuge; it would be easier to run if I hadn't already started a conversation with him. I grabbed Curtis's hook, surprised to find some squirming bait on it. I swallowed hard and wrapped the mouth of the fish around the hook. I pulled down so the barbed end erupted through the lip, making a gristly noise. I gagged, gave the line a couple tugs, and stood back.

"Yoo hoo! Today's a good day for Curtis Poling! I knew if I switched bait that I'd get a bite. C'mon, baby, c'mon!" The voice above me was ecstatic, and the pole waved back and forth, the line going up and down, in and out. If I wasn't standing on land below him, I'd swear Curtis was really catching a big one. In water.

"That does look like a nice catch, Mr. Poling," I called up to the legs.

"Unless you got a net, I got no need for you right now!" the voice called happily. There was a big jerk, which I imagine was Curtis setting the hook. The rest of the reeling was fairly uneventful. When the fish and legs disappeared, I waited.

It was about four minutes before I saw a face appear over the railing above, its teeth gone and its hair not far behind. "Well, I'll be dipped in hot honey," Curtis said, peering down at me. "Who woulda thought? What're *you* catching?"

I pursed my lips. "Panfish, mostly," I said, wondering exactly what they were. I had heard the word used around the social table at the Turtle Stew.

"Well, how deep you fishin'?"

"Pretty shallow."

"Me, I was fishing deep, about a foot off the bottom. Leech for bait. And you know what I caught?" He let out a whoop before he hung my store-bought fish over the side. "A salmon. In Clitrull Lake! Wait'll the guys hear about this!" Curtis danced a little jig.

"Hey, Mr. Poling, could I talk to you?"

He stopped dancing and looked over the ledge, patient exasperation in his eyes. "Well, of course, missy. I've caught my limit. You don't expect me to sit out here and keep fishin', waitin' for the DNR to haul me away, do ya?" He shook his head at me like a father explaining a simple concept to a child. "Meet you by the garden."

I shrugged and walked back to the garden. I was pleased to notice that it was not nearly as far along as mine. In fact, it hadn't even been tilled since last year, and the brownish tendrils of old squash pulled themselves up the skeletons of tomato plants. "Not much to look at, is it?" a voice asked. I turned to see Apron Lady, the one who had come to the library for Mrs. Berns's tour. "We never get it tilled up in time for an early planting. Drives me crazy every year."

I nodded my head, understanding completely her need for order, even in a ten-by-twelve-foot area. Behind Apron Lady stood a shrunken woman, her bearing the human equivalent of a dog perpetually putting its butt out to be sniffed. "I'm Ida," Apron Lady said, and then moved to the side. "And this is Freda. They call us the 'Da' sisters."

I wished I had brought some old-people suet or some such to give them, but I was empty handed. "Nice to meet you both," I said. "My name is Mira, and I'm meeting Curtis out here in a couple minutes. If you don't mind, I'd like to talk to him alone."

They both got a knowing look, obviously thinking they understood more than I knew there was to understand. They backed away, returning to the door to sneak smokes with Mrs. Berns. I took the opportunity to pull out the field book and write "till the garden at the Sunset" on my to-do list.

Curtis came out minutes later, naked except for his blue crinkly pants and white tank top. I assumed by the yelp he got at the door that he had either flexed his sagging muscles or goosed one of the ladies. When Curtis reached my side, he smelled clean and strong, like my grandpa in his Old Spice. I had expected him to smell fishy and sour. He held out a hand. "Curtis Poling. What can I do for you?"

His grip was firm.

"My name is Mira James," I said, "and I'm writing an article for the *Recall*. I was told that you could answer some questions about the history of Battle Lake for me."

Curtis looked at me with clear blue eyes, that startling cerulean shade so vivid those born with it look otherworldly. "I've lived in this town for ninety-three years, most of my life spent as a hired hand. I did construction, farm work. Jack-of-all-trades. You get to know a lot of people and a lot of things when you work that way." His eyes faded a little as he thought to his past. "I'll tell you what I know, but it may not be what you want to hear."

"I can decide that, Mr. Poling. I specifically want to know about the Jorgensen land."

Curtis sucked air in his mouth, an effect made more dramatic by his sporadically intact teeth. "Lots of people want to know about the Jorgensen land lately. Just answered questions for that nice Wilson boy the other day."

A fist punched through my chest and squeezed my heart. "So Jeff *was* here! What'd you tell him?"

"I told him that if you want some psychic unrest, you go to the Jorgensen land. There's Indian burials all round this town, enough to give you bad luck for two lifetimes. But at the Jorgensen farm, you can touch it. Drive a man straight crazy out there. I think Mrs. Jorgensen died just because she couldn't think of no other way to deal with that land. She didn't leave no heirs. You mess with that land, you got the devil to pay. It's bad luck from now until the end of time. That's what I told him, and now I'm tellin' it to you."

I felt a little ill. Curses carried a lot of weight with me due to my generally high paranoia level, and there seemed to be pretty stiff evidence to support this one. Jeff was dead, and not long after having been warned about the land. "Did you tell him anything else, Mr. Poling?"

"What two men talk about may not be any of your business," he said, his loquacity stemmed by the talk of the Jorgensen land. The subject had that effect on people.

"So is the curse why everyone shuts up when I try to talk about the Jorgensen land?"

"You don't call someone's name unless you want them to find you. Same thing with a curse." He signaled to the ladies standing near the door, and Ida ran over with a lit cigarette for him. "People been around long enough know what happened there. So many Jorgensen kids dying of croup, Jorgensen mothers dying in childbirth, Jorgensen fathers dying in freak farming accidents. No one likes to talk about that, or they might bring it on themselves. That's why the land is bare right now. Ella didn't want to pass it on to anybody she loved." He set his shoulders and blew out a perfect smoke ring. "It's no mystery. Just no one around here wanna associate themselves with the Jorgensen land or name, that's all."

I was thinking I might want to be added to that list. "Well, thank you for your time, Mr. Poling," I said. I had heard enough. None of it was particularly enlightening, but all of it was scary. "One more thing. Do you know if Jeff Wilson has any family around here?"

Curtis took a bottomless drag off his cigarette and looked deep into my eyes for the first time. Despite my best intentions, I felt a little sparkle of electricity and thought I might know what the old broads were attracted to. Then I felt my stomach fizzle. I wasn't willing to let teeth become a negotiable requirement in a partner. "He was an only child, and his parents left town about the same time he did. The only family he got around here is his second cousin. You should know him, missy. He's your boss over at the library. Lartel McManus."

TWELVE

I DIDN'T KNOW IF I was more surprised that Curtis Poling knew who I was or that he had just told me my boss was related to my murdered lover. I didn't see the resemblance, as Lartel had struck me as a fairly creepy loner, which suited his job perfectly. I had no idea he had any family, particularly not a dashing young archaeologist cousin. Besides, Lartel was on vacation in Mexico for another week. Another dead end. I sighed. "Well, thank you, Mr. Poling. It's been nice talking to you."

He raised an eyebrow, and for a second I was sure he was going to goose me, too. "You know where to find me."

I nodded and walked off, halfway to the door before I heard him say something so soft I might have imagined it: "Thanks for the fish."

I tipped my head glumly toward the ladies at the door and didn't notice when Ida and Freda followed me. I was almost out the front when Freda tugged at my shirt. I turned to look at her, and she pointed to Ida.

"We overheard your conversation with Curtis," Ida said. "We thought you ought to know that Kennie Rogers was also out here asking questions about the Jorgensen land. She was with Curtis, in his room, for nearly an hour." Ida seemed indignant, obviously thinking Kennie had brought her own brand of tuna to the table.

"When was that?" I asked.

"Saturday sometime, because it was the day Freda and I got our hair set, and we always get it rinsed and set on Saturdays." Freda nodded vigorously in agreement, looking at her shoes. I was thinking that old people in nursing homes made great narcs. If only they could get some sort of network set up, they'd be a secret force to be reckoned with.

"Thanks, Ida," I said sincerely. I scribbled down my phone number on the corner of the sign-in sheet, ignoring the attendant's skimpy-browed glare. "Call me if you think of anything else, OK?"

"OK," Ida said happily, turning with a swish and walking back down the hall. That swish was beginning to grow on me.

As I walked out the door and toward the Village Apothecary, the May sun shining warmly on my head, I struggled to fit all this together. The Jorgensen land was cursed, Jeff was dead, and Kennie was asking questions, hot on Jeff's heels. I didn't know when Jeff had talked to Curtis, but it had to be Saturday because he was with me Friday and hadn't mentioned it then. So Kennie visited shortly thereafter. And she could have been the mystery woman Jeff met Saturday night. Yuck. I didn't want to go there. It was much more palatable imagining Jeff had screwed around on me with a glamorous, big-city type than a former-prom-queen-cum-mayor who couldn't let go of high school.

I walked into the Apothecary, a stock-two-of-everything drugstore, hoping they sold costumes. I was pleased and a little surprised to find a wide selection of masks in the corner. They weren't cartoon-emblazoned kids' masks either, although I was disappointed that I couldn't be Wonder Woman, replete with glittery tiara and bullet-repelling bracelets. Instead I found tasteful Mardi Gras half-masks with embroidering elaborately sewn around the eyeholes, or full masks with Harlequin faces. I picked a full mask because I didn't want to be remotely recognizable and headed up front to pay. "You have a great selection of masks," I said to the teenage cashier. "Why so many?"

"Because we sell lots." She snapped her gum, the unspoken "Duh" hanging between us, looking for a source and a place to land. She had dishwater blonde hair hanging in strings around her face, and her cornflower blue eyes were intolerably bored.

"Don't you think it's weird that you sell lots?" I asked, making my eyes as big as hers.

She looked at me, her face saying, "Don't you think it's weird that you're asking me stupid questions?" She rang up my purchase, and I fought the petty urge to ask for a pack of condoms from behind the counter. It would be a wasted effort at making her feel inferior, because I knew I wasn't going to get laid and she could probably guess. In fact, she was probably having better, more frequent sex then me. I exhaled noisily, took my change and my bag, and trudged back to the library.

The after-lunch crowd was pretty brisk considering that the summer people hadn't arrived in full force yet and the locals didn't normally set much store by recreational reading. As an unfamiliar group of people browsed, I realized I was witnessing a continuation of the library ambulance chasing. There were older men in feed caps, bills perfectly straight, hats barely resting on their heads. A good number of housewife types had also appeared, some brazen enough to bring their children as cover, and even some of the rare breed known as "young male professional" were around. They were considered exotics in this town. All in all it was a full and diverse crowd, everyone drawn by a need to solidify their lives by verifying death.

"Minnesota nice," that uniquely Midwestern quality that keeps natives from confronting anything directly or expressing any emotion deeper than a kind smile, stopped most of the women and younger men from asking me any outright questions, so I appreciated it when two men in feed caps invited me into the local information dance.

"I remember that Jeff Wilson playing football with my son back in the day. Heckuva good ball player, and an even nicer kid," began a man with a brown and used-to-be white Cenex hat, leaning his elbow on my counter. His hands were clean, but I could smell car grease on him.

"Yup," his John Deere friend said. He switched his toothpick from one side of his mouth to the other while he fiddled with the short pencils on my desk. I looked at his yellowed fingernails, each thick enough to unscrew a rusty bolt.

"Damn shame," Cenex continued, "especially in a small town like this. We don't have room for murder."

I wondered how many animals he had killed in the past year. Murder is a sanctioned sport in Otter Tail County. As a meat eater, I appreciated my hypocrisy as well as his. I was having a hard time staying out of the conversation, though. I had learned the unspoken rules of this game from the social table at the Turtle Stew: they were trading me what they knew for what I knew. I just had to pick the right time to jump in, because once I entered, I would stop receiving any information and would have to start supplying.

"Lartel is going to be surprised when he comes back, then," John Deere said.

"Oh ya," Cenex shook his head sadly. "His star player killed in his library."

"What do you mean, 'his' star player?" I was in.

Cenex had the good grace not to acknowledge how little prompting it had taken for me to cash in. He acted like he just noticed I was

106

there. "Lartel was the football coach back in the days Battle Lake was good. They went to state that year with Jeff. 1982. Would have won, too, if Jeff had played. Yup, Lartel stopped coaching that year."

"Hunh," I said, sitting back in my tall chair. Lartel's name sure was coming up a lot today. When I had applied for the library position, he had been the picture of politeness, yet there was something slightly off about him, some smell or color that hinted at food about to go bad. It wasn't his shiny head or his swishy pants, either, though those didn't help.

Come to think of it, those swishy pants were a red flag. Of course he had been a high school sports coach. No other adult male wore swishy pants. Although his demeanor pegged him more as the wrestling coach type, what with the sport's promise of leotards and constant touching, I supposed football would make sense, too.

I realized I wasn't holding up my end of the conversational bargain. "Jeff didn't talk about his football career when I interviewed him." Both men relaxed slightly. "Why didn't he play that last game?"

Cenex sucked something invisible out of his front teeth. "Depends who you ask. Everyone agrees it had something to do with Gary Wohnt, though. He was a good player, but it was hard to tell with Jeff shining so hard. Yup, that Jeff Wilson could play ball."

"Like I said, he didn't mention his ball playing when I interviewed him. He just talked about the Jorgensen land and the theme park they were thinking of building here. We were supposed to meet Monday night so I could, um, interview him some more, but he never showed up. And then I found his body here Tuesday morning."

"That finding a body can be tough," John Deere said, twirling his toothpick with his tongue. He was a regular oral circus attraction. "I found my grandma in her bed when I was about eleven. I can still see her lying there, *Reader's Digest* stuck in her hands . . ."

I would never understand this Norwegian relish for conversation. I knew these men would talk all day about everything and nothing if I encouraged them, and anything up to and including picking my nose would be seen as encouragement. Personally, I'd rather be alone with my thoughts. I mustered my best "sudden library emergency" look, directed it over their shoulders, whispered, "Oh, darn!" under my breath, and excused myself from behind the counter.

I escaped down the nearest aisle, hoping for privacy so I could sort through what I had just heard. Lartel McManus was my boss, and I had learned more about him in the last two hours than I had since I started the job. He was Jeff's cousin. And he had been Jeff's football coach back in the glorious eighties. And he was on vacation in Mexico while his star football player had been murdered, said player's body turning up in the S section of his library. It occurred to me that I had no proof that Lartel had actually gone to Mexico, nothing but his word.

I was thinking it might be time to call Lartel back early. Unfortunately, he had not left an emergency contact number, which I suppose made sense. This was a library in Battle Lake. The closest thing to an emergency here had been years earlier, when the one copy of V. C. Andrews's *Flowers in the Attic* had not been returned, setting the waiting list back weeks.

"Excuse me," a voice behind me said.

I turned to see one of the semi-suited young men I had noticed before. "What?" I said.

"I was wondering if I could check this out." He held a large paperback toward me.

"You can have it," I said. I walked away from him and down to the next aisle so I could do some more thinking.

"Really?" he said, following me into the next aisle. "I'll need to get a library card first."

I wanted to assemble this new information, and I was irritated at his interruption. I put my fists on my hips and stared at the poor man while I tapped my foot impatiently.

The man looked at the paperback in his hands and back at me. "Um, I'm not from around here. I just moved to town and was hoping I could get a library card and check out a book or two on my lunch hour so I'd have something to do tonight. Are you the librarian?"

I rolled my eyes and snatched the book from his hand, walking toward the counter. "Of course I'm the librarian. I'll need two forms of picture ID." I hoped I turned fast enough that he couldn't see me blush. I was pretty sure I had a special kind of Tourette's that made me be rude to perfectly nice people when I was on a mental bender and then rendered me incapable of apologizing. It was a tough cross to bear.

I was happy to see the front area empty. John Deere and Cenex had moved on to greater distractions. I stepped behind the desk, punched the enter key on the library computer's keyboard, and then looked at the screen, expecting to see the flashing sign-in prompt. Instead, a note had been taped there, an ominous message written in large, slanting pencil:

STOP SNOOPING. UR GOING TO FIND
THE SAME TROUBLE AS WILSON.

I read it twice. I was pretty sure it was a threat, but my skin was crawling so loudly that it was hard for me to concentrate. I sat down hard on my chair and tried to make some spit.

"Are you all right? Ma'am, are you all right?"

I turned my head to the noise and found myself looking at the young professional. He had called me "ma'am," which was way worse than being called "lady." I had never been called "ma'am" before, and short of finding myself at a point in my life where my boobs brushed my knees and you could see my pink scalp like some cloud-covered ant farm through my thinning white hair, I thought it was completely uncalled for.

"You know what, I'm not all right. I just got laid right for the first time in my life by a guy who could actually converse and was sensitive, and the next thing I know, he's dead. And now I have a threatening letter on my computer. And the icing on this cake is that you just called me 'ma'am.' So no, I'm pretty far north of all right."

He looked at me like I was something itchy he had found in his pants. I stood up on my chair and cupped my fingers around my mouth. I figured it was time to take the bull by the horns before I started yelling at kids and pulling hair. "Library closed! Everyone out!" I was not discouraged by the surprised glances. "Out! Out! We will reopen at the same time tomorrow." Still nobody moved. "OK, people, I didn't want to have to tell you this, but there is going to be a private viewing for the deceased this afternoon, and we need to start setting up. Come back tomorrow."

This drew understanding nods, even from the out-of-towner I had just verbally accosted. These people understood funerals. Anybody who chose to live in a place where the wind chill could reach sixty degrees below zero without causing a hitch in the daily giddy-up respected the great circle of life. Plus, funerals were another opportunity to talk about other people, or nothing.

As the crowd filed past me, I studied them for beady weasel eyes. I was sure anyone who made death threats must have clear and shifty animal features, but no such luck. For the most part, the looks I got were reassuring or sympathetic, all the eyes clear blue or brown.

When they were all gone, I locked the door and went back to the note. I imagined the police could have it fingerprinted, but I didn't think they really did that stuff around here, and if they did, it would take a really long time. Besides, at this point I had suspicions about Chief Wohnt since discovering he had known Jeff pretty well back in high school.

I ripped the note off the screen and looked at it closely. Nothing telltale except the cutesy "UR" in place of "you are." Stuff like that bugged me. If you're going to threaten someone's life, you should probably take the extra twenty seconds to spell out all the words. Jesus.

All this was really starting to get my goat. I had felt I was to blame for Jeff's death. The article I wrote came out the day before I found his body, and I was worried that somehow the article had killed him. At first, it scared me. Now I was getting pissed. Wasn't it enough that the murderer had taken away the one man I was starting to trust, not to mention the only decent recreation I'd had in longer than I cared to remember? Now they were threatening me directly.

I folded the note and tucked it in my pocket. It took me about fifteen minutes to close the library up, and then I headed to the liquor store. I found myself with a case of Rolling Rock in my hands, knocking on Gina's door with my foot. It was midafternoon. If she had worked the early shift, she would be home.

"Christ, Mira, I was wondering when you were gonna stop by!" She pulled me in and locked the door behind me.

I flopped on her couch and reached for the open beer she handed me. "You heard?"

"I heard about Jeff's death yesterday on my lunch break. I didn't hear about you snaking him first until I was almost done with my shift."

I grimaced. "What is up with this town?"

"It's the seven degrees of sexual separation, Mir. You live in Otter Tail County long enough to get laid by a native, and I can guarantee you're no more than seven degrees from having slept with everyone in the county. A new member in the club is a big deal. Word's gonna spread." She shrugged her shoulders and chuckled, taking a pull off her beer.

I shuddered. That meant I was likely only one degree from having slept with Kennie Rogers, and that slippery slope could lead anywhere. "What do I do, Gina?"

"About what?"

I filled her in, beginning with the first meeting with Jeff, our excellent sex, the article I wrote, him standing me up, Kennie's weird treatment of me at the café, Karl telling me who Jeff really was, finding Jeff's body, finding the invitation and checking it out in the yearbook, the interview with Curtis, finding out about Lartel's connections, and finally the note on the computer today. It was a great relief to say it all out loud at once. The only detail I left out was about the petroglyphs I had found. I still felt protective of that information for a reason I didn't know.

"Hoe-lee shit," Gina said.

"I know." And suddenly, I was crying so hard I was hiccupping. Since finding Jeff's body, I had made a point of being busy to the point of crazy, but talking about it with another person, and one who cared about me, was too much.

Gina rushed over to the couch and put her arms around me. "It's not your fault, Mir. None of it is."

"But the article came out the day before I found his body, and . . . and . . ."

"And nothing. No one even reads that rag, and for sure they don't kill over it. Jeff had something going on that you didn't even know about."

I tried to wipe the hot tears from my face but managed only to blend them with the snot gushing from my nose. "Yeah, he had lots I didn't know about going on," I said darkly.

Gina pulled back a little but kept her arm around me. "You tell him about your dad?"

"No."

"Then you've got no right to be upset at him for not telling you about growing up in Battle Lake. He used to date Kennie Rogers, for chrissake. That's worse than being Manslaughter Mark's daughter any day of the week."

I sniffled and laughed a little.

"Here, have another beer." She handed me my third, along with a box of Kleenex from off the coffee table. "You know, I've heard about those class of '82 parties. I don't think it's a reunion thing."

I blew my nose hard. "What is it, then?"

"I don't really know. People never answer you when you ask them straight on. I think it's one of those direct sales things, like Tupperware or lingerie parties in your home. Better bring some extra cash."

"I don't think I'll be buying anything. I just want to check it out. Why would there be an invitation to the party right by where I found Jeff's body?"

"Who knows? Why do I have the body of Nell Carter when I have the personality of Cameron Diaz?" Gina laughed her throaty, contagious laugh, and I felt myself loosening up.

"You know," I said, "beer can be so delicious. It makes me want to smoke cigarettes again."

"But don't," Gina said, firing up a Marlboro Light 100. "If I could quit, I'd never start again. By the way, what're you doing for lunch tomorrow?"

"Nothing. Wanna meet?"

Instead of answering me, she charged me with another question. "So what was Jeff like in bed?"

My hiccups were gone, and the beer was lubricating my joints and my tongue. "Mmm, you know how he's an archaeologist?"

Gina nodded, leaning forward.

"Well, let's just say he knew how to use his digging tools, and he was definitely into finding value in things discarded by past civilizations." We both laughed at this until tears came out of our eyes. Gina knew the story of my first boyfriend, a clitoriphobic bass player in some lame garage band based in the Cities. I should have known better when he told me their name was Ancient Chinese Penis. I misread his quietness for intelligence and confidence, and we were together for four months. I pretended that it was OK that he thought foreplay was rubbing an erection against my leg, and he pretended that he had a personality. It was enough that we were both not lonely for a while, and then I moved on. It was that being-happier-with-my-own-thoughts thing.

By the time Gina's husband, Leif, got home, we were both completely in the bag and playing the "Would You Sleep with . . ." game. He offered me a ride home, but I chose the couch instead. I didn't want to be at the mercy of someone else's wheels the next day, even though I knew her husband to be a reliable man. I woke up before sunrise, a bad habit I'd developed this past week, and drove home to shower and change. My head was only slightly throbby, and I shoved aside my guilt about getting drunk.

The Thursday morning library crowd was a lot more reasonable than the Wednesday afternoon one had been, and some of those who showed up even dropped off memorial cards in the basket at the front counter that held slips of scratch paper. I had forgotten about the "viewing." I was reaching for the phone when it rang. It was Ron Sims, the *Battle Lake Recall*'s editor, desktop publisher, only full-time reporter, photographer, and salesman, and I hadn't called him back after he had left a message telling me to come up with an article on Jeff's murder.

"Mira." Ron wasn't one for small talk. "I got good news. We've had a staff illness, so I have some extra work for you." The only other people besides Ron on staff were me and Betty Orrinson, who wrote the "Tittle-Tattler" and "Hometown Recipes" columns. If you wanted to know who had dined with whom and whose relatives were visiting from where and what to cook them, you read her stuff. She apparently had a good following and actually had to turn down tidbits and recipes from readers on a regular basis.

"Betty's sick?"

"Sick of writing the recipes. She says there's nothing new out there. The job's yours. I need one recipe a week, starting tomorrow, and make it original with a Battle Lake feel. Questions?"

Only a hundred. "What do you mean by a 'Battle Lake feel'? Where do I get the recipes? How long do they have to be?"

"You'll figure it out. I'll be in the office all day today. Get me a recipe before lunchtime." Click.

Ron had come at me so quick that I'd forgotten to tell him I was working on the Jeff article. This recipe mandate was Battle Lake's version of cutting-edge, push-the-deadline journalism; I would have complained if Ron hadn't hung up on me.

Instead, I plopped myself in front of my computer, fired up Word, and made a sign advertising a contest for "Homegrown Minnesota Recipes. Winners will be published." I printed the sign and stuck it on the other side of my counter, where it would stay, at least until Lartel returned. I folded another sheet of paper in half and stapled the edges, making a pocket for people to slip their recipes into. I visualized it full and plump.

Being a realist, I also went online and punched "Minnesota recipes" into a search engine. A lot of wild rice and game recipes, along with carb-heavy hotdishes, popped up, but none of them spoke to me like the recipe for "Phony Abalone." Some clever woman had discovered that if you marinate chicken breasts in a bottle of clam juice overnight, wake them up and pound them between wax paper, roll them in flour, corn flakes, and egg, and cover them in tartar sauce, they taste just like fish. To me, this had a Battle Lake feel. I especially loved the phrase "Fool your friends and family!" at the top of the recipe. I retyped it and e-mailed it to Ron.

Then, I returned to what I had been doing when he called. It took me twelve minutes of wait time to track down the Fergus Falls coroner. When she got on the phone, I explained who I was and that I was writing an article on Jeff Wilson's death for the *Battle Lake Recall*. She placed Jeff's time of death at sometime Sunday evening. She said his corpse had been in surprisingly good shape but that there wasn't enough fluid to do a toxicology report. She told me that's common in a shooting. Something about the heart pumping after the person is dead.

The strange thing is I didn't feel anything when she told me all of this. I filed it away with the rest of the information, knowing that I was going to have to schedule a full-blown nervous breakdown in the near future. For now, there was too much work to do.

After I hung up the phone, I tried to chase down more information about building on sacred Indian land. I had no reason to doubt Karl, but it would be my name on the *Recall* article I was working on, and I wasn't in the habit of using secondary information. After some Internet searching, I found out Minnesota had a state archaeologist, and I tracked down his e-mail address. I wanted to know what the rules were. I was pleased with the quick reply but disappointed to find what Karl had told me corroborated:

M—

Non-burial archaeological sites (incl. petroglyphs), and non-burial-related archaeological artifacts are private property if they occur on private property. There are no restraints on sale/use/etc. of such property/sites/artifacts by property owner. E-mail with any more qs.

MD

So it was true. The petroglyphs wouldn't slow Trillings down. On a hunch I decided to see if the company had a website. I clicked on the blank bar at the top of my computer screen and was about to type in the address for my favorite search engine when my eyes caught on the word *Trillings* in the list of addresses that dropped down. I knew I hadn't typed it in before. I opened up the whole list and didn't see anything else familiar—just some doll sites, a couple links to state casino home pages, and the URL for WebPALS. I clicked on the Trillings address and looked over their bland home page, trying to figure out what Lartel had been looking for. It had to be him who had gone to the site before. He and I were the only ones who used this computer.

After finding nothing of note on the page, I opened up the field book and jotted down a contact number for the company, which was located in Pennsylvania. I didn't know what I was going to do with that number, but it seemed like a good thing to have. I imagined they would begin building soon. Jeff had said he was going to give them a report on Saturday, and Karl said they had called him Monday to say that they wanted the land, so that seemed like a done deal.

I was so caught up in researching that when the tall, salt-and-pepper-haired man with deep brown eyes stood at my counter, it took me ten beats to notice him and another ten to figure out who he was.

"Mira?"

"Yes, I'm Mira." My heart was beating fast and deep, like a techno beat in a smoky club. I wasn't just playing dumb.

He held out his hand. "I'm Jake. We were supposed to meet for lunch?"

Gina. The big, hairy hagasaurus had e-mailed the Moorhead State professor with an online ad and set up a lunch date for us, and here he was, squiring me at the Battle Lake Public Library. That's why Gina had asked me if I was free for lunch today. I thought quickly. "Sure. Right. I have some things to shut down. Can I meet you at the Turtle Stew, the diner right on the corner?"

"Absolutely." His smile revealed an underbite that hadn't been apparent in his online picture, and his hands were small and soft, the hands of an academic. He was cute, but the last thing I wanted to do was date someone. Apparently that hadn't been of concern to Gina. I told myself she must have set this up before she knew about Jeff and me, but that didn't make me dread it any less. I abhor small talk, and the thought of mining someone for compatibility instead of responding to the natural thrust of chemistry was repellent, particularly in the wake of my most recent lover's death. Sigh. But this wasn't the professor's fault, and I didn't need to make this any harder on him.

I put up the Out to Lunch sign and pouted all the way to the Stew. When I got there, Professor Jake was waiting, his bark-brown eyes eager as a puppy's. He was around six foot one and wore a suit, vest, and button-down-collar shirt, and his hair was close trimmed and neat.

"I hope this booth is OK."

"It's fine," I said, in what I hoped was a magnanimous voice. I took the menu out of the waitress's hand and scanned it for the quickest items. "I only have a short lunch break today. So sorry. How was your drive?"

"Fine, thank you." He had a soft accent, maybe Mississippi. "What's good?"

"I always get soup and a sandwich," I lied.

"Deal." He closed his menu and ordered for both of us. Lunch was quick and not memorable. He was pleasant and attentive, asking me about my cat and my friends and college. Actually, he was remarkably easy to talk to for a man, but I found myself spending most of forty-five minutes counting the ways he was not Jeff, and the rest of the time counting the number of times he mentioned his mother. Eleven. I wondered from a distance how odd that was. I could go whole months without mentioning my mother to another living person, and here this environmental sciences professor had mentioned his eleven times.

"I really enjoyed our lunch. Can I see you again?" he asked politely when he paid the bill.

"Sure. E-mail me." I stepped back from what was looking like an attempted cheek kiss, scurried out the door, and cursed my weakness. I couldn't turn him down to his face. I didn't look behind me until I got to the library, and by then Professor Jake was gone.

My lunch date, by making me miss Jeff even more, only gave me one more reason to solve his murder in record time. Someone was going to pay for his death, and I had to find out who. The rest of the day I actually spent doing library-related duties. They say that idle hands are the devil's minions, but for me it's the opposite. When my hands are busy with mentally untasking duties, my mind plays. That's what I blamed for the plan to case Lartel's house—working and a bad date. If I had been doing anything else, I never would have come up with something so asinine.

Lartel was caught up in all this somehow. He was related to Jeff, he had been Jeff's coach in high school, and he had been researching Jeff's employer shortly before the murder. If nothing else, Lartel would be the easiest to eliminate as a suspect. I just needed to verify that he wasn't in Battle Lake at the time of the murder and only pretending to be in Mexico. A quick peek into his windows would tell me that. If I couldn't get enough proof that Lartel wasn't involved by spying from the outside, the way I figured it, I had done a pretty good job getting into the Battle Lake Motel. How hard would a house be? Most people around here didn't lock their doors anyhow.

THIRTEEN

As I DROVE UNDER the cover of night to Lartel's house, I marveled at how much television had prepared me for life. A *Charlie's Angels* fan from the word go, I had seen every episode at least twice, sometimes three times thanks to Nickelodeon reruns. I was a fan of Sabrina, of course. She had the name and the smarts and didn't have to do all that ridiculous fawning over the men, as her hair was short and her boobs small. Sabrina used the downtime to figure things out and get the real work done. She taught a whole legion of underdeveloped and underpopular girls how to lie, spy, and detect.

And I had been a willing pupil, as evidenced by my about-to-be second break-in in three nights. Tonight I was wearing a black turtle-neck and black jeans, dark hair pulled back, flashlight strapped onto a makeshift utility belt next to my spider knife. The spider knife was a purchase I'd made a few years back at Midwest Mountaineering in the Cities before a solo road trip to Colorado. I figured a woman needed protection, and it felt cool to whip open the three-inch blade with a flick of my thumb.

I had spent the first night of the road trip alone in my tent tossing the opened knife from one hand to the other just like bad guys in old cops-and-robbers movies, trying to look menacing. Apparently I was doing one thing too many because I fumbled the knife early on. It nicked the edge of my shin and started a solid bleeding bout. Since that time, I just relied on the knowledge that my secret inner superhero would know exactly how to use the knife should the need arise.

Lartel's house was about ten miles north of Battle Lake off of County Road 78, sandwiched somewhere between Ottertail and Blanche lakes. The night was beautiful and clear, the air crisp with the sweet threat of a winter past. The stars seemed low and bright, like they always do in the spring, and the lazy off-season traffic allowed me to take a couple wrong turns before I happened upon the black mailbox with the name McManus etched onto a plain signboard swinging below.

I killed my lights (Sabrina would be proud) and rolled in stealthily. I felt the excited vibration brought on by elective fear. Lartel's driveway was relatively short for a country home in this area—no more than three-quarters of a mile—hedged by oak trees on each side. I saw the glowing yard light as I neared the house, but I couldn't make out the house itself until I turned the last bend in the driveway.

The outside of the residence was pretty much as I had envisioned it, except for the alabaster Doberman pinscher statues on each side of his front door. I figured he would be more of a frolicking-lawn-trolls kind of guy, but this wasn't the first time he'd surprised me this week. The house itself was painted a pristine white, with green trim on the windows and matching green shingles—a standard country home. I guessed that the bottom floor had about three main rooms, all small, one bathroom, and limited closet space and that the upstairs had three main rooms, all with low ceilings that slanted in on the sides.

I followed the driveway to the back of the house and was pleased to find that there was a little turnaround where I could leave my car. I knew I wouldn't be visible from the road even in front of the house, but I didn't want to take any chances. When I got out of the car, the thick buzzing of frogs surprised me. There must have been a slough or swamp nearby. I put one hand on my knife and the other on my flashlight for reassurance and took a deep breath of the untainted air.

The sound of my feet chewing the gravel brought on a wave of reality. If Lartel was in his house, or if there was evidence of him having been in his house recently, he was either weird enough to lie about going on vacation or a murderer, and I would be dragging my clumsy fly body right into his web. Knife or no, I was just a librarian in black clothes with a big attitude. Before common sense could get the better of me, my brain flashed me a picture of my unremarkable lunch with the droning professor and then kindly supplied previews of hundreds of lame dates with faceless men lining my future. I had a strong feeling Jeff had been my one chance at happiness, and I wasn't going to take his death lying down. My vision narrowed, and I concentrated on my mission.

I swiveled my head and counted the outbuildings. This had been a farmhouse once, but the barn and silo had long been removed, leaving two smooth cement surfaces, one rectangular and one round. Two sheds, both painted white and green to match the house, stood on each side of the cement slabs. There was no garage.

I walked toward the house on the balls of my feet, noticing that the cement path that led to the door didn't have a single dandelion poking up through it. The grass was trimmed perfectly on each side and up to the house. I hadn't even mowed mine yet, and here Lartel's looked like a golf course green. I first peeked in the back windows, the play of light and shadow making it hard to see anything beyond the kitchen I was looking at. The table I could make out in the center of the room appeared spotless.

As I crept toward the side windows, I heard a twig crack in the woods a hundred or so yards behind me, and every other one of my senses melted away as I froze and tuned in to that one sound, waiting for the second snap that would indicate deliberate movement. My hair was the first thing to acknowledge fear, followed by my body and soul. My physical focus became superhuman at the cost of my mental ability. I looked at my car, closer to me than the woods, and then I peeked at the white and green house alongside me. The dwelling suddenly seemed malevolent and cocky. "Don't run," my brain whispered in my ear. Or maybe it was the house talking. I waited for more input, but none came. No more sound broke from the woods, and as my peripheral sense returned, I once again registered the noise of cars on the tar miles away and the melody of frogs and crickets. My breathing slowed. I walked the remaining sides of Lartel's house and saw no sign of recent inhabitance. I had to go in.

When I returned to Lartel's back door, I looked for the telltale faux key rock. He had one "hidden" at the library, so I figured he would have one by his house also. Sure enough, the big, exotic-looking lava rock was behind one of the two bushes guarding the rear door, a bright silver key clipped neatly into its underside. I unlocked the door and returned the key; I wanted to be primed for a quick, undetected getaway should it be necessary. My short hairs were telling me it would be, and adrenaline rushed into my fingers.

It was thrilling to enter his house, the same way it is thrilling to be kissed when you have to pee really bad. It was the same combination of excitement and restraint, and it made my breath come shallowly. It was a bright night, but I kept the flashlight on and took in the perfectly ordered kitchen. There were no just-washed glasses or plates in the dish-drying rack, and a glance into the fridge showed condiments lined up like lockstep soldiers but nothing with an expiration date. The room had the faint but reassuring smell of Lysol and sugar cookies, and I wondered if I'd prematurely judged Lartel.

Maybe he wasn't hiding anything and really had just gone on vacation coincidentally at the same time his second cousin was coming to town, and maybe he had been looking Trillings up online for some completely unrelated reason. He could very well just be a quirky bachelor, reliving his glory days in his head while he freaked out the younger generation. Of course, that would make me the freak for breaking into his house. Better I find something incriminating.

I glanced around the shadowed kitchen with its white ruffled curtains and blue-and-white-trimmed cupboards and was relieved to see that there was no basement door. Old Minnesota farmhouses often had root cellars, but you usually had to go outside to access them. And a basement would have been just too creepy. If I stayed in the main part of the house, I could pretend I was on an adventure, secret spy chick for a night. If there was a basement, I would have to consider that I might be in a *Friday the 13th* movie.

I walked into the room off the kitchen, disregarding what looked like a pantry. I wanted to see pictures of Jeff and Lartel together, and I wanted information on what sort of terms they had parted on. If I was lucky, I could also find some dirt on Chief Gary Wohnt. I figured any guy who had a yearbook section in his library must have a decent-sized scrapbook or two in his house.

With that in mind, I cruised through the living room that went off one door of the kitchen and made only a peripheral inspection of the dining room at the front of the house. Both were immaculate and spartan, like the kitchen, the only decoration a multitude of live plants in all sizes and shapes. The lack of TV on this floor was the only thing that stood out. I admired Lartel's housekeeping. My mom always taught me to clean my house when I went away because the only thing worse than coming home after a vacation was coming home to a dirty house after a vacation.

The stairs led off the dining room and were breakneck steep, so I had to make an effort not to bump my knees on each riser as I ascended. The creak of the third stair started my heart yammering. I really wasn't supposed to be here, and even an empty house carries the energy of the people who've occupied it. It's a scary thing to amble through, and years of media conditioning were screaming that something was going to jump out and grab me.

I slid my spider knife from my belt and held the reassuring weight in my hand. When I got to the thirteenth step, I felt a whisper at my neck. It was that essence that had turned me off of Lartel since the first day I met him, and if it was a smell or sound, it was just below my radar. Maybe it was only that I was on the second floor now, and getting away would be harder. Or maybe it was because the second floor is always the personal floor, and I finally felt like I was trespassing. Whatever the reason, I felt my nipples get hard in a bad way, and I had to fight the urge not to turn tail and run. For a moment, my breath came fast and loud enough that it echoed in the stairwell, the sound of two animals hunting each other.

When I planted my foot on the top step, I saw that I had guessed right about the layout of the house—there were three rooms up here. The one to the left looked like a bedroom, the one straight ahead looked like a den, and the one to the right had a closed door. Outside shadows from the trees played across the floors and walls, making it difficult to focus on the solid details of the house.

I forced myself into Lartel's bedroom directly off the landing and clicked my eyes at the ruffled bed buried under dolls. My head turned farther to the right, and I saw a doorless closet full of dresses, all swimming in moonlight. I had a moment of vertigo as I tried to remember where I was. I looked behind me and saw the stairs I had just come up, the corner of the reassuringly masculine wood dining room table visible from my perch. I shuffled my feet toward the bed and touched one of the dolls. They were all alike, all of them cheap little Ben Franklin dolls decorated by the same kind of ladies who baked fruitcake and had knickknack shelves.

I willed myself to relax and move on. Obviously this wasn't Lartel's bedroom, so I had no reason to look further in here. He must have a niece or some other relative who visited him regularly. Maybe he had a lover who had her own room in his house. I shook off the sweet-sick feeling and headed into the next room. It was a sparse den dominated by a computer and a couch. It occurred to me that I hadn't seen any bookshelves yet. A librarian without books in his home would be a strange creature.

There was one room left in the house, and I knew it was the room I had come to see. It must be Lartel's bedroom, and I was sure that I would find the box I was looking for under his bed or in his closet, or maybe there would be a whole shelf of clues. I returned my spider knife to my belt and shined the flashlight on the doorknob, an old-fashioned glass knob with ornate clusters of flowers etched in metal around it. Protruding from the keyhole was a highly wrought skeleton key, which I grasped and turned. I took a breath and pushed, ready to use my flashlight as a weapon if need be.

I expected the door to creak like the stairs, but I wasn't surprised when it didn't. Everything about this house called out high maintenance and cleanliness. When I stepped in the room, I was confused by the sudden darkness around my flashlight. A black shade had been pulled over the one window, and no moon or starlight shone in. This was good, because it also meant no flashlight leaked out. I closed the door behind me and panned the room with my beam. A bile of pure horror rose in my throat as my eyes processed the spotlit vignette.

The room was a shrine to the past, but not the sort I had expected. The same dolls I had seen in the bedroom took up all available shelf and floor space, but in here they had a purpose. It was a tiny city populated by cheap, soft-bodied Shirley Temple wanna-bes. Every doll had an activity, and all were dressed for it.

Near the door was an open-air café featuring a waitress doll complete with apron and customer dolls talking and eating. One even had her head thrown back in an eerie imitation of laughter. Under the covered window was a dance club full of suggestively dressed dolls cutting a rug, drinking, or just being wallflowers. To my left was a baby doll beauty pageant, and it looked like they were currently judging the swimsuit competition. To my right was a strip club diorama set inside a glittery cardboard box with "Gentleman's Club" written across the front with a Sharpie. Inside was a walkway with tiny metal poles that looked like they were made out of knitting needles. Dolls in bikinis straddled the shiny metal, and I marveled at the intricacy of the tables in front of the stage, little martini glasses and ashtrays glued to most of them. There were even stamp-sized posters on the wall of the strip club.

In the center of the room stood a miniature football field with white chalk lines traced across the green felt surface every ten centimeters or so. This was the only tableau with men in it, and there were only two of them: the first was a Ken doll standing tall in the center of the field, a baseball cap on his head and a coach's whistle around his neck. He held the hand of a much shorter generic female doll in a cheerleader's uniform. They both stood over the second male, an unidentified brand of doll lying on his back with one of his legs bent under and back, wearing a football uniform with the number 17 on it. At least I think that's what number it was—it was hard to tell with the red paint splattered all over the front.

I was willing to bet my safe bed—the very bed I wished I was in now—that Jeff had been number 17 in high school. I felt narrow sheets of ice slip between my skin and muscles as I stared around the small room, beyond the doll fantasy world clamoring for my attention.

Where the wall showed through, I could see picture on top of picture of a woman who looked very familiar. It took me two blinks to realize they were all pictures of Kennie Rogers back when she was Kennie Jensen. She looked exactly the same as she had in the yearbook, perfect doll face and perfect doll hair. Some were publicity posters from her Miss Teen Minnesota and homecoming queen days, but most were obviously taken without her knowledge. A whole series on the far wall featured her and a man who looked like a young Jeff, though it was hard to tell because he was in the shadows of any photo he was in.

My stomach was in my throat and my ass was out the door. *Charlie's Angels* had *not* prepared me for this. I took the stairs three at a time, which is never a good idea in an old house. I clipped my head on the overhang from the landing and found myself flat on my back on the nubby carpet of the dining room. The carpeting scratched at me, and I could feel cold cement under it. I heard the sound of thousands of mouse feet scurrying toward me and away from me as I stared at the smooth ceiling above, immobilized by fear and pain. I forced my body up, dazed, and ran through murky grayness, only to realize I had imagined my escape. The floor was still holding me. Blind, clawing hands pulled me down, and I couldn't get a scream past the dark closing in. I thought I heard a creak at the top of the stairs, but it could have been the sound of the sealed door of my hysteria opening.

I thrashed at the paralysis tying me to the floor and pictured myself standing again, and again, until finally a scream broke free of my mouth and I was on my feet and running for real. And of course there's nothing like running to make a person feel like they're being chased, so I ran even faster, my only thought getting to my car safely.

I flew into my Toyota and locked every door hard before I turned the engine, refusing to look at the house. I was sure I would see dolls in the upstairs window beckoning for me to come back and play, their smiles serene and their waves beauty-queen perfect. The feeling that I was being watched was tangible, ghost hands stroking my neck and laughing at me.

I peeled out of Lartel's driveway and drove so fast down the gravel that I didn't need lights until I got back on County Road 78 and saw the normal traffic whizzing by. My hands were still shaking, and needles of nausea pricked my body. I felt my utility belt and was relieved to see that I had the flashlight and the knife. All I needed now was a really hot shower in a really safe place. I guess I now knew why Lartel made my skin crawl. And unless he had a room in one of the sheds, that first bedroom filled with dresses and ruffled bedding was where he slept.

My boss was a creepy, cross-dressing, doll-loving, Kennie-obsessed, superclean freak of nature. And it was looking more like he was also a murderer. Good Christ. This is what desolate, solitary winters do to a person. There was only one place I could go to cleanse myself.

FOURTEEN

Bonnie & Clyde's was jumping. Thursday night is close to the weekend for a reason, was the saying. At least that's what they were saying at the bar. I needed a crowd of people around me, so this was ideal. I wanted a vodka cranberry, but that meant that I would have to swallow some Clitherall ice, and besides, Ruby would probably have to go to the store to get the cranberry juice. I settled for a shot of tequila and a beer and leaned against the bar, wondering if people could tell where I had been. Something as dramatic as Lartel's little doll shop of horrors should leave a mark.

"Hey, girl, drinking two days in a row! Welcome home!" Gina was loud enough to be heard from ten feet away, but nobody turned to look. Yelling was expected here. She pushed her ample girth through the crowd, her platinum hair glowing in the smoky light.

"Gina! Come with me," I said urgently and pulled her toward the back.

"Hey, hey, heeeyyy now! Where's a hi?" slurred a voice next to me.

"Hi, Hal." I waited until we were in the relatively quiet recreation area, then told Gina what I had done. Spock looked down at me sagely from the back of the pinball machine as I filled her in. "I swear, Gina, it was the creepiest thing you've ever seen. Dolls everywhere, and they were *doing* stuff. I think I even saw a doll massage parlor in the corner of the room."

Gina's eyes were perfectly round. "Jesus H. Christ. You know, there's been stories about Lartel, but he mostly keeps to himself." She smacked my arm. "I can't believe you snuck into his house! If you do that again, I'm going to fucking kick your ass."

"I didn't even tell you the worst part. There was a doll dressed up like a football coach, holding the hand of a cheerleader doll, standing over a murdered football player doll. Lartel used to coach Jeff in football in high school, and Karl told me Kennie used to be a cheerleader. What does all this mean?"

"I think it means he's a freak," Gina said. "And I'm a nurse, so that's a medical diagnosis. Shit. He must have had something going on for Kennie back in the day. Were there any recent pictures of her?"

"None."

"He must have coveted her pants right off." Gina did a full body shudder like only wet dogs usually do. "You know who you should talk to is Bev Taylor. She works mornings at Ben's Bait, and she used to be a cheerleader in the eighties. She for sure knows Kennie, and there's no love lost between those two, so she could fill you in on all the dirt from back then."

I was beginning to calm down, soothed by the safety of numbers. Lartel's house started to feel like something I had imagined, light years away from the sounds of beer mugs clinking on tabletops, pool balls clacking together, and raucous bar laughter. "I wouldn't mind making some sense of this."

Gina nodded understandingly. "So you're pretty sure Lartel had something to do with Jeff's death?"

"I don't know. His voodoo room is the definition of suspicious, but I don't know how he could have, unless he came back from Mexico, killed his cousin, and then ran back to the beach."

"Maybe he never went."

I looked at her, but she was leering off in the distance, her eyes bouncing off her husband to the back end of the man he was talking to. "Do you see that tight ass on Tony? Too bad he still wears acid-washed jeans."

"Do you think Lartel is still around, Gina?"

"I was just kidding, Mir. I'm sure Lartel went to Mexico. Why would he lie about that?"

"So he'd have an alibi while he killed Jeff."

"How could he know Jeff was coming? Nobody knew."

"But Lartel was family. Jeff might have told his family. For all I know, he's the reason Jeff came to town. He had been looking up some info on Trillings online."

"Maybe," Gina said doubtfully. "But Lartel has been planning this trip for months. That's why they hired you, you know. It's the first vacation he's taken since he started at the library. Besides, why would he want to kill his own cousin? Playing with dolls doesn't make him a murderer."

"I don't know, Gina. Obviously he's unstable, and he's got a thing for Kennie. Maybe his perpetual jealousy finally snapped. Or maybe he is holding a grudge because Jeff wouldn't play in the last football game at state."

"A high school football game is not a reason to kill, Mira. Tony's ass, on the other hand . . ." A smile played at the corner of her mouth.

I rolled my eyes. Gina had expended all of her available serious attention.

"Hey, Gina, you're up!"

"Oops, back to darts. You wanna play?"

"No thanks. I think I'll go home, take a shower with some steel wool and lye, and get some rest. I suddenly feel very exhausted."

Gina gave me an impulsive hug. "Promise me you won't go back to Lartel's house. And you know, you should probably tell the police what you know."

"Yeah, probably." I gave her a wan smile. For all I knew, Gary Wohnt had made the death threat against me. I was going to lie low until I had something more substantial, something that I could take to the real police.

"Bye, chickie!" Gina started to wander back into the writhing mass of beer-greased hormones, but I remembered something important and pulled her back.

"Not so fast, chickie." I looked her in the eyes, and hers were blood-shot. "Don't you want to know how my date with the Moorhead prof went?"

She didn't even have the grace to act sheepish. "I know he wants *more head.*" She put her hand over her mouth and giggled.

"I think he'd have to ask his mother first. Do you know he mentioned her eleven times over lunch? *And* he talked about the diet he was on? What sort of man diets? He was not right."

"Hmm. You're so judgmental, Mira. Most people wouldn't even notice that stuff. He's a college professor, for gawd's sake, and it's not good for you to wallow in depression. Anyhow, you'll have a chance to let him down easy over lunch on Saturday. He'll pick you up at work at noon." She winked at me, and as she walked away, she said over her shoulder, "He really likes you, Mir. You should see the e-mails he sent. You must remind him of his mother."

I imagine she was cackling, but I couldn't hear her over the bar din. I thought about navigating through the crowd to pull her hair, but I suppose this was my instant karma. I should have told Professor Jake that he wasn't my type when I had the chance, and that would have been that. I pulled out Jeff's field book and put "dump professor" on my Saturday to-do list.

I bought a bottle of vodka on my way out.

"Hello?" I had the cordless phone in my hand before I was fully awake. There was no immediate answer on the other end, and I felt a surreal jolt as I tried to place myself. For a second I thought I was still jammed to the thinly carpeted floor in Lartel's house, struggling to pull myself upright. The obnoxious sound of birds singing, coupled with the squeaky springs of my bed, assured me that I was safe in Sunny's doublewide. "Hello, hello, hello!" I said. I hate crank phone calls and usually just say my one hello and wait. It always throws freaks off. Their kick is altering the norm, so if you do it first, they have nothing left.

"You *are* still answering the phone, eh Mira?"

I sat back on the pillows. "Hi, Ron," I said, recognizing the voice of the *Battle Lake Recall*'s editor in chief.

"Hello, Mira! So how about it? 'Murder in the Midwest'? 'Former Star Battler Loses the Big Game'?"

"Hunh?" I looked at the digital clock next to my bed. It wasn't even six a.m.

"Your article! What are you going to call your article on the Wilson murder? It's a scoop, you know. I have papers as far away as Duluth asking me what I know, asking to run whatever story we write."

I ran my fingers through my hair until I got to the snarls. I must have tossed and turned all night. "I'm working on it, Ron. I've got some leads I'm following up on."

"I have to have something by tonight for the Monday paper, Mira. We need to get something in the paper, some details. What luck, that you interviewed him before he died, and then his body turned up at your work! What luck!"

I scowled. "With luck like that, I should stay in bed most days, Ron. I'll have something for you by tomorrow, 'kay?"

"OK," Ron said, "but no later than tomorrow. I'm saving half the front page. And get me another recipe. That phony abalone was delicious!"

I hung up without a goodbye. Ron wasn't much for small talk and neither was I, which suited our relationship but didn't really help us as reporters. Fortunately, the *Recall* was just a small paper. I thought about the article I was working on appearing in newspapers around the state. It didn't excite me. At this point I needed to find out what happened for peace of mind.

I stretched and heaved myself out of bed. I hadn't actually taken a shower last night because Lartel's dolly land had rattled me enough that I didn't want to be naked for a while. I still felt that way this morning, so in lieu of a shower I splashed water on my face and pulled my hair up and back in a ponytail bun. I darted a toothbrush over my teeth, dabbed some sandalwood oil in my armpits, got dressed, grabbed a banana, and was out the door.

I was in my car before I remembered that I hadn't filled the bird feeders since last weekend, and here it was Friday. Now was not the time to let the bird kingdom turn against me. I walked back to the feeders, the frost-tipped grass crunching under my feet. I could actually see my breath this morning.

My poor garden. I had gambled that there wouldn't be another freeze until fall, and I had lost. Tonight I would have to do some serious green nurturing.

Once in back of the house, I took the brick off the garbage can that held the feed and seed mix and hoisted the bag up to fill the feeders. I envisioned the birds watching me in the trees, *Godfather*-style, shaking their heads.

Back at my car, I had to use the side of my hand to scrape the rime off the window. I had an ice scraper in the back somewhere, but I was not going to use it out of principle. It was not unheard of for there to be a last frost or two in May, even snow in June, but I wasn't going to legitimize it with an ice scraper.

My radio turned over with my engine and startled me. I must have left it cranked when I shut the car off last night, and now Robert Plant was trying to convince me that he really did have a whole lotta love. I believed him, but I wasn't in the mood. I clicked the radio off and headed out the driveway. I was actually just being proactive, as my radio has a tendency to pick up screeching static pockets on cold mornings, usually just as I envision myself slinking to the beat in a cat suit through an admiring crowd. I cranked the heat, putting the still-icy hand I used to scrape the windows in front of the registers.

It was early enough that I hoped I could catch Bev Taylor at Ben's before she got busy. It was still a week shy of fishing opener, so the bait business would be pretty slow, but Ben's rented videos and sold newspapers, tourist trap toys, T-shirts, souvenirs, and fishing and hunting gear, so they appealed to a diverse crowd. The danger of coming here over my lunch break was that the front would be lined up with old-timers or part-timers telling stories, and I didn't want an audience for my questioning.

Fortunately, the only car in the parking lot when I got there was a battered Chevy pickup, the rust accenting the original green paint surprisingly evenly. I assumed this was Bev's truck. I pulled my old Toyota in next to it, thinking the two vehicles would have a lot to talk about if they could get past the language barrier.

The bell tinkled merrily as I entered, and the unique and inviting smell of bait welcomed me. Fish stink; bait smells like a warm, clean aquarium. It's one of the mysteries of Minnesota. I walked straight over to the bait tanks and peered at the wriggling sacrifices. The little minnows were my favorite. I couldn't look at them without feeling a tickling flutter in my hand. Holding a minnow is like holding a butterfly with the lease to its life. I strolled to the end of the bait tanks, the denizens getting progressively larger until the bait began to look like keepers to me. I should have come here for Curtis Poling's fish.

I always wondered what people caught with the big shiners. I looked around at the mounted fish lining the store, the muskies snapping their razor teeth into perpetuity, the walleye so big they looked like googly-orbed sea monsters, and even some sunnies that seemed ready to explode with their own superfish girth. I had never seen fish this big actually caught, so I preferred to view them as illusions to titillate the tourists, similar to the jackalopes at Wall Drug in South Dakota or the uni-goat at the Renaissance Festival. These glandular mounted fish, I surmised, were just the biggest bait in the store, set up to catch vacationers.

A short, solid woman in her late thirties with black hair cropped close to her ears, thick glasses, and a questioning smile came up from the back room. "Can I help you?"

If this was Bev, I bet she was always at the bottom of the cheerleading pyramids. They always stuck the chick with glasses at the bottom. "Are you Bev?"

"Ah-hunh. What can I do for you?"

I considered asking her what she thought of the name Norman's Baits for a bait shop, but sometimes my humor only served to make people uncomfortable, which was the opposite of what I was after. "My friend Gina Sorensen said I should talk to you. I'm looking for some information on Kennie Rogers." I figured I'd start out small.

Bev dragged a stool underneath her, plopped herself on it, and put her elbows on the cracked glass of the counter. She rested her chins in her hands and looked at me eagerly. "What do you want to know?"

I could tell this woman and I were going to get along just fine. "I'm not sure exactly. I'm doing a story on Jeff Wilson, and I know he and Kennie dated back in the day. I also know that he had some conflicts with Gary Wohnt and his coach back then, Lartel McManus. And people say Kennie and Gary are 'together' now. I just don't know any details or how to piece it all together."

Bev played with the masking tape holding one of the bigger counter cracks together and studied the reels in the case below her. They needed dusting. I could see a smile push at the corners of her mouth, and I knew she had been waiting a long time for someone to ask her this. She was going to tell it right. A waxworm peeked at me out of its sawdust container by the cash register and then tucked its shiny slug body back under. I looked away and pretended not to be nauseated.

"Where to start?" Bev asked the waxworms rhetorically. "Well, Kennie was a royal bitch. She had that perfect blond curled hair, perfect teeth, perfect blue eyes, perfect little body. That was fine—she couldn't help what she was born with. She just let it go to her head, is all. First day of cheerleading practice, she told all the big girls that they best get used to being on their knees."

Mmm-hmm, I said to myself. Big girls with glasses on the bottom. This is why I had avoided cheerleading in high school. I was never overweight, but I was never particularly popular either, and five pounds one way or the other could make or break you if you were in the fringe crowd. No reason to exploit myself even further by putting on a short skirt, tight sweater, and fake smile once a week. Part of me always bought into the myth of the cheerleader mystique, though. Thank God I could hide it under my natural sarcasm.

"But that was a long time ago," Bev said, as if reading my mind. "I try not to hold grudges. Jeff, on the other hand, was the nicest guy in the world. I don't know what he ever saw in her beyond her good looks. I think he saw a potential in her, some real person under all the makeup and hair, and figured he could help her. They just kind of fell in together when they were freshman and stayed together after that. It made sense, what with him becoming a star football player and her being the beauty queen."

"Did she really do all that beauty pageant stuff?" I was grotesquely fascinated.

"You know it. Her mom carted her off to all the local contests. She had a regular makeup chest that she carried everywhere, and I hear she got real good at twirling a baton." Bev let out a raucous laugh. "She did pretty well, too. Got as far as Miss Teen Minnesota the year before we graduated."

"Did Kennie have any other admirers?" I asked, thinking of Lartel.

"Just every guy in school and most of the gals as well. Gary had a real thing for her, though, moping around after her, sending her 'secret' love notes."

"Gary Wohnt?"

"But Gary 'Will' for Kennie," she said, laughing again. "That's what we always used to say."

"So Gary and Jeff were rivals?"

"That's just it. Jeff was too nice a guy for that. He always bent over backward to be nice to Gary, inviting him out and to parties or whatever. Shit, he even bowed out of the last high school football game of his life so Gary would have a chance to shine."

"That's why Jeff didn't play for the state title in '82? Because he wanted Gary to have a chance to play?"

"Gary would have played regardless. He was a real good running back, it's just you couldn't tell with Jeff doing everything better than right. Jeff knew he already had a full ride to college, he knew it was just a high school football game, so he pretended he was sick so Gary would have a chance to shine out of his shadow." Bev tapped the side of the waxworm container and Sleepyhead, or it could have been Sleepybutt, looked out at her again. "Everyone knew he wasn't sick, though. Everyone knew why he did it. McManus was furious."

Ick. Hearing that name made me feel like I had just found a blond hair in the last bite of my supper. Make that a yellow toenail. With a piece of Band-Aid stuck to it. "So Lartel and Jeff weren't real close at the end?"

Bev looked at me. "How much do you know about Lartel McManus?"

"I know he was Jeff's second cousin and football coach, and I know he is one weird dude."

"You don't know the half of it," she said. "He's related to Jeff, and really wasn't much older than us back when he was coaching. He was our math teacher, too. He was hell on wheels as a coach, and I saw it when we would practice our cheers while the players were practicing. We used to call him 'Lartel McMeanest.' He just couldn't control his temper, or his eyes." She paused for dramatic effect.

"He had a wandering eye?"

"I wouldn't say it wandered. It always landed pretty good on Kennie. After that last football game, he just lost it. They didn't win, of course, not without Jeff. Lartel was furious and rode home alone. He stopped coaching and teaching end of that year. The official word was that he quit, but everyone knew he was let go. We just didn't know why. It had something to do with Kennie and Jeff, though. Jeff moved away right after graduation, and Kennie stayed behind. She was supposed to go with him, to some cosmetology school out East, but she never went. She started hanging out with Lartel, of all the people in the world."

"Kennie and Lartel?" I was incredulous. I had never once seen them together.

"Oh, that was a long time ago. Then something must have happened, because Lartel just dropped out of sight. No one saw him for over a decade. He showed up about five years ago and started work at the library. Him and Kennie don't interact that I can see. He doesn't interact with much of anyone, and if you have kids, you tell them to avoid Lartel McManus like the boogeyman."

Sound advice, I thought. "So would any one of those three have a reason to kill Jeff?"

Bev sucked on her teeth. "Killing I don't know about. This was just high school stuff. Who hangs on to high school stuff that long?"

The doorbells jingled behind me, and in strode a gruff-looking man. "Hey, Bev. How much for some large leeches?" Apparently he was used to interrupting women, because he didn't even acknowledge my presence.

"Same as it was last weekend, Mike," Bev said, laughing flirtatiously. "We don't got no leech sales going on."

Mike winked. "A man's got to be ready. Why don't you give me one large."

Bev turned to the fridge and pulled out a see-through plastic container, the kind Chinese restaurants use for carryout soup. It was full of leeches dancing their worm dance, struggling over each other's bodies to get to the top, just to end up on the bottom again. Ah, the life of the leech. There could be something philosophical about it if they weren't so damn repulsive.

The worst part was that during walleye season, you could find a container in most fridges around here. If you were at a friend's house and they offered you a beer, you let them get it or risked seeing black bloodsuckers squirming next to the margarine and eggs or, worse, next to the thawing hamburger.

Mike and Bev were chatting it up, so I walked over to the candy. Ben's Bait is a treasure chest of unique candy. My favorite was the Lemonheads. I sucked the gritty, sour yellow coating off and spit out the tasteless white ball in the center. I grabbed two boxes of those and one bag of old-fashioned Tart-n-Tinys. When I got back to the front, Mike was on his way out.

"If you hear any new gossip, Bev," I said, lining up my purchases on the counter, "can you give me a call over at the library? Otherwise, you can call me at home. I'm staying at Sunny Waters's farm, and I haven't changed her phone number."

"I thought I recognized you," she said. "Yeah, I can call. Don't quit your day job, though. This town has gotten pretty quiet since the murder. Don't anyone want to believe it was one of us."

I nodded and slid her some cash. "Thanks for your time. Say, did you get *Snatch* in yet?" I asked, eyeing the racks of videos.

"Nope, one of the Christianson boys took it out and hasn't returned it. I need to give him a call. We're going to have to order another copy if we don't get it back soon."

"Have a good day, then," I said, sliding into my best Minnesota accent. On the way out the door, I popped a Lemonhead in my mouth. If I just pierced the coating with the tip of my eyetooth, I could ration the sour bursts for nearly ten minutes.

"Hey, Bev," I said, turning as I remembered one last question. "What number was on Jeff's football jersey?"

"That I can't tell ya. If you stop over at the high school, though, it'd be easy enough to find out. They have his jersey framed in glass in the trophy case up front. You can see a bunch of pictures of the team, too, if you're interested."

The sun was shining down on my car when I got outside, and I smelled a loud hint of summer despite the late frost this morning. It was going to be a warm day, warm enough to start my farmer's tan if

I had lunch outside. I felt pretty good as I drove the half mile to the library. Some pieces had fallen into place, and everything I knew was pointing at the class of '82. This party tonight was going to be very illuminating.

I pulled into the library parking lot, ready to devote my day to the reading arts and starting the article on Jeff. I had some backed-up paperwork and shelving that needed my attention. Plus, the library needed cleaning and the plants needed watering. Lartel had a thing for plants, as I had seen at his house, and he especially liked the high-maintenance ones that needed regular attention. I didn't mind watering them.

I unlocked the door and strode straight to the windows, pulling up the shades with a zip. I returned to the door and flipped the sign to Open. I walked toward the computer and nearly tripped over a doll on the floor. I shook my head. The magazine inserts were bad enough, but now kids were leaving their dolls. I picked it up and turned it over, then dropped it like a burning book. It was the cheerleader doll from Lartel's dark room, her expression bland and her hair impeccable. I backed up to a wall and surveyed the library. I couldn't see down any of the book rows, and the back room was dark.

I could smell my sandalwood-laced sweat, and one word raced through my head: *Lartel*.

When the library door donged open, I squealed like a pig. Kennie Rogers strode in and chuckled. "Did I catch y'all playin' with dolls?" She walked over and took the cheerleader from the floor. "Well, isn't that the sweetest thing. Y'all takin' up arts and crafts? These ain't easy to sew, these little outfits. I am plum impressed with you, Mira." She laughed again. The good-looking get a lot of slack in our society, and though Kennie's looks had faded, the air of privilege they had given her had not.

I was sure my eyes looked like two fried eggs, sunny-side up, and my back was still pressed against the wall. "Some kid left it." I willed myself to relax, which at this point consisted of breathing again and releasing the wall from the vise grip my ass had on it.

It didn't matter, because Kennie didn't seem to be paying attention. She sauntered behind the front counter and flipped the computer on. "Whoo, y'all got a bad smell gone worse down here. You might want to empty your garbage."

She walked back around to the front of the counter, halfway between the children's area and me. She stretched dramatically, her arms reaching toward the ceiling and her back to me. I eyed the wolf's head airbrushed on the back of her denim jacket. Her wide behind was stuffed into Chic jeans, which were in turn stuffed into fringed white ankle boots covered in faux-southwestern metal studs. It reminded me of a cascading pork sausage in tight casing, and when she turned around, I was sure the front of her jeans would display a perfect camel-toe. I returned my eyes to shoulder level before I was called upon to verify that.

"I used to work here, you know, Mira. Used to be the head librarian back about a coon's age. That was before y'all came to town, even before Lartel came back. Of course, I've moved on to bigger and better things." She turned back to face me with a dramatic flip to her hair. "I will just be skinned alive, Mira, you look like you seen a ghost! You keep starin' at me like that, I'm inclined to get the wrong message from y'all."

I closed my mouth with a snap and went behind the counter to put some physical space between Kennie and myself. I set the doll on the counter. "You know anything about these dolls, Kennie?"

She strolled back to the counter like the aged beauty queen she was. "I know you can buy 'em at the five and dime. A kid's toy." Her eyes glittered at me.

"I suppose. I'll put it in the lost and found." I feigned nonchalance and tossed the girl-Chuckie into the cardboard box overflowing with widowed mittens and ratty hats. "What can I do for you, anyhow?"

"Not much, honey chile. I heard Lartel may be comin' back early is all, and I wanted to welcome him home."

My blood turned cold like leech water, and I swallowed some of my own bile. Liquid burp, we used to call them in my partying days. "When did you hear that?"

Kennie smiled and shrugged her shoulders innocently, looking for all the world like Little Orphan Annie would if she had grown up in a luxury trailer park and dyed her hair platinum. I could tell she was playing with me, but I didn't know the game. "Coulda been today, coulda been yesterday."

I was feeling cornered, and the metamorphosis into bitchy Incredible Hulk began. "Well, you know what I heard, Kennie? I heard that you and Lartel used to date. I heard that after Jeff dumped you back in high school, you went straight into the arms of the coach and stayed there. Then he left town, too, just like all your boyfriends, and next anybody sees of him, he's a crazy librarian. So maybe if we're going to talk about what we heard, we should talk about that."

Kennie's color drained from her skin, making her peach-toned foundation and deep red blusher stand out like clown's makeup. "Or maybe," she purred, "we could talk about how you screwed Jeff his first night in town, you little slut."

Shit. I was way out of my league here. I consciously relaxed my body language and changed my voice to what I hoped was a soothing tone. "I can't help what you heard, Kennie."

"Hmm. Does that mean you also can't help what I heard about a Mr. Mark James, suicidal murderer and your dear, departed father?"

There is a space, after the click of the camera and before the flash dissipates, when every sight, sound, and smell is suspended. I now found myself in that space, but there was no relief coming. Mark James. Manslaughter Mark. My father. The spring of my sixteenth year, he fell asleep at the wheel driving home from grocery shopping and veered into another car. He killed himself and the driver of the other car, along with her infant son, in the head-on collision. His body had been mangled beyond identification; the autopsy revealed that he had been driving very, very drunk.

The accident happened on Highway 23, the main road through Paynesville, and it was weeks before the black tire marks and sparkling windshield glass completely disappeared from the shoulder. Shortly after, the driving instructor at the high school landed the now-mangled car my dad had been driving, our '73 Chevy Cordova, and installed it in the shop as a warning of what happens when people drive drunk.

My mom and I really didn't talk about it much. We didn't talk much, period. The overriding emotion I remember from that time is relief that school was almost out for the summer so I wouldn't have to face my classmates. The irony was that after the accident, I no longer had a face in Paynesville. I became the countenance of a series of unfortunate events instead of a person. And now, I was at risk of that happening to me in Battle Lake. I didn't want to be erased again.

"Is it true? Are you the daughter of a killer? Maybe the apple doesn't fall far from the tree."

"Fuck you, Kennie." There was no strength in my words. I was suddenly bone tired. "It's none of your business. And it really doesn't matter anymore. My dad is dead. Jeff is dead."

"Maybe your dad is dead, little Mira the Murderer's Daughter. Or maybe he's like Elvis, and he faked his death. Could be he killed Jeff to protect his virginal daughter?"

Kennie was way out there, talking crazy, but like a child in a tantrum, she was oblivious to the pain she was inflicting. She tried to stare me down, alpha female to alpha female. "Did you sleep with him? Did you and Jeff sleep together?"

I shook my head and turned my face to the front door, using the time away from her stare to put my dad back in his cage. His life and death were not going to follow me to Battle Lake. It was bad enough they had chased me out of Paynesville. My voice came out neutral, that icy quiet of bridled fury. "All I care about now is finding out who killed Jeff. If you have any information on that, then we can talk." I forced myself to pick up the returned books and walk past her. I swear she had to stop herself from sniffing my butt and growling. I started to put the books away, making surreptitious glances down each aisle as I passed it, on the alert for a sinister doll-leaver.

Kennie stood up at the front with her back to me for the whole time I put books away. I took advantage of her presence to make a quick run through the back room. All clear. Kennie and I were the only two people in the library. I returned to the front counter, bracing myself for more venom, and picked up on the bad smell Kennie had caught earlier. I turned to her, ready to defend myself. To my surprise, Kennie looked like she had been crying, her face even puffier than normal, her eyes rimmed in crimson. Maybe she was just trying not to sneeze.

"I loved that boy, you know," she said softly, her southern accent rubbed out. "I was going to marry him, have his kids, settle down to a nice life in Battle Lake after college. That one night with Lartel was a mistake. I was just a girl, really, trying to get back at my boyfriend for letting me down in the big game, but Jeff caught us and turned Lartel in. It's bad form for coaches to sleep with cheerleaders. Jeff left for college shortly after. He never returned one phone call, not one letter. When I heard he was back in town, it was my happiest day since high school."

She wiped at her eyes and looked at me. "You don't care. You didn't even know him. I'll give you a little bit of advice, though." She leaned toward me, her eyes bright but her mouth slack. "I'd steer clear of Lartel if I were you. Just ask your friend Karl at the bank about him. Lartel has a 'special' relationship with Karl." She turned abruptly and walked out of the library, her shoulders and head so straight I could have balanced a book on her.

I watched her walk out, surprised to feel sorry for her. That woman was one emotional roller coaster. "That's what you get for living in the past," I said to no one in particular.

I sighed and checked out the garbage. There was a whole but unidentifiable fish in the bottom of the canister, happily decomposing. The doll-leaver was apparently into creating a multisensory fear experience. I pulled the bag out and looked up pensively as the door chimed again.

In walked Mrs. Berns. "Whew, girl, that smells worser than week-old garbage! What do you have in that bag?"

"Somebody left a dead fish as a prank, Mrs. Berns." I tied a knot in the top of the bag and held it at arm's length.

"You know what'll get rid of that smell? A bag of shit. Works every time." Mrs. Berns cackled and walked to the magazine rack.

I smiled shakily at the back of her head. These old people were beginning to seem like the only sane ones in this whole town.

FIFTEEN

I SLID ACROSS THE booth from Karl, grateful he had agreed to meet me for lunch. I was surprised at how hungry I was. Fear and confusion must burn a lot of calories. There was some consolation in that. If I was going to be a stupid chicken, I was at least going to look good in a swimsuit this summer.

"You don't look so good, Mira," Karl said.

"Thanks, Karl."

"Really, Mira. Have you been sleeping lately?"

"I guess so, as well as a person can sleep with one eye open. Jeff's murder just has me walking on eggshells."

"You two got to be pretty close over that interview." It was a statement, not a question, and I was grateful that I wasn't going to have to explain my unflagging interest in solving his murder.

"That, and Ron's asked me to write a story on it. So far all I have is some high school gossip on Kennie, Jeff, and Gary Wohnt. Oh, and let's not forget Lartel."

Karl snapped his menu closed and leaned close to my face. "Mira, if I can give you any advice, it's to steer clear of Lartel. He's not a good person."

"Well, it's kind of hard to avoid your boss," I said. "Anyways, he's still in Mexico." I thought about what Kennie had said about Karl's "special relationship" with Lartel. "How well do you know Lartel, exactly?"

"Back in high school, I was the football team gofer. I got to know him as well as anybody. Now, I'm his banker."

"Why haven't you ever brought him up before? You know I work with him."

"Nothing to be done about that, Mira. I didn't want to worry you unnecessarily. He seems to be fine in the public eye. It's when he's alone that the problems start."

"What have you heard?"

"Things that I wouldn't repeat, ever. But enough to tell me he's not a person you want to associate with. I do business with him because I have to, but if it were up to me, he never would have come back to town. And I'm not the only one who feels that way."

"Why did he come back to town?"

Karl rubbed his thumb on an imaginary spot on the table. "People say he didn't really have anyplace else to go. I suppose he figured the scandal he caused back in the old days had blown over. He hadn't done anything illegal, so why not come back to the town he had grown up in, the town where he had once been a hero?"

I didn't buy it. There was more to the Lartel story. "Have you heard if he's coming back from vacation early?"

"No, nothing like that. And it'd be around pretty quick if he was."

I studied Karl. He looked the same as always—bland and kind. Kennie must have exaggerated his relationship with Lartel. It wouldn't be the first freaky thing she'd ever done, that's for sure. "He's not the only wacko in this town, you know. Kennie stopped by the library today and gave me the third degree about Jeff. I'm starting to wonder what everyone thinks I know."

"Kennie's harmless, Mira. Like I told you before, she's just harboring some jealousy."

"You might be right." I shook my head. "So how's the sale of the Jorgensen land coming without Jeff in the picture?"

"It's coming. They're going to send someone out next week to sign the papers, and it should be a done deal. This time next year, we'll have a new attraction at Battle Lake." Karl didn't sound any more excited about it than me. "You know," he said, "people are saying that Jeff was killed by a homeless man. They're holding him in Otter Tail County Jail."

"What? Why haven't I heard this?"

"He hasn't been charged yet. But he had the right kind of gun on him, and he has no alibi."

I shook my head. No. No, it wasn't a homeless man who had killed Jeff. It made no sense. Why would a homeless man kill him and put his body in the library? This couldn't all be over so quickly, could it?

Before I could speak, our waitress sidled up to the table. "What can I get you, Karl?"

Karl smiled up at her. "Hi, Chrissy. I'll take a patty melt and a salad, and twenty dollars worth of pull-tabs. What're you hungry for, Mira?"

I found my voice, and with it, my appetite. "I'll take a grilled chicken sandwich with fries, and what's your soup?"

"We have chili, navy bean and ham, or Wisconsin cheese."

"A cup of navy bean and ham, please, right away."

Karl laughed quietly. "You're not eating for two, are you?"

I gagged on my own spit. Talk about being dragged from one emotion to another. "I better not be. That's all I need right now. Nope, I'm a good eater, always have been. I'm going to the bathroom—be right back." I scurried to the restroom. Once in there, I felt my boobs and my stomach. They felt normal, both sticking out about equally far from my body. I splashed water on my face and walked out.

I took my time getting back to the table. On the way, I overhead snatches of conversation: ". . . the blackest beaver I ever seen. I never skun a beaver before, but it was easy as pie until I got to the feet . . ." ". . . you betcha, that's the last time I ever let a Watermeller girl babysit my kids . . ." ". . . really hot last night . . ."

I was starting to feel faint. When I got back, my soup was waiting, and I dug into it as a distraction. Karl and I visited about this and that and managed to stay away from the equally toxic topics of murder, pregnancy, and high school. He bought for us, I left the tip, and we both headed back toward work.

When he was out of sight, I ducked into the Apothecary. I was hot, dizzy, and ill, and I recognized the symptoms—I-might-be-pregnantitis. Thanks for putting it in my head, Karl. That would explain why people were being so weird to me, though. They could smell a breeder in the herd. I shuddered. It would take more than both hands to count the number of pregnancy tests I'd bought in my life. I was mostly really good about using protection, but I heard on some morning news show that an alarming number of condoms have pinholes in them. All it takes is one tenacious sperm.

Since that show, I usually ended up taking the pregnancy test right in the Kmart, Wal-Mart, Target—you name it—bathroom the next day. This obsessiveness was certainly a sign of a mental illness. How many women peed on a pregnancy stick in a store bathroom? Multiple times? It's always a humbling experience, but so far I was batting a hundred, and I figured a little self-respect was a small price to pay for immediate peace of mind.

I wasn't too excited about buying an EPT at the Apothecary since certainly I would see someone I knew in there, and the whole town would be buzzing with the news by the end of the day. "Jeff Wilson lives on!" But once I had it in my head that I was pregnant, it was best just to take the test and turn off the voices before they really got to me.

I walked straight to the front counter and was not pleased to find the teenage girl who had sold me the mask the day before, her dishwater hair in a ponytail. Why couldn't they have the decency to sell pregnancy tests in bathroom vending machines, like tampons and condoms? My culture had always taught me that anything related to the vagina was not supposed to be talked about or acknowledged in public, and here it was letting me down. "Hello!" I said. I wished I had come in disguise.

"Hello," she said, flipping the page on *US Weekly*.

"I need one of those EPTs."

"Those what?"

"The pregnancy tests. Behind you."

She turned around. "Which one you want?"

"The EPT one. It has the letters 'EPT' on it. On the front. That one."

She put her hand on the generic one. "These are cheaper."

"Right. The EPT, please." Like I was going to trust my urine and my entire future to a generic brand.

She smacked it onto the counter and rang it up. "$16.99."

It never failed to amaze me how expensive these were. I suppose silencing crazy voices in your head doesn't come cheap. And of course, if I was sane I would just rely on the fact that Jeff and I had used a condom every time and that my period wasn't even late. If I was sane. I handed her a twenty and waited for change.

On my way out, she called after me. "I like your coat, hey."

"Thanks." Unplanned pregnancy—the great unifier of females across all ethnic, age, and attitudinal boundaries.

I scuttled back to the library, peed on the stick, and was relieved to find no pink line. I knew perfectly well that it was probably too early to tell if I was pregnant, but I didn't humor my psychosis that much. I got back to work, and my first job was to snoop in Lartel's desk.

It was one of those cool roll-top numbers, all the wood glossy and deep red. It was locked, but I had come to see locks as a negotiable inconvenience in the last couple days. About twenty minutes with a metal nail file slid the top off, and once the top was open, all the side drawers opened, too. I wasn't surprised to find a doll catalog amidst all the library-related papers. After all, a grown man in swishy pants can only buy so many dolls in person before his motivation is rightfully questioned. Actually, the only surprising thing I found was a letter to Karl. It was so smooth it looked like it had been ironed. It featured the letterhead of the Shooting Star Casino, a gambling club on an Indian reservation about a hundred miles north of Battle Lake. The letter was short and politely worded:

Dear Mr. Syverson:

I'm afraid your credit has been extended as far as we can allow. Your $59,000 debt to our company is payable immediately. Please contact our financial counselor at extension 4536 for assistance in making payment arrangements.

I felt witch fingers on my lower back. A debt that large in a town this small could really start people talking. If one was a banker, it could end one's career. Lartel must be blackmailing Karl, which would explain Karl's deep dislike and distrust of him and why Kennie fingered Karl during our encounter in the library. Whatever was going on, my friend wasn't looking so good anymore. In fact, I was wondering if there was anyone left in town I could trust.

I put the papers back where I had found them and carefully closed and locked the desk. I went to the computer to write the article on Jeff. As soon as I started typing, I could smell the faint cedar of his soap and feel the warmth of that soft spot under his earlobe that he loved to have kissed.

On our second date, he had come over to the doublewide and showed me how to bake vegetable lasagna. We laughed and drank Chianti, and as he baked, he sang "That's Amore" and talked in a corny Italian accent. The food was delicious, and afterward, as he washed and I dried the dishes, he told me funny stories about his travels in Europe.

I remembered thinking that I could listen to him forever. Instead, I was writing a combination murder investigation and eulogy. My eyes got cloudy, and I decided it was time to switch to some low-impact recipe hunting. Too bad no one had put recipe ideas into the envelope I had put out. As I went to Google, I speculated about what reporters and researchers had done before the advent of the Internet. I couldn't get my head around it. After a brief search of online Minnesota cookbooks, I had my two candidates for the tasty Battle Lake recipe of this week.

The first contender was "Fluffy Fish Tacos," Minnesota style. The "taco" was actually white bread, toasted and buttered. On top of that, one spread the fish of choice, sautéed in butter with parsley. The two ingredients that actually would make this dish Mexican—chili pepper and salsa—were blessedly optional. It was simple and weird. It was Battle Lake.

The second contender was the disturbing "Deer Pie." The crust of this pie was meaty ground venison sprinkled with rice and salt and scalloped at the edges like real piecrust. Into this bloody shell, one placed a layer of thin potato slices, a layer of Velveeta cheese, another layer of thin potato slices, another layer of Velveeta, and finally, as decoration, coins of venison sausage. Cook the whole pile for forty-five minutes at 375 degrees, take it out and garnish it with parsley for those health nuts who like some green with their woodland meat, and you have a feast worthy of a caveman. The whole concept and the name were clearly some hunter's wife's plea for help. I couldn't save her, but I could introduce her gory invention to the masses. Deer pie it was.

As I was finishing up my shift, I decided I needed to do a little more sleuthing before I went to the class of '82 party. I was feeling exposed, and I needed to find out who my friends were, or at least clarify my list of enemies. I was going to the cop shop to feel out Gary Wohnt, and then to the high school to verify that it was Jeff's number I had seen bloodstained in Lartel's creephouse of a bedroom.

When I walked out of the library, worn field book in one hand, flashlight in the back pocket of my jeans (even though it was still light out), I realized I was starting to feel like an actual sleuth. Before I started to buy into my own myth, I went back to the lost and found and retrieved the horrific doll. It wasn't as scary as when I first found it, but it was definitely disturbing.

I had the urge to fashion a noose and hang the doll out front of the library as sort of a reverse warning, but nobody had ever taken the time to teach me knot making. Besides, it might turn off the clientele. I decided I'd take the high road and dash over to the nursing home while the library was empty. I set the cheerleader outside the front door. I was sure some old person would take her in and give her a nice home. Out of sight, out of mind.

The cop shop was a block up from the Senior Sunset, located directly behind the municipal liquor store. It was a red brick slug of a building that you could huff and puff and still not blow down. I didn't know what Wohnt's hours were, but I assumed he was around all the time. I had this vision of the law as omnipresent. It was only four o'clock on a Friday, so I was hoping to catch him inside.

Sure enough, when I walked in he was at his gray metal desk, staring at the product of two overhead projectors. They each displayed a four-foot thumbprint on the far wall. This passed for technology in Battle Lake. I stared at the bristly side of his thick neck and swallowed hard. The blue uniform and gun belt didn't help me relax any.

"Chief Wohnt?"

"Yah." In lieu of turning around, he leaned over and turned the knob on the right projector, clarifying the fuzzy whorls of the far thumb.

I realized I didn't have a plan for talking to him. I really wanted to ask him if he was one of the bad guys, but I had to find a stealthy way to do it. "I was wondering if you'd found anything more about Jeff's death?" I shifted my weight from my right foot to my left.

The Chief rubbed his eyes and turned to stare at me. He looked like two miles of bad road. "No, Ms. James, we haven't found out anything more. Do you have some more information to give me?"

"I just heard that you had arrested someone, a homeless man."

He stared at me sideways with his sharp eyes until I had to look away. "Do you have some more information to give me, Ms. James?"

Except for the shiny lips, this was not the loquacious man who had interviewed me immediately following Jeff's death. He had seemed very animated then; now, he looked like he was fighting some serious demons.

I shook my head. I suddenly didn't feel like a grown-up. I heard the radio cackle out some numbers in the next room and saw the Chief's back stiffen. He stood up, grabbed his blue jacket and hat, and strode toward the door. "You'll have to excuse me."

Abruptly, I was alone in a police station. Weren't there prisoners or something who needed guarding? I tiptoed to the back room with the radio and saw it was a standard break room—dorm-room-sized fridge, hot plate, crusty coffee pot, and filing cabinet upon filing cabinet. I tried the top drawer of the closest one out of spite. It was locked. I went back to the main room and tried the two other doors. One was locked and the other was a dingy bathroom. I glanced over my shoulder, certain I was being watched. The room was still empty.

I looked at the Chief's gray desk and felt my bad judgment kick in. I slid the top drawer open. I pulled it harder than I needed to and caused an avalanche of paper clips and pencils inside. I pushed the detritus around and saw nothing of importance. I had my hand on the cool grip of the left uppermost drawer when I heard a heavy foot outside the front door. I snapped the drawer shut and jumped down to my knees.

"What in *the* hell are you doing?" The Chief's frame ate up the doorway and spilled inside. Every heavy breath he wheezed pumped him up a little bit larger, and if I didn't say something smart real soon, he was going to explode all over me.

"I'm tying my shoe." Jesus. Thank God I was wearing shoes that actually had shoelaces, my recently washed tennies, a fact I hadn't bothered to verify before I bald-face lied.

I felt the air move as he swung his head from side to side, looking for something to disprove me. His body had stopped expanding, and now only his neck was swelling. He reminded me of one of those African lizards that run at the National Geographic camera, legs splayed and gills flying.

"Get out of my office. Now."

"Good idea," I said. I had slammed the drawer shut before he had charged back into the room, but not before I saw the silver invitation with the words "For Your Eyes Only" embossed in green on the front.

SIXTEEN

I WALKED THE MILE to the high school, taking the long route and running my hands along the edges of the lilac bushes on the way. Hidden water drops slipped onto my fingertips. If the Chief had an invitation to the party, that meant I hadn't found his invitation in the library. Maybe nobody had lost their invitation; maybe it had been intentionally left there to get me to the party. I was going to find out one way or another in a few hours.

By the time I got to the Battle Lake High School, it was almost five. The original architect must have had a bomb shelter in mind when he built it. The whole structure cried out, "I'm sturdy, not pretty!" Fortunately, a wealthy patron and 1954 Battle Lake graduate—the same one who had sponsored the library—had donated a million dollars to the school a couple years back, and an innovative art center, library, and new gym had been added on. That section looked like something out of Epcot Center, but it was all done in the same shade of puce for continuity.

There weren't any people out front of the pale building, so I went to the doors of the original section. There must have been some sort of extracurricular practice going on, because the green doors opened with a sigh. My hair lifted up slightly as a gust of pheromones, fish sandwiches, freshly copied paper, and some syrupy Calvin Klein imposter cologne kissed my cheeks. Aaah, the smell of high school.

The front lobby had a few vending machines, recycling bins, and droopy ficuses. This space was the bottom leg of a T, with the head being a gigantic trophy case and the arms row upon row of gray lockers. The entire layout of the trophy case was set up to display the crucified green and white football jersey with the number 17 emblazoned on the back, underneath the name WILSON in all caps. The fallen football player effigy in Lartel's creep room had been Jeff.

I walked closer to the case and was alarmed and validated to find a group shot of Lartel, Kennie, Karl, and Jeff. Karl and Lartel had on coaches' clothes, Jeff was in full football uniform, and Kennie was a cheerleading princess. Their arms were on one another's shoulders, and the caption read, "The Good, the Bad, the Ugly, and the Beautiful. Division Football Championship Game, 1982." I wondered which one was which, and where Gary Wohnt had been when that picture was taken.

I eyed the halls to my left and then to my right. They were identical except for an open door at the far end of the right hall. I thought I could hear faint processional music coming out of it, and I walked in that direction. My soft shoes made no sound on the tiled floor. I smiled at the sameness of all small-town high schools. The lockers were papered with "Go Team!"–type stickers, and there were cheerleader-painted pep posters on the open walls—"We've got spirit, yes we do, we've got spirit, how about you!"

It brought me back to my high school days. I had always gotten along OK with my classmates, but I hadn't made any lifelong friends. The people I thought I knew the best faded after my dad's accident.

In my senior year, a new doctor moved to town and brought along his large Irish Catholic family. His oldest daughter was in my grade, and she was in track with me. She had red curly hair, glasses, sporadic acne, and cool clothes. We happened to sign up for job search on the same day and both ended up in the closet of a room set aside for determining our future. The file cabinet was full of career likeliness tests, and the walls were lined with Occupational Outlook handbooks.

While I was cracking some joke about what a waste of time it all was, Mary sneezed and farted at the same time. We both laughed so hard it hurt. I went to the bathroom to get some Kleenex, and when I came back, a girl whom I had gone to school with since kindergarten was in my seat whispering to Mary. They both got quiet when I walked in, and I knew they had been talking about my dad. It rotated between me being the daughter of a drunk or the girl whose dad had killed a mom and her baby. It didn't really matter what they called me. It all worked the same. Mary didn't have much time for me after that. Manslaughter Mark strikes again, this time from the grave, to devastate his daughter's life. Having a dead person tied around your neck is a horrible way to live.

The gray Battle Lake High halls probably had their own stories to tell, probably housed their own broken kids. Thank God high school lockers can't talk. As I got closer to the door I could hear music coming out of, I had an *Alice in Wonderland* moment. The closer I got, the smaller the door got. I was fifteen feet away before I realized it was one of those miniature access doors that usually lead to a furnace room or utility space.

This doorway was about three feet high, and the actual door was thin metal with an indent in lieu of a handle. The siren song of curiosity tapped at me. I looked quickly over my shoulder at the empty hallway, pushed the door open all the way, and crawled in. I felt my way over empty boxes that smelled like mothballs. There was enough light slitting through to show me that I was in some sort of theater storage room and that all the boxes contained costumes.

I inched my way forward to a little barred window. I looked down and realized I was in a storage room attached to the old gym, which now served as the theater for school performances. I knew there must be a way to get from where I was down to the gym, but I couldn't see it in the darkened space.

The music was much louder where I was, and I could see it was coming from a boom box down by the stage, about thirty feet from my hiding spot. The black stereo scratched out a tinny version of "Love Lift Us Up Where We Belong." I wondered what play was being rehearsed, and I was about to leave when I realized I was listening to the class of '82's theme song. I looked back through the slits and was unsurprised to see Kennie emerge from the cheap-looking velvet curtains that covered the stage.

She wore a tight, peach-colored chiffon gown, floor length and strapless. I could see pointy heels snaking out from underneath, and they were dyed the exact color of her dress. Her makeup was visibly thick, even from this distance. She had a glittery tiara on her head and a "Miss Battle Lake '82" banner over her shoulder and wrapped around her waist. She walked strongly from one end of the stage to the other, her chin tipped forward and a brilliant smile on her face.

At first I thought she was waving the parade wave to an imaginary crowd, but then I caught movement out of the corner of my eye. I pressed my face against the cold metal bars, but I could only see the right shoulder and what looked like a head with a hat on. I was clearly looking at a man, but I didn't know which man.

I had to see who had come to watch Kennie's disturbing beauty pageant for one. I leaned back and looked at the vent. In the slit of light from the open door behind me, I saw that only one Phillips head screw held it in at the top. I pulled out the Swiss Army knife attached to my key chain and used the tip of the nail file to turn the screw lefty loosy. I turned slowly and quietly, my movements lost under the music blaring from Kennie's stage.

The screw was out three-quarters of an inch when I realized that the loosened vent was falling into the gym, not onto my lap as planned. It clattered the twenty feet to the floor and froze Kennie in mid-wave. She stared right into my eyes, and I was halfway down the hall before I realized there was no way she could see me in the half-lit space.

I finished running outside and through a couple alleys before I forced myself into a walk. I didn't want Kennie or her mystery audience to discover my spying. Who was watching her, besides me? Right now, I figured it was Gary Wohnt or Lartel, but it could just as well be Karl, the way the cards were stacking. I got to my car unaccosted but couldn't shake the feeling that I was being followed. I decided my safest time passer would be to go home and wait for the class of '82 party. I had a feeling I would find familiar faces at the gala event.

On my way home, I stopped at Swenson Nursery to pick up a flat of annuals. I needed to relax and clear my head, and gardening was my drug of choice after liquor and Nut Goodies. The spicy green scent comforted me on my drive.

When I walked in my front door, Luna at my heels, I did an extra careful eyeball and nose scan of the place. I wanted to make sure there were no dolls or fish waiting for me. The front room was just as I had left it. There was a sectional couch in early tacky-cabin print, a small color TV that got channels 7 and 29 if I had the rabbit ears and tinfoil just right, a bookshelf high on the wall and another on the floor, and plants lining the windows. I didn't like clutter. The more you had, the more you had to clean.

The kitchen was divided from the front room by an island counter. My spices and oil neatly lined the countertops, and there was no bad smell that I could discern. I strode to the fridge, its front covered with pictures of people I knew and places I had been, and reached in for some string cheese. I moved to the table to read through the mail I had grabbed on the way in and saw that it was two bills and the community newsletter. I paged through the newsletter. It was mostly community ed classes—volleyball, computer basics, lefse making.

I walked over to the office and spare bedroom, which I normally kept closed. Both rooms were stacked wall to ceiling to wall with Sunny's stuff, and both appeared untouched.

I stepped over to my bedroom and was gratified to see Tiger Pop sprawled on the bedspread in a fading sunbeam. When I was five, my dad told me I could be anything I wanted to be when I grew up. "Then I want to be a cat," I said. My cat reminded me daily why that had been one of the best ideas I'd ever had. I ran my fingers over his sleek calico fur, pausing to scratch his favorite spot by his tail. The rest of the room was in order—a dresser, a closet, a mirror, and a nightstand.

The main bathroom looked good as well, except for the telltale rust stains made permanent by well water. I wondered what that orange would do to my hair over a period of time if it stained plastic and porcelain so profoundly. I could also smell Tiger Pop's litter box. I was thinking about training Luna to be one of those poop-eating dogs to take care of that problem. If you pass a problem off for long enough, it sometimes really does fix itself.

I stripped off my clothes into a pile on the floor and pulled on a gray T-shirt from a bluegrass festival over a bikini top and some weathered jeans, their knees permanently freckled with dirt. It was time to garden, and Tiger Pop followed me outdoors. Outside, I knelt in the sun-warmed dirt, hands on knees, and closed my eyes. I shut out Jeff, I shut out the birds, I shut out my dad, and I shut out fear.

When I felt myself fully in the moment and the dirt, I dragged my fingers through the spongy soil and released the rich smell of the earth. First, I would weed. This was mostly cosmetic, as few of the bad guys had had time to grow since I was last here. The little sprigs I did find were so close to the earth yet that I had to dig my fingernails down and hook them at the base to pull them out whole. They came up smoothly, their roots white and tender. I laid them on the dirt to be sacrificed to tomorrow's sun. If it was cruel to let them die slowly, so close to the salvation of the moist dirt, I didn't think about it. There would be order in my garden.

Despite its appearance, gardening is rigorous work if you do it right. I was sweating from the concentrated activity, and stripped off my T-shirt. The sinking sun felt purifying, and the dirt was warm and solid in my hands. When pictures of Kennie's disturbing beauty pageant began to sneak in, I moved from vegetables to flowers. I cleaned out the twelve scattered flower/weed beds that Sunny had started last spring and never really followed through on. This gave the late tulips and daffodils a new blush and allowed me to plant the eight packs of annuals I had bought on my way home.

My heart started to triphammer at the thought of crashing the party tonight, so I moved to planting, patting down the cooling soil around the spicy orange and gold marigolds, white alyssum, and sweet red and deep purple petunias in the well-lit areas. In the shade gardens I planted wax begonia, impatiens, and coleus. The red and white begonias made excellent edging with their glossy bronze and green leaves. The impatiens were pink and lavender and framed by the greens, whites, and burgundies of the coleus leaves. I also dug down to worm level to plant dahlia bulbs and scraped the earth to seed some zinnias.

When the sun began to set around eight, I realized I had been in the dirt for a couple hours. My hands were rough, and I knew it would be at least a week before I got all the dirt from under my fingernails. I smiled at my cat, who was sucking up the last bit of sun next to me, eyeing the dog warily. I patted his side, leaving little dirt balls to irritate him. I rolled my stiff shoulders and pulled myself up, my legs creaking from all the time kneeling. My two gardening tools—a little dirt fork and a hand spade—went back to their home by the front steps. After my outdoor cleanup was done, I sat on the front porch, which was really a splintery reddish picnic table with some steps built into it. I put my chin in my hands and looked down at the lake, and then back at the very neat rows of flowers I had planted. My mind, body, and heart were reconnected.

"Come on, Tiger Pop. It's time to fill our empty heads."

Back in the kitchen, I washed my hands until the water ran clear and then cracked a Dr. Pepper, poured a couple fingers of vodka into it, and popped some homestyle butter popcorn in the microwave. I rarely drank pop, as it made me weird, but I thought I deserved a treat. Plus, I didn't know how late I would be staying up tonight, and the caffeine would do me good. When I had my snacks ready to go, I invited Tiger Pop to watch TV with me. He was meditating on my bed, and I felt rude for addressing him directly. I flopped on the scratchy couch and grabbed the least-used remote in the county. When I saw I was only getting Fox, I put it down and sat back to watch an old episode of *Star Trek: The Next Generation*. Sometimes I really liked my life.

SEVENTEEN

It was spring and dark came around eight p.m. I didn't know what time was appropriate to arrive at a masquerade, but ten seemed like a safe bet. Any earlier and I might be one of two or three awkward people in masks trying to make small talk.

Come nine-thirty, I couldn't wait anymore. Fox's Friday night lineup was stultifying, reinforcing what society had been teaching me since I was old enough to get my ears pierced: anyone worth their salt will be out on a Friday night meeting people and being exciting. Well, I could take a hint.

I changed into my now-standard spying outfit of black jeans, black turtleneck, and tennis shoes and headed out the door. Eagle Lake, the site of the party according to the invite, was approximately ten miles south of where I lived. If there wasn't too much farm machinery, tourists pulling boats, or deer on the way, I'd make it in under fifteen minutes. I planned to drive straight to the public access boat landing about a mile from where the party was supposed to be. I would park my car there and walk so I wouldn't be recognized by my vehicle when I arrived.

When I reached the divided highway, I took a left on Eagle Lake Road. I drove about two miles before the road changed from tar to gravel, and another three-quarters mile until I saw a yard light obscured by trees. It reminded me of Lartel's house, except the mailbox was white and I could see peeks of a blue house through the white oaks. There were lights blazing and cars in the driveway.

I drove a little farther until I passed by an approach. I turned my car around and drove back to the public access. There were seven other cars parked there, which was a lot for 9:47 p.m. Plus, none of them had boat trailers hooked on. Looks like I wasn't the only one who wanted to hang low, though I didn't recognize any of the vehicles.

The blue house was a straight one-mile shot through the woods on the south side of the road. Given the number of cars in the access lot, I decided it would be best to wear my disguise from the word go, though I felt like a dork traipsing through the moonlit forest in a Harlequin mask. I couldn't get the picture out of my head of me stuck in a bear trap, passed out from pain, found all in black and masked. I was so engrossed in this potential shame that I almost walked straight into a tall man, back to me, peeing.

"Sorry," I said. It was the knee-jerk apology of someone who has accidentally walked into a bathroom stall they thought was empty.

He quickly shook, zipped, and turned to me. Everything below his eyes was covered in an elaborate feathered and sequined veil, but it didn't disguise his dark beard and mustache. What I thought were black pants and a shirt turned out to be belly dancer trousers and a bikini top under a transparent blouse. It looked like something Barbara Eden would wear on *I Dream of Jeannie*.

He looked away quickly. "Not a problem." He jogged ahead and out of sight.

I looked around and behind me. I didn't see any other hairy, peeing Bedouins, so I continued on. I was much more alert now, but the only sounds I heard were branches snapping under my tennis shoes and the breeze in the tops of the trees.

I was nearly out of the woods when a dark shape swooped at me like a pterodactyl. It knocked off my mask and scratched at my shoulder. I ducked, hands over my head, and waited for the next attack. I heard a heavy shape land on a nearby branch and risked a peek.

"Whoo whoo."

Shit. An owl. The birds were turning on me, just like I knew they would. I scrabbled around on the forest floor until I felt my mask and hunch-walked toward the house. I tried to move completely unlike a mouse, but it's hard to seem ominous when you're crouching. When I got to the clearing, I fought the urge to stand up straight and run. If that owl was going to get me, he was going to work for it.

I heard subdued music coming from inside. I checked to make sure I still had my keys and some money in my pockets. If this was some kind of direct sales party, like Gina had said, I wanted to have some cash on hand so I would blend in.

I circled the house, but all the windows had shades covering them so I couldn't see in. In the front lawn were those wooden ornaments that look like big ladies leaning over and exposing their butts, and an excited white poodle was tied to the lone oak tree in the lawn. My feet crunched on acorns as I walked to the door. It looked like the only way to go was in.

I reached for the doorknob and entered, confused by the dim light. From all the blazing lights in the yard, I had expected it to be much brighter inside. A firm hand grabbed my wrist right inside the door. "Invitation."

I turned to the voice and saw a man in an exact replica of my outfit—black shirt, black pants, and tennis shoes, topped by a full-face

Harlequin mask. He was thick-necked and large and had a faint vanilla odor about him that I couldn't place. I pulled the invite out of my back pocket and handed it to him. He glanced briefly at it and returned it. "Which room do you want to go to?"

What kind of party was this? I couldn't see anyone but this guy, and the music was no louder inside that it had been outside. I played with the idea of mumbling something, but I took a chance and revealed my newness. "This is my first time. What are my choices?"

His neck muscles relaxed a little, and he pulled a tiny white pot with a black and yellow cover out of his back pocket. He applied a generous slab of Carmex to his lips without lifting his mask, and then nodded toward the top of the stairs. "First-timer. We're glad to have you. You want the Red Room, first door on your left at the top of the stairs. They'll take care of you there."

It was Battle Lake Police Chief Gary Wohnt dressed as my disguise doppelgänger. Was he doing off-duty security work? I nodded my head, not wanting to use my voice any more than necessary, and walked up the stairs. Something was not right about this. I had felt less anxiety walking into Lartel's house. I heard a click behind me, and suddenly a disco strobe light began orbiting color off the walls on the bottom floor.

When I got to the top of the stairs, the music was slightly louder but still muffled. If memory served, the tune was the Waitresses' "I Know What Boys Like." I stood in front of the first door on my left at the top of the stairs. It was a very ordinary entrance, and next to it was a very ordinary table with a doily and a bowl of mixed nuts. I opened the door and walked in with feigned confidence.

EIGHTEEN

No one was startled to see me. On the contrary, it was me who acted like she had just walked onto a Broadway stage when she meant to go into her bathroom. It took me a good three minutes to register what I was seeing, due to the black light flickering in the center of the room, the psychedelic free love posters, and the large quantity of smoke, most of it smelling too sweet to be from cigarettes. It looked for all the world like one of the basement parties I had attended when I was in college at the U of M, except for three important differences: everyone here was wearing masks, hardly anyone was wearing clothes, and most of the bodies I was getting a gander at were a good fifty years past their prime displaying age.

In fact, I couldn't see a body that looked under seventy, though I hadn't had any experience judging naked old people. I had always gauged them with their clothes on, and the sheer amount of loose skin and hair everywhere but their heads overwhelmed my senses. Most of the aged partiers were lounging and talking, and it looked like a group in the back was passing a bong. I heard the telltale gurgle from my post at the door, and I'm pretty sure I caught a glimpse of Mrs. Berns as she pulled up her mask to get a better hit.

I sensed a small pocket of hardcores to my left redefining what it meant to bump uglies, but I wasn't going to look too closely. I thought I could hear papery skin chafing. Over all this floated mild Ravi Shankar–esque tunes.

"Welcome to the Red Room."

I turned to my right to see who had spoken. Frankly, I was hoping by the lack of reaction as I entered the room that I was invisible. This was scary. "Thank you," I said to the little old man with the Batman mask, a green plastic lei around his neck his only other cover. I tried to keep my eyes on his, but I couldn't help running a quick glance down to the genitals tucked under his paunch. He looked like I imagine Mickey Rooney would look naked about this time in his life, if I had ever imagined Mickey naked. Which I hadn't.

"Are you here for the smoke, or could I interest you in a tall cool one?"

"A tall cool one would be great." The smoke in the room had already made my mouth dry. I needed a minute to catch my breath, and it would be good to have something to focus on besides breasts and balls that hung at about the same latitude.

Batman grabbed my hand and led me to a chair by the window. This really was a large room. Now that my eyes had adjusted to the strange light, I saw that a wall had been knocked out, the little divider left at the top covered in stenciled grapes. I sat in the chair, and Batman called over his shoulder, "Arnie, she wants a tall cool one."

Arnie appeared out of nowhere and stood in front of me, the picture of aged aloofness. He had a half-mask that allowed him to suck on the cigarette that he undersmoked, snitching and snatching at it like it was an annoyance. His pork-and-bean eyes glistening through the eyeholes stared at something far away. However, what really drew my attention was the large erection he held at about eye level, mere inches from my face. My mouth clamped shut in automatic safety mode, but I couldn't help marveling at the unwrinkled length of it. The whole man's body was a monument to extra skin with built-in pockets, and here was this immense, smooth penis stuck in the middle of it all like a banana on a Shar-Pei.

"Here's your tall cool one," he said in a bored voice. I swear if he had a watch on he would have looked at it.

I stared at his penis, and it stared back at me. The only thing I was blowing tonight was my cover.

The door to the Red Room suddenly slammed open, and I had to quell my latent high-school-bred urge to jump out the window. But it wasn't the cops; it was Kennie Rogers. Her face was amazingly unmasked, which somehow made her seem the most naked in this room of geriatric bacchanalia. "Where's that first-timer?" she trilled. "Come on out, don't y'all hide from me!"

Her arrival took the wind out of Arnie's sails, and now it was just me, him, and his sleepy snail by the window. How quickly the mighty do fall. I suppose he needed the extra blood to keep his heart going. I raised my hand.

"There you are! Come on now, come with Mama Kennie. You gotta tour all the rooms, darnit, before you get too comfortable in the ever-lovin' Red Room. The rest of y'all go back to business. Free love is the best love!"

She grabbed my hand, and God knows I was thankful to be led out. I think I saw a tube of KY jelly as we passed a grouping of high-backed chairs in the center, but it could have been denture cream. Once in the bright light of the hallway, Kennie let go of my hand and turned to me. She had on her usual heaping helping of makeup, and her frosty hair was trained under a tiara. Her costume was identical to what she had been wearing in her strange beauty pageant just hours before, except that she no longer had the "Miss Battle Lake" banner. A bouquet of roses would not have looked out of place in the crook of her arm, but her expression was icy.

"Mira, Mira, Mira. Y'all just don't give up, do you, honey chile?"

Shit! I thought my disguise was at least as good as anyone else's. Under her imperious eye, I felt dirty and trapped after what I had just seen. The hallway closed in on me. I thought of running, but I could see Gary Wohnt, still masked, at the bottom of the stairs with his arms crossed bodyguard style. It must have been him watching Kennie at the high school earlier, though I couldn't shake the feeling that it might have been Lartel. I wondered what current reasons Kennie had to spend time with either man.

Kennie pulled out a pocket mirror from some secret fold in her dress and clicked it open. She pushed her eyeliner around and puffed her hair. All the movement scared up a cloud of drugstore perfume. "I wondered where Jeff's invitation had gone. It wasn't found on the body, at least that's what I heard. I didn't see it when I came to the library yesterday, either." She snapped the compact closed. "But that's because y'all had it, isn't it?"

I bet none of this would have happened if I had on a Wonder Woman mask. When in doubt, attack. "What the hell kind of party is this, Kennie?"

"This is the only kind of party, sweetie. What you think, we all just fish and crochet around here? A person's gotta stay warm. Better yet, a person's gotta make money." Her tone was beguiling and her smile was sly.

"Money? But I wasn't charged anything."

"That's because you stole your invitation, now isn't it? Everyone else here paid fifty dollars, and does for every party they go to." She made a grandiose wave with her arm to indicate the house and its horny inhabitants.

"Fifty dollars? Isn't this illegal?"

"Not if you're over twenty-one, my dear, as all my clientele are, and then some. What the adults do once they get to my party is their own business, though we like to provide various forms of entertainment so no one gets bored. I'll give y'all the tour."

If I didn't know better, I would have said she was proud of all this. She grabbed my hand in her meaty paw and dragged me to the door across the hall. The runner on the floor was a flowered Victorian rug in pale creams and yellows. I felt like I was in my grandma's house, but on the dark side. Or at least the lubricated side. I wondered whose house this was during the day and if they just rented it out for the parties or if it was just a dedicated orgy site.

This door opened to a shadowed room lit by candles and thick with Nag Champa incense. In the center a belly dancer in her mid-sixties gyrated suggestively. At least she had clothes on, as did everyone else in the room. They were all wearing belly dancer outfits, and they were all trying to follow the lead of the woman in the center, to varying degrees of success. The hairy guy I had seen peeing in the woods was directly in front. He had lost his transparent blouse and now looked like a gorilla in a bikini top and puffy pants. He danced the jerky, off-balance ballet of the white male farmer, but his concentration was admirable. Kennie shut the door and pulled me to the next one.

This door thankfully opened to a well-lit room. Unfortunately, there was wall-to-wall nudity, all the clothes in a heap by the door like coats on a bed at a dinner party. The ten or so elderly, masked inhabitants were all holding a piece of wood and sharing paints. The instructor at the center of the room was illustrating a technique while she spoke, her dried-up breasts resting against her stomach. "The definitive characteristic of rosemaling is its ability to blend colors while still making them distinct . . ."

Kennie shut that door as well and led me to the stairs. "Y'all are gonna see our newest room. It's the first time it's been at a class of '82 party, and it's a big hit." She glared at masked Gary Wohnt when we passed him. He stared at her with a cock to his head that I recognized. *He* had been the audience for Kennie's beauty pageant at the high school.

I followed her into the kitchen, preparing for the worst. But then, based on what I had seen so far this evening, I had redefined the word *worst*. That's why I was pleasantly surprised to find myself in a homey kitchen with masked seniors playing bingo. A new game must have just started.

"B19!" the caller shouted. The twelve or so people at the card tables scoured their playing cards. Some of the players had as many as seven to look through. I heard a couple squeals of joy as people placed tokens on what must be B19. Then, to my horror, those same people took off an article of clothing and tossed it on a pile in the center. Strip bingo. Was this the gambling I had overheard Kennie mention to Gary Wohnt?

"The best part," Kennie said into my ear, "is that the winner gets ten bucks and gets to put on someone else's clothes."

This was too much. In my world, old people come permanently clothed. You can't undress them any more than you can remove their hair or teeth. I suppose, though, that pretty much everything comes off or out of an old person if you pull hard enough. Kennie grabbed my hand and pulled me back toward the stairs before I could finish my train of thought.

"That's about all we have goin' down this week, sweetcheeks. There's a Nintendo room in the basement, and I think there's a game of Twister goin' on somewhere, but you seen the meat of it."

I shook my head, unable to comprehend all of this in Otter Tail County, right under my nose. I probably passed these people in the grocery store. I wondered if I had gotten a contact high from all the smoke in the Red Room. "Why is everyone so old and naked?"

"Why shouldn't they be, honey? Old people got a right to be naked, too. Besides, old is where the money's at. You should see my business boom when the tourists start coming in. Whoo-eeee, it's like greasin' a pig! I'm an entrepreneur, doll, and this is where it's at." Kennie really did seem to be in her element here. Supreme cruise director—screw the shuffleboard and bring on the sex, drugs, and old folks.

"Why'd you give Jeff an invitation?"

Kennie's shoulders slumped, and she sighed. "I don't know, honey. I wanted him to see how successful I was, what I had made of myself. It doesn't matter now, does it? Jeff is dead, and he never even knew what kind of party he was missing."

Her eyes were sad, and I felt a connection to her for the first time. Maybe it was all the seasoned hormones floating through the house like pollen and bringing people together. But then I had a thought— the cutesy "CU there!" on the class of '82 invitation, and the same annoying word abbreviation in my death threat: UR GOING TO FIND THE SAME TROUBLE AS WILSON. "Did you leave the note on my computer at the library, threatening me?"

She nodded her head dismissively. "I had hot flashes that day, honey chile. I don't always think so clearly when I have hot flashes. No harm done, right? Just a little kitty fight."

"What about the doll and the dead fish?"

She shook her head and smiled. "I don't play with dolls, and the only dead fish I touch have tartar sauce on them." She slapped her knee and laughed. "So you gonna stay, baby? You're welcome to. Some of these old folk like fresh meat every now and again." She winked.

I shuddered. "I don't think it's my crowd, Kennie. If you don't mind, I'm going to make it an early night." I turned and began to walk away. "Say," I said, turning my head just enough so I could see her, "you see much of Chief Gary Wohnt around these days?"

To her credit, she did not look at the man at the bottom of the stairs. "I'm the mayor of a small town, hon. I see the police chief every day."

I nodded my head. The door was held open for me as I walked out. "Thanks, Chief," I said. I was going to visit the Senior Sunset. I had a very important question to ask my friend Curtis Poling.

NINETEEN

I HAD A SINKING suspicion Mr. Poling was back at the party, but I knew there was no way I was going to stay and start lifting masks. I'd give him the benefit of the doubt and go to the nursing home in the hopes that he was sleeping. I parked a block up from the Senior Sunset. I was right by the police station, but I knew where the head cat was tonight, and it made me cocky. I strapped on my flashlight and made my way to the one-story Sunset. I counted off windows until I saw what I thought was 11A and peeked in. Through the cracked shades I saw Curtis Poling wrapped in a hospital blanket and sleeping like a baby. Or a really old guy.

I rapped my knuckles on the glass and waited. Nothing. It occurred to me that he might wear a hearing aid during the day that he took out at night, or that he maybe just slept really hard. I tapped the glass again, this time with a pebble I picked off the ground. Curtis opened one eye and looked toward the door. I waved my arms and he glanced toward the window. He squinted his eyes, nodded his head, and was out the door.

I strolled over to the garden and waited, enjoying the moonlight and the sound of crickets. Residential Battle Lake went to bed early, even on Fridays. I was wondering about old people. There was a lot about them that I didn't know. I had previously viewed them as a sort of wrinkly garnish: I saw them around and didn't mind that they were there, I appreciated their decorative purpose, but I never really thought they had nutritional value. Here I was finding out they were as clever, horny, and inclined to party as the rest of us. It was a little reassuring and a little disturbing. Oh well, it gave me some hope for my future. If I couldn't get laid again in what was left of my twenties, I still had another sixty or so years to work on it. Curtis was out in the blink of an eye, naked except for boxers and work boots. Given what I had seen tonight, I was grateful for the boxers.

"Aren't you cold?" I asked.

He pulled a cigarette out from behind his ear and a lighter from his boot. "Nah. It's darn near fifty degrees out here! I got the blood of an ice fisherman." He sparked the lighter and held the flame to his smoke. I could see a flash of his vivid blue eyes in the temporary light. "I was wondering when you'd be back."

"Sorry to wake you up, Mr. Poling. Why did you think I'd come back?"

"You got curious eyes, missy, and they didn't look satisfied when you left. I suppose you got the right questions to ask this time?"

I did. "Jeff came to talk to you on Saturday. You told him to watch out for the Jorgensen land. Did he tell you about the Indian etchings he found that morning?"

Curtis smiled. "That he did, missy. And that's when I told him he can't build there, no matter what, no matter how. I told him that Mrs. Jorgensen never did want that land sold, and it's because she knew what was on it. You find her will, you find out all about that. That land is about as sacred as it comes to the native people."

"And when Kennie talked to you later that day, did you tell her that Jeff needed to find some different land in this area to build on?"

I think Curtis may have blushed at the mention of Kennie, but given what I knew about him, it was probably just a trick of the moon. "That woman can make the dead talk, I tell you." He shook his head in disgust. "I told her that Jeff was smart enough to figure out the Jorgensen land wasn't no good. She asked me what I knew about Skinvold's acreage over by Glendalough Park, and I told her I knew about as much as she did. And that was the end of that."

"Thank you, Mr. Poling. You've been very helpful." My head was dancing. I knew Herbert Skinvold was selling a good-sized chunk of prairie on the north side of town. I had seen the flyer on the library bulletin board.

"I believe you're going to find who killed that Wilson boy, missy."

"I believe I am too, Mr. Poling." I smiled at him, took one last whiff of his Old Spice and tobacco smoke, and walked back to my car.

Talking to Bev that morning and then stumbling into the geriatric hedonism fest had clarified some things. The first was that Jeff was about as decent as they come. I had never wanted to believe that he would have OK'ed building on the Jorgensen land after he found the petroglyphs, and Curtis had proved my faith justified. A visit to the Skinvold farm would verify that Jeff never had any intention of approving the Jorgenson purchase for Trillings and that Trillings was never going to buy the Jorgensen land, which meant Jeff's death was unrelated to his archaeology work.

His murderer was clearly someone with a grudge, and my guess was that it was either Lartel, who was also blackmailing Karl, or Gary Wohnt, who maybe loved Kennie enough to murder the man who had done her wrong in high school and could win her love back in the present. I didn't have all the pieces yet, though. I was hoping Herbert Skinvold could fill some in for me the next morning. What he couldn't tell me, a travel agent could.

TWENTY

BEFORE THE SUN HAD fully risen on Saturday morning, I made a quick call to Ron's machine telling him to hold the front page space for a last-minute article that revealed who Jeff's killer was, and I hurried out to Skinvold's. Based on the directions I picked up at Ben's Bait on the way, the farm was close to Lartel's house, which was also relatively close to the land over by Glendalough State Park that Skinvold was reportedly selling. That concentrated a lot of weirdness in one place, and I wondered how much time I had wasted barking up the wrong tree by focusing on the petroglyphs and the Jorgensen land.

When I turned west off 78, I found myself on a familiar dirt road. Blocking it were two pickup trucks, one pointing east and one pointing west. The drivers were holding a conversation that included leaning out their windows to make energetic one-armed gestures. I sat impatiently, knowing that it wouldn't do any good to rush the road-exchange of farmers. After about four minutes, they waved at each other across the three-foot space between their vehicles and pulled forward in opposite directions. I drove through the middle and did the pointer-finger wave, avoiding eye contact. In my rearview mirror, I saw them back up to their original positions and begin conversing again.

I drove past Lartel's and on to the Skinvold farm. Herbert Skinvold was a small-time dairy farmer, a dying breed. I knew he would be up bright and early; when animals are your business, there's no such thing as time off. Sure enough, when I pulled into his bumpy, one-and-a-half mile driveway, I could see the barn lights in the dawn glow. I pulled up in front of the red building and inhaled the earthy smell of manure as I got out of my car. Before I knew it, three ratty dogs jumped at me and sniffed my crotch, and a mewling cat crawled into my tire well. I held my hands up so I didn't get dog tongue germs and waded through the squirming bodies to the barn. I pulled the wooden door open and squeezed myself in while keeping the dogs out.

The interior was huge and stuffed with cows in stalls, some of them bawling but most of them eating hay and licking their snot with thick pink lizard tongues. A few looked at me with morose brown eyes, but most continued to contemplate their cowness and the far wall. The drone of machinery was pervasive, and I couldn't see any humans.

"Mr. Skinvold?" I tried to stay equidistant from the rumps lining each side of the cement walkway. I wasn't going to get kicked by a cow—it'd be a bad way to go.

Three cows up on my left, there was a black-and-white heifer pooping, and I was amazed to see the used food get carried away on a permanently turning belt housed in the trough behind the cow's back legs. I wondered if I could get Tiger Pop to use one of those. I found a man I presumed to be Mr. Skinvold on the end of the row, hooking the shiniest metal tubes to the teats of a bored cow. Once on, they sucked her baby's milk to a faraway place where it could be sanitized for human consumption.

I self-consciously adjusted my bra and made thanks that I hadn't been born bovine. I also pledged to keep drinking soy milk and stop eating cheese. I wasn't a big fan of the booger-eating poopers, but they deserved better than this.

I raised my voice to be heard over the humming of large machines and the muttering of cows. "Mr. Skinvold, I'm Mira James with the *Battle Lake Recall*, and I'd like to ask you a couple questions about the land you're selling."

The man glanced at me, nodded, and went back to what he was doing. He wore pinstriped Carhartt dungarees under a frayed denim jacket, knee-high green waders, and a feed cap with greasy salt-and-pepper hair curling up around the edges. I noticed the roughness and strength of his hands as he adjusted the suction tubes on the dangly cow boobs. I bet in the winter his hands got deep cracks from his hard, cold work. I turned my back to his cow molestation and feigned an interest in barn trusses.

"We can talk outside," he yelled, then walked down the clean cement path that had led me to him. He even slapped a cow butt on the way. I cautiously followed him outside and was relieved at the noise reduction. Dog noses pushing between my legs quickly repelled my respite. I tried to pull my coat in front as a shield and wondered if I should consider douching. They were treating me like I was packing a Milk-Bone.

Herbert Skinvold spat on the ground. "What can I do ya for?" His brown eyes had pleasant crinkles around the corners, and his posture was relaxed.

"Like I said, I'm writing an article about Jeff Wilson for the *Recall* and was wondering about that land you're selling over by Glendalough. I heard he looked at it on behalf of the company he was working for, Trillings Limited."

"Damn shame about that boy. They know who killed him yet?"

"Not that I've heard."

"Yes, ma'am, he was interested in that land. I got two-hundred-plus acres over there that I'm getting too old to farm. These cows keep me too busy, anyhow. Some of it's flat farm land, been growing corn on it for years. The rest is woods and such. Part of it even touches on Blanche Lake. Right beautiful over there."

"Did he say anything about not buying the Jorgensen land?"

"We didn't talk specifically about that, but Ms. Rogers made mention that the Jorgensen land wasn't going to work for what he had in mind. When we drove—"

"Kennie?"

"Yes, ma'am. Ms. Kennie Rogers, the mayor of Battle Lake. She and Jeff drove out here together. Then the three of us drove over to my land for sale. Spent a good three hours out there looking around. Jeff seemed pretty pleased when he left."

"This was Sunday?"

"Sunday morning, bright and shiny. Jeff said he had to talk to his boss and tie up some loose ends but that my land was looking real favorable. Said he'd get back to me Tuesday. Of course, he wasn't alive no more come Tuesday."

"So you only had that one meeting with Jeff, and Kennie was there? You never heard from him before or after?"

"No, ma'am. George, down!" The black-and-white Springer-something cross continued to pump my leg, but I was too caught up in my thoughts to notice.

"Well, thank you, Mr. Skinvold. You've been very helpful. Can I call you if I have any more questions?"

"Sure you can. I got a phone in the barn, but sometimes you need to let it ring for a while before I hear it." He smiled and tipped the corner of his feed cap.

"Will do. You have a good day."

"You bet I will!" And he returned to the barn. I tried to shake my leg lover, but he had a good grip. I dragged him to my car, leaned over and pulled the kitty out of my wheel well, and peeled the dog off as I got inside. I closed the door and checked for wet spots on my pants. Give me an arrogant, aloof cat any day. I wondered how long a creature had to go without real sex before a stiff leg came across like a pinup. I hoped it took at least a year, because it was looking like I was in for a dry spell myself.

My next stop was Karl's house. Skinvold had told me what I had expected. Jeff was no longer interested in the Jorgenson land at the time of his death. He had been killed because of jealousy, and I needed to drill Karl to find out more about the person who had called him earlier in the week impersonating a Trillings rep. That caller was Jeff's killer. I was sure of it.

Karl's house was a neat little clapboard two-story over by the Battle Lake Public School. I hoped he and his wife would be up this early. I drove by twice, parked out front, and got out. Karl's Chevy pickup was in the driveway, and a light was on in what I figured was the kitchen. I had never actually been in Karl's house before. We didn't have that kind of friendship.

I walked up his orderly walk, taking in the absence of kids' toys. Karl really seemed like the kind of guy who should have at least two kids. I'd have to ask him what was up with that. I pushed the doorbell and waited. Karl appeared promptly, wearing sweats and tennis shoes. His hair was tousled, but his eyes were bright. "Morning, Mira! Come on in. Can I get you coffee? Tea?"

I walked through the door he held open for me and looked around. It was exactly like I had expected—fancy country decorations on knick-knack shelves, comfy flowered furniture, and plenty of doilies.

"Come into the kitchen."

I followed him to the next room and found myself in Martha Stewart's dreamland. Everything was blue, white, or blue-and-white checked. The few containers on the counter were lined up and clean, and the only dish to be seen was a coffee cup that had been scoured and was drying in the rack in the sink. I think I now knew what kind of wife Karl had.

"I hope I'm not waking you, Karl. Is your wife still asleep?"

"You betcha. She's always been a night owl, and I'm the early riser. 'Dear Abby' says we can make it work, though." He smiled. "What do you say to some coffee?

"I'd love some tea if you have it. I'm afraid I have some bad news."

Karl kept his back to me while he busied himself with tea. "What's that, Mira?"

"Trillings isn't interested in the Jorgensen land. Jeff found some petroglyphs out there and wasn't going to recommend building. He was looking into the Skinvold land."

Karl turned to me. "I knew about Jeff's interest in the Skinvold land. He told me that when he called last Sunday afternoon. But Mira, like I told you, a Trillings rep called on Wednesday to tell me to get the paperwork ready. Where are you getting your information?"

"Lots of places. How do you know it was really a Trillings rep? Couldn't anyone have called and pretended to work for Trillings? Couldn't Jeff's killer, for example, have called?"

Karl got a concerned look in his eyes and sat across from me. He put his warm hand on mine. "Mira, I know you're shook up by this. The whole town is, and you got a little closer to Jeff in the couple days he was here than the rest of us had a chance to. But I don't think there is some big conspiracy here. Why would someone impersonate a Trillings representative? It would be a very short time before I'd call the company with questions about the sale. That lie wouldn't hold up long, and what would be the point?"

I pulled my hand away stubbornly. "The point is that it would be a distraction from the real murderer's motive. What did the rep sound like? Did he say anything unusual?"

Karl opened his mouth and closed it again. He looked out the window and then back at me, a look of parental resignation in his eyes. "He didn't sound familiar, if that's what you're asking. He had a regular man's voice, a little deeper than average, and he talked like his lips were tight, like he measured every word. Typical eastern accountant type."

Tight lips and measured words. A perfect description of the local chief of police. "Did he give a name?"

"Yes, a Tim something or the other. Do you want me to go into work to get it for you?"

"No thanks, Karl. You could do me a favor and get a copy of Mrs. Jorgensen's will, though. I have a bet to settle."

"That's not public information, Mira."

"I just need a peek, Karl. I'll stop by the bank in a couple hours. You're a great help!" I kissed the balding top of his head and was out the door before he could argue.

I was home in seven minutes flat and on the phone to Trillings not long thereafter, glad I had gotten the number off the Internet. Too bad they were closed on a Saturday, though the robotic female voice on the machine encouraged me to try back Monday during regular business hours. I didn't have that long.

I tapped my foot impatiently, then remembered the original "Call Trillings v.p." note I had found in Jeff's field book when I'd discovered it under my bed. I scrambled to my bedroom, found the tin I had stored the loose pages in, and whipped through them until I came up with the phone number. I dialed it immediately, hoping against hope that it was a direct line, or better yet, a cell number. Luck favored me. I had reached the Trillings vice president on his cell. When I explained who I was and why I was calling, he was understanding and said they were all saddened by Jeff's death. He confirmed what I already knew, which was that no representative had called the First National Bank in Battle Lake since early April.

The company had only received one short note from Jeff since the time he arrived in Battle Lake. The vice president read the message Jeff had e-mailed one week ago today in lieu of the report he was supposed to send to Trillings. It said, "Jorgensen's land won't work—looking for other options in area. Have a great idea to make this work, but need a last bit of research. Expect report Monday."

The next the company heard, Jeff was dead. The vice president and I exchanged sympathies, and I hung up and went to pet Tiger Pop. That usually helped me to concentrate. He purred as I stroked his calico fur and scratched at the base of his ears, and my head began to clear. I had already crossed Kennie off my list of suspects because she really had cared about Jeff. That left Lartel, on account of pure weirdness, and Gary Wohnt, due to jealousy. From Karl's description of the Trillings rep impersonator's voice, Wohnt was my number one candidate. But why pretend to work for Trillings and call Karl? Why not just murder Jeff? And why put his body in the library? That sounded like something purely irrational and creepy, AKA Lartel McManus.

A call to Lartel's travel agent in Minneapolis would tell me whether the man was really in Mexico. If he was, Gary Wohnt was going down, once I could figure out how to pin all this on him. My brain was full again, so I got myself ready for work and headed back to town to begin the first day of the rest of my life.

TWENTY-ONE

FORTUNATELY, THE TRAVEL AGENCY was open on Saturdays. My phone call took only a minute. I had found the number listed in the Rolodex I had borrowed off Lartel's desk. Once I explained who I was and that a close member of Lartel's family had died and I needed to contact him, the agent was happy to help. She confirmed that Lartel had bought the tickets to Mexico, but she did not know if he had actually gotten on the flight or checked into his hotel. She said she would look into it and get back to me. I hunkered down for an excruciating wait.

The library was busy, and my mind was energized by anticipation. Today, I would find out who had killed Jeff Wilson. I finished the article on Jeff, all but the ending, and spent the morning alternating between crabby/hyper and manic/helpful. Before I knew it, it was noon. I emptied the library and hung the Out to Lunch sign on the door. I had no intention of leaving my post lest I miss the travel agent's call, but I did want some quiet time to eat chips and think. On my way back to my desk, the front door donged, and I realized I had forgotten to lock it.

"We're closed," I said, turning to see who had come in. My stomach flipped when I saw it was Professor Jake. Damn. I had forgotten about our lunch date, made via e-mail.

"Hi, Mira! Ready for lunch?" His thick-lashed black eyes sparkled, and he looked so hopeful. I hated hurting nice people's feelings only slightly less than I hated leading on nice people.

"Um, Jake, there's been a little misunderstanding."

His face fell far and quick. Clearly, this wasn't the first time he had received this speech.

He cleared his throat and stopped me from continuing. "I understand. I really do. This can be an uncomfortable thing to talk about. I assumed from your e-mail that it wouldn't be a problem, but . . ."

He trailed off. The flutter in my throat told me this was not the conversation I had planned in my head. Professor Jake had obviously revealed something about himself in an e-mail that had never gotten past Gina, my evil matchmaker. The professor's apologetic and depressed manner told me he thought it was a dump-worthy secret. My curiosity overrode my better judgment.

"Yeah, well, you know, things like that can be really surprising." I figured if I played dumb, he would tell me what he thought I already knew, and it would let me off the hook. How often is it that life makes it easy to dump someone nice? This day was going well for me, and it was early.

"I understand. I thought I would gamble that you wouldn't mind."

"Yeah, well, you know how it is."

"Believe me, I certainly do."

"Yup." This was like pulling teeth. "So what reaction do you usually get when you tell people that?"

"It really depends."

Gawd. "So what for you is the hardest part of telling someone?"

"Their reaction."

"Mmm-hmm."

"Well, Mira, it was nice meeting you. I felt really comfortable around you, and I'm sorry this isn't going to work out." Jake shook my hand and turned to go. He shook hands like a girl. I looked into his eyes. He had eyes like a girl. I replayed our date. He talked about dieting like a girl. No. Way. I took a stab.

"Jake, what did your name used to be?"

"What? Oh. Jessica. But I always made people call me Jake, even when I was little. I knew I was male from day one, so the hormones and surgery just set things to rights."

Super. A post-operative transsexual, living in the Midwest, attracted to me. I felt worse for him than I had when I had to dump him. Geez. Then I started to feel deceived on a biological level, like a dog caught humping a raccoon. I didn't have a lot of hard and fast rules for a good date, but at least one of us had to have a factory-standard penis. This dating wasn't all it was cracked up to be. Score another point for the vibrator industry.

He started to look away. "Like I said, Mira, you're neat. Really neat. I just thought I'd take a gamble."

I watched him walk away, all six feet of him looking manly from behind, when it clicked for me. It clicked so loud that Jake even turned questioningly on his way out. I waved him on. I suddenly knew who killed Jeff, beyond a doubt. "Neat. Really neat." I said it under my breath, over and over again. "Just thought I'd take a gamble. Really neat. Like Jeff's body. Neat and clean, on the library floor."

Jake let himself out, and I saw my hands were trembling. Lartel's house had been really neat. Too neat. And the high-maintenance plants in his home, the kind that needed to be watered every other day, were thriving when I had snuck into his house. Really neat. Just thought I'd take a gamble. The irony was, Curtis Poling had practically handed me Jeff's murderer on a silver filleting knife a couple days ago, and I had been too blind to see it.

The phone rang rudely in the stillness of the library. I glanced over at the caller ID on the handset and saw it was a 612 area code. The Twin Cities. I didn't recognize the number, but it could be the travel agent. I calmed my hands as best I could, grabbing the phone a nano-second before the machine got it.

"Mira. Lartel. I'm at the airport."

My heart pounded in my ears like it used to when I was in track and waiting for the gun to start the hundred-yard dash. I recognized Lartel's clipped speech, but his voice seemed a lifetime away. "What?"

"I'm in Minneapolis. I got called back early. I'll be at the library tomorrow. You should meet me there at nine o'clock to catch me up."

"Tomorrow? That's Sunday?"

"Nine a.m." Click.

I stared at the window in the phone and watched the call length counter continue to reckon the seconds. I pushed the end button to turn it off and sat down in my captain's chair. I looked at the dappling of the sun outside the library window. Lartel was somewhere in the 612 area code, which meant he would be in Battle Lake in under three hours.

I looked at the wall clock. 12:37. I had until 3:00 for sure to get to Lartel's house and find the proof. I turned off all the lights, changed the message on the answering machine in case someone called to see why the library wasn't open on a Saturday afternoon, shut down the computer, grabbed my coat, and was out the door by 12:42.

TWENTY-TWO

I NEVER INTENDED TO cross the threshold of Lartel's house again. That first visit had been enough for me. But I knew from the caller ID that Lartel wasn't in the county, so I was out of harm's way for at least two more hours. When I drove up to his tidy farmhouse, I felt ill. My body and mind reminded me of the drive to the hospital to hear the official story on my dad. He had only been dead for a couple hours, and the meeting was a comedy of gruesome errors as the police officers and doctors tried to figure out if his body was identifiable. They decided it wasn't. It was scorched beyond recognition. They sent my stoic mom and my quiet self away to plan the funeral. The last time I would ever be with my dad's whole body had been the morning before, when I said I wished my mom would divorce him so I wouldn't have to see him and his drunk face ever again. That whole life of mine was surreal and timeless, and I watched it from well outside my body.

That familiar detachment was with me as the Toyota and I crunched into Lartel's driveway. It didn't look like anyone was around, but fear still punctured my skin like spears of ice, infecting my heart and filling my veins, bringing me back into my body and the moment. I couldn't turn back now, though. I hadn't found what I was looking for in Lartel's office, so the answers to my questions were in that house.

Adrenaline forced my legs out of my car and to the front door of Lartel's house. Everything appeared as I had left it two nights before, except now it was all washed in garish daylight. I retrieved the key from under the faux rock. Like a sleepwalker, I inserted it in the lock and pressed the door open.

"Hello?"

Reverberations of silence answered me. I forced myself inside and eased the door closed. The whispered warnings of the house started up immediately. "Do you really want to do this twice?" it asked me.

"You know, I really don't," I answered. I knew what creepiness lay here. I was actually turning to leave when I saw a manila file folder with a black tab on the kitchen table. That hadn't been there two nights ago. I tiptoed over and touched the smooth and cool paper. My curiosity got the better of me. I let the bright light of daytime soothe me.

At first glance, it was obvious the thick file contained a lot of bank matters. I studied the papers, feeling like a recovering alcoholic at a bar—a bar that gives you a free drink in exchange for your sobriety chips. I couldn't stop reading. It took me a couple pages before I realized I was looking at the deed to the Jorgensen land. It seemed innocuous and wasn't what I had come for. The next document was pay dirt: Ella Jorgensen's will. Curtis told me it had the answers, and I'm sure he had told Jeff the same thing.

The will named First National Bank executor of the Jorgensen estate, with Karl Syverson as acting representative. If there was an outstanding mortgage at the time of Mrs. Jorgensen's death, the bank was to pay it off in installments with proceeds from her CDs. When the CDs reached their minimum investment period, the bank was to cash them in, pay off any remaining mortgage, and hand the rest over to the Department of Natural Resources. The DNR would use the money and land to construct a wildlife refuge. My head swelled like a sponge in a bathtub.

I flipped open the last item in the folder, Mrs. Jorgensen's investment portfolio. Fortunately, it was hick-friendly and I could make enough sense of it to see that Mrs. Jorgensen's investments had been gradually withdrawn at stiff penalties over the seven years since she had died. There were no more CDs. That would explain why both Karl and Jeff had said the property was in arrears. That left no income with which to pay the mortgage, which clarified why the property was now up for sale even though Mrs. Jorgensen had made crystal clear in the will that she wanted the land donated, not sold.

My mind flashed me a picture of the casino letter I had found among Lartel's things at the library. Karl owed the Shooting Star Casino $59,000 in gambling debts, and I had assumed that Lartel was blackmailing Karl with this knowledge. I had been wrong. Karl had robbed the estate to pay his gambling debt. When there was no more money left, he put the land up for sale. Jeff must have demanded the will, so Karl had killed Jeff rather than ruin the life he had meticulously built in Battle Lake.

"I was going to make a clean start," he said softly, his voice high, almost womanlike. "I was going to sell the land and pay off my debt. Then I would be done with it. I could start over."

My intestines constricted, and my face stuck in mid-blink. I couldn't turn around. Although I had had enough clues relating to the Jorgensen estate to point to Karl as the killer, I had been too caught up in our friendship to even consider him in that light. He was kind and welcoming to me when I first came to town and had always been a good listener and lunch buddy.

His kind front had blinded me, until my conversation with Professor Jake had triggered a convergence of clues. Jeff's body had been spotless, its clothes changed, with a book placed precisely over his eyes. Karl, the neat freak of Battle Lake, couldn't make a mess even when he was murdering.

"Karl?"

"Mira?" he mocked, chuckling softly.

I could feel my fight-or-flight mechanism kick in, and adrenaline bum-rushed my brain. Why didn't it go to my arms, like it did for Popeye? "Who else knows that the land is supposed to be donated to the state instead of sold?" I asked in a thin voice.

His left hand slid onto my left shoulder, making me jump. Karl massaged me softly, delicately. "No one. At least not anymore. There was a time that Rob Winston, Mrs. Jorgensen's lawyer, knew, but he died almost five years ago, well before the CDs could be withdrawn without penalty. Mrs. Jorgensen didn't want it to be a big deal." His voice deepened. His right hand connected with my right shoulder, and the massage intensified.

"She said she wanted the curse of the land to rest. Batty old lady. And she wanted to pay back the town's debt to the Indians. But she didn't want to stir up trouble, so she asked Winston and me to keep it quiet. No problem, I said.

"Winston said the same thing, but he was a lawyer, so he was a weasel. By the time the information chain he started got back to me, it was pure rumor. People said that the land was haunted and that that was why Mrs. Jorgensen never wanted it sold. I thought that all the truth to the rumor had died, but somehow Jeff got wind that the land was supposed to go to the state."

I thought of Ruby calling Curtis Poling "the town's memory."

"I just took a little off the top at first," he continued. "I paid the mortgage, and whatever was left over I considered my pay as executor.

But then, you know." He pulled my shoulders up, forcing me to shrug for him. "The gambling got the better of me."

"So you killed Jeff? Because he knew the land was supposed to go to the DNR and he wasn't going to let you sell it for your own profit?"

He abruptly took his hands off my shoulders and strode to the other side of the table. The curtain-covered sunlight shadowed his face like a mask, but his body was plain to see. He was wearing his loafers, and I could see pant legs sticking out, but above that he was clad in an ankle-length gingham dress, his nails painted pink, his receding hair covered by a platinum-blonde wig. His eyes glowed in the shadows like a wolf's. When he stepped forward, his pink-tinted lips were pulled back in a fierce, pained smile.

"What are you staring at, Mira?" His voice switched to a falsetto southern accent. "Don't ah look pretty? Gotta be ready for Lartel to get home. Y'all do know how he likes his house clean and his food cookin.'"

Hiccups of panic were pushing up from my diaphragm. "Who are you?" I whispered.

Karl giggled, but his voice returned to normal. "We're not talking about me. We're talking about your boyfriend. He had a hunch about the land. A pretty good hunch. That guy always had good instincts." Karl's eyes were on fire, threatening to burn this horror house down around us. "Even back in high school, he always knew what to do—when to throw the ball, when to run. Back then, I looked up to two people: Jeff Wilson and Lartel McManus.

"But that was a long time ago. I'm successful now. It was actually me who contacted Trillings about the Jorgensen land months ago. Jeff was going to see what kind of person I had become. Then he called me at home on Sunday afternoon and asked how much was left on the mortgage, and I told him. He said he was thinking of some big PR stunt, some ludicrous idea for Trillings to donate money to pay off the mortgage so it could be handed over to a land conservation group. He knew Mrs. Jorgensen never wanted it sold, but he didn't know about the investments or why the mortgage hadn't been paid. Yet. Said he needed to see the will to make all this work.

"I told him I was interested in learning more but that I was house-sitting for Lartel so he would have to meet me out here."

Housesitting. Karl was the one who had been watering Lartel's plants while he was on vacation, and apparently he was also a surrogate Kennie in Lartel's twisted world. The real Kennie had warned me about the connection between those two, and damned if that woman hadn't been dead on. I felt myself going numb, probably from my heart overexerting itself. My own fear was poisoning me. Soon, I would collapse to the floor and be unable to run. Would Karl clean my body up before he planted it somewhere? Would he dress me in my own clothes or borrow some of his play clothes?

Karl rubbed his nose absently, then pulled out waterless disinfectant and squirted a dime-sized drop into his palm. The alcohol smell hit me like a slap. "Jeff wouldn't have given up, Mira. He didn't when he was in high school, and he hadn't changed."

My hands were sweating viciously, and I tried to buy myself some time while I fought for control of my body. "I won't tell anyone, Karl."

Karl laughed again, but not the kind of laugh you'd want to join in on. "No, you won't, Mira James. You're absolutely correct right there." He rubbed the disinfectant into his hands vigorously and popped the plastic bottle into a pocket of his dress.

Then, he tensed up like an electric bolt had zapped him. "You know, it was Kennie who messed it all up again, just like the old days." Karl spit her name out as if it burned his tongue. "She told Jeff about the Skinvold land. He met with her on Saturday night to talk about the acreage. Sunday he met with Herbert, and then he came to me to tell me about that PR coup bullhockey for Trillings."

I was not pleased by the distracting surge in my emotions. Jeff had met Kennie on Saturday night, not some mysterious lover, and he had only gotten together with her to look at some land. He hadn't slept with anyone else. I struggled to get back on track. "But since Jeff didn't know about all the debt, couldn't you just make something up?"

Karl's eyes became distant and unfocused. "Lartel warned me about women like you, Mira. He always talked about how manipulative you can be, women like you. Nosy, unclean, disorganized. Best avoided. I knew when I saw you snooping through his house on Thursday night that you were a sneaky one. I was a couple steps behind you that whole night, you know. You thought you were so clever, tromping through here like a bull. When you landed on your back in the living room, I almost took advantage.

"But I didn't. I thought that doll and the fish I left later at the library would have discouraged you, but females like you don't discourage easily. Lartel would have caught on to that right away." Karl tilted his head back like he was trying to catch a voice in the next room, and he switched his own tone up a notch, back to his falsetto. "Yes, Mr. McManus, you're always right. Always."

Salty bile ate away at the back of my tongue. Clearly, Karl had spent a lot of time with Lartel, and it wasn't happy healthy time. I didn't want to know what sticky string connected those two. I needed out. Karl's calm insanity had kept me frozen like a rabbit in a wolf's stare, but my most feral instinct, the urge not to let others control me, was cracking the spell.

Karl picked up where he had left off, too caught up in his own confession to notice my change in posture. "Jeff would have figured it all out soon. All it ever would have taken to blow my whole plan was someone asking to see Mrs. Jorgensen's will. And nobody ever would have if Jeff had just done what I brought him to town to do and not gotten so curious. All he had to do was survey the land for Trillings, sign the papers, and maybe entertain our mayor a little, bring her back East with him so Lartel had more energy to focus here at home. But that was too much to ask of Jeff, to do things right. He was always one to ruin everything." Back to the falsetto. "Y'all were right about that, too, Mr. McManus. Yes, you were."

His eyes refocused on me. "I could have sold the land free and clear. I could have been free." He blinked. "So, you will keep my secret, Mira?"

His hand reached under the table, and I smelled acrid smoke in the back of my brain. My escape appeared for the briefest moment. Before thought could act, I jumped at him, my fingers gouging at soft skin and wet surfaces. I might have growled as I dug at his face, deeper and deeper, down to the black dirt below. There would be no more weak men hiding behind addictions and anger in my life. Something popped under my fingers and yanked me out of my bloodlust. I couldn't make sense of what I was seeing, so I spilled through the front door and tried to slip into the shadows between dimness and solid things. My echoing heartbeat chased me and kept me fast.

I had prepared for this run ever since my dad had died. Sometimes, it had been monsters in the night, and I had to save my mom before I could flee. As I got older, it was burglars or crazy boyfriends or escaped prisoners, and I had to save my cat as well as myself. When the nightmares were at their worst, before I went to sleep I mentally mapped out the route from my bed to the nearest safe spot, always disregarding the car that likely had been disabled by my pursuer, the yard lights of neighbors who might be his accomplices, roads that would leave me too exposed, and loud noises that would point at me.

It felt exhilarating to really run, like touching something so hot that at first you think it's cold. I was a purely physical animal doing the one thing I knew how to do. I didn't know this area well, but I knew how to run in the woods, and I was certain that if I kept running, I would end up in one of the many resort communities that lined the forests and lakes here.

Paths appeared in front of me whichever way I turned, small openings in the brush that would be missed by preoccupied, human eyes. I could smell the pine needles crush under my feet and hear the soft whump of my soles on the forest soil. There were occasional explosions of noise and rushes of air around my head, but to this day I don't know if Karl shot at me, or even if he chased me.

It didn't take me long to reach Madsen's Resort, where I was welcomed like the crazy lady I appeared to be. When I explained what was happening, the police were called immediately. That's how I had always expected it would be, of course, except that in my head I always imagined making all the people I encountered run with me, because once you've felt absolute terror, no place is safe to stand still.

TWENTY-THREE

THE STATE, NOT LOCAL, police arrested Karl in a cabin down the road from Lartel's house. I had gashed his face pretty well but not done any lasting damage. Apparently, after I had broken out the door like a crazed animal, Karl had taken his bloody face to the cleaning supplies and arranged and sanitized everything in Lartel's space. When that was done, he moved on to the cabin down the road, broke in, and was busy alphabetizing the contents of their cupboards, first by type of food and then brand name. Fortunately, they were summer people and not yet around in the middle of May.

Karl didn't confess to the crime directly, but he never moved the file of evidence that told the story. The police found Jeff's bloody clothes buried out back of Lartel's house, covered in synthetic hairs from a platinum-blonde wig. They released the homeless man, who was never officially charged with any crime. As for Lartel, he really had been in Mexico the whole time and was coming back early because Karl had called and told him there was an emergency, specifically that his cousin had been found dead in his library.

I prefer to think Karl had wanted to get caught, even though the police never did find the gun he had shot Jeff with, either around the house or in the woods. Regardless, he clearly was deeply disturbed. The police surmised he had kept Jeff's body in Lartel's root cellar for over twenty-four hours before deciding what to do with it. He sanitized it and transported it to the library Monday evening, using a key Lartel had given him long ago. It chilled me to realize Karl had probably come from dumping the body at the library when I bumped into him outside the Turtle Stew, freshly stood up by a corpse.

The word around town was that Karl was pleading insanity as well as spilling some of the town's dirtier secrets, including the facts that his wife had left him more than a year ago and that Lartel McManus had been stalking Kennie for over five years. As a direct result, I think, Lartel packed up shop and disappeared before anyone even noticed he was back from Mexico. His clean, creepy little house is for sale, and I'm the interim head librarian. A promotion is a promotion.

I also got my article published as widely as the *Star Tribune* in Minneapolis. They edited a lot out that appeared in the *Recall*, but I suppose we were catering to a different audience in Battle Lake. Writing and publishing the article was good experience, and I was happy to make Jeff look like the hero it turned out he was. I celebrated my first statewide publication by dumping out the half-empty bottle of vodka I had bought at Bonnie & Clyde's.

The doublewide was now officially liquor free again, and when Sunny called to tell me Alaska and Rodney were still wonderful and to ask me how I was doing, I could truthfully answer, "Just fine." And it was time to go out and see how the world was treating me.

The Turtle Stew has tater-tot hotdish on the lunch menu, and that's about as good as it gets. A side of green beans and whole chocolate milk, a quality pen and a virgin crossword puzzle, and I'd be that much closer to mental health.

The bell jingled as I entered, and conversation stopped momentarily. I passed around the bland, "how ya doin'?" smile I had been practicing, meant to reassure and soothe while keeping others at a distance. I sat down in the only open booth by the window, the electric red naugahyde cover feeling alive next to my naked calves. I had decided to wear a skirt this morning, another part of my master plan to blend for a while. I had ruffled enough feathers and was feeling moderately spanked.

"Hello," the waitress said, sliding a menu over to me.

"Hi," I said, sliding it back. "I know what I want."

"Tater-tot hotdish, green beans, and chocolate milk?" She smiled openly at me.

I smiled back, this time a genuine grin showing my teeth. "Sounds perfect." As she walked away, I debated the merits of being considered a regular in Battle Lake. Before I could get my list past one ("save time ordering food"), Kennie slid into my booth across from me, a full-sized cardboard-backed poster in her hand.

"I know what y'all did, and I have to say I am so proud of you, honey chile. You saved the town."

I blinked loudly at her, willing her to be uncomfortable in the silence. Like most beauty contest types, she was immune to negative body language. It really is hard to shame the ignorant. She lowered her voice and leaned across the table, air escaping the negative space between her thighs and the naugahyde in pained squeaks.

"And I know you called Trillings and told them what Jeff planned to do with the land. That's right good of you." She nodded her chin firmly. "The DNR has started looking into making it a wildlife refuge." A playful smile highlighted by bubblegum pink lipstick and makeup-caked wrinkles tugged at the corners of her mouth.

"But y'all ain't the only humanitarian." She slowly turned the poster around. Mrs. Berns's full-body, swimsuit-clad picture beamed at me, her skin going one direction, her varicose veins another. "Elderly beauty contests! Countywide!" Kennie grinned.

In a distant way, I noticed how the whites of Kennie's eyes were as milky as her teeth, a startling contrast to her heavy blue eyeliner and dark red rouge circles. "That's gross, Kennie."

She laughed heartily, but it was a reflex instead of an acknowledgement. "Beauty doesn't stop at any age, and we need to prove that. We're gonna fight the good fight in Otter Tail County, you mark my words, honey chile. These old people just plain ol' need more extracurricular activities." Her fingers clacked the beginnings of "The William Tell Overture" on the plastic tabletop. Her wide smile wilted, and she pouted like a child. "Well, I can see y'all ain't gonna get excited. And here we were gonna ask you to be a honorary judge, bein' a town celebrity and all. Y'all change your mind, you let me know."

"Don't quit your day job, Kennie."

She laughed her belly laugh again and darted out to place the poster in the entryway. Gary Wohnt was leaning against his new police Jeep across the street, perfecting his Frank "Ponch" Poncherello look. He had on the requisite mirrored sunglasses, glossy hair, and jaunty toothpick. It appeared as though he was even cultivating some facial hair, and for a grotesque second, I pictured him offering free mustache rides at the next class of '82 party.

I watched Kennie strut out the door and toward the Chief. His gleaming lips cracked a smile, and he opened the passenger door for her. Apparently she had a chauffeur for her poster-hanging run. I mentally made it a mission to not find out anything more about those two.

I sighed, thinking that geriatric beauty contests were probably a healthy improvement over geriatric orgies. One small step for Kennie Rogers, one huge step for humankind. The waitress plunked my food in front of me. One of the many beauties of tater-tot hotdish is that it's quick; at the time you order it, it's already cooked and just needs to be heated. I peppered the pile and dug in.

I reached into my back pocket to pull out the note from Jeff I had found yesterday in my bottom dresser drawer. He must have written it after our last night together, intending for me to find it while he went to the Cities.

Mira,

You're one of a kind. I am looking forward to spending a lot of time getting to know you better. Beware closed minds and open mouths while I'm gone, blood brother. This town can trap you!
Jeff

My eyes got a little hot reading it, even though this was the fourteenth or fifteenth time. He had been a note writer, and I hadn't even known it until he was dead. I loved note writers. I wondered what he meant about this town trapping me. I would have to spend some time with that one.

But first, I needed to do two things. I had to haul Sunny's draconic garden tiller over to the Senior Sunset and get their garden ready for planting. It probably wouldn't hurt to pick up some seedlings for them on the way. Next, and most importantly, I needed to go out to the Jorgensen land and say a farewell prayer for two men, Jeff and my dad, who were going to miss out on a lot of good things in life. I knew just what flower I was going to leave as a memorial—a bloodroot. I only hoped Jeff and I hadn't plucked the last one.

ACKNOWLEDGMENTS

Big love and thanks to Holly Hassel, who is a fantastic teacher, editor, friend, and wordsmith. Her encouragement and faith kept me on track and have earned her a place in a future Battle Lake mystery. Mom, I literally couldn't have done it without you; my kids and I are forever grateful for the time you take out of your life to make our lives better. Thank you also to Mom, Suzanna, and Rondi, whose feedback to early drafts was energizing. Andrea, Christine, Kellie, and Jenny, your confidence in me is worth a lot. Grandma, I'm sad you aren't here to thank in person, but I'm doing it on paper and in my heart—you would have been first in line for this book (I know because you told me so), and I miss you.

Many thanks to my agent, Kristin Lindstrom, for choosing not to be the 294th person to reject me. Thank you also to Barbara Moore, first for thinking it would be a good idea for Llewellyn to branch out into mysteries, and second for deciding I was worth a shot. Lisa, Alison, Wade, Brian, and Jennifer, thank you for your hard work on *May Day*, and Jed, thanks for being a great web designer. Laine Cunningham and Jessica Morrell, thank you for your help.

Finally, thank you to my kids. They make it really hard to write, and frankly, they can be a lot of work, but what's the point without them? Zoë and Xander, you're fabulous and perfect.

Read on for an excerpt from the
next Murder-by-Month Mystery by Jess Lourey

June Bug

ONE

In my dream, I walked days and nights through the woods to get to the clear stream. There was a tower at the edge of the water built to look like a silo, and I knew I was home. The creek gurgled, the moon shone, and the frog sounds of night sang to me. I laid down to rest and was swept with serenity. There was warm breath on the back of my neck and a comforting hand on my shoulder. I felt protected, covered in the safety of night and cozy warmth. But when the hand crept purposefully lower, and I smelled digesting Schlitz on the tepid breath, I knew I wasn't in paradise anymore. My body lurched awake, and I was standing before I even remembered I had been lying down. The vertigo caught up with me, and I clutched at a bedpost as I blinked rapidly.

"What!" I yelled.

"Sunny?" slurred the voice in my bed.

I shook my head, and some REM-spun cobwebs fell out. I wasn't in my apartment in Minneapolis, where I had lived for nearly ten years—a little loft on the West Bank where I shared a bathroom with a sexy, blue-eyed horn player in his sixties and a compulsively clean law student. I had moved out of there in March, leaving my career as a waitress and grad student in the University of Minnesota English program, and had been housesitting for my friend Sunny ever since. I was in her little doublewide on the outskirts of Battle Lake, Minnesota, and there was a strange man in her bed. My bed.

I flicked on the cat-shaped lamp and angled the lit ears toward the intruder still laying in my bed on top of the handmade Amish quilt I had lucked on in the Fergus Falls Salvation Army. I yanked it from under him and covered up my nakedness. I was usually comfortable with my five-foot-six, 140-pound frame, but I wasn't a flasher. I pulled my disheveled hair away from my face and stared down my pointy nose at the relaxed drunk.

"Sunny isn't here." I was hoping to come up with a magic verbal vanishing potion, but my heart was still pummeling my ribcage, and my voice shook. "Who are you?"

"Mira?"

I squinted. Happy Hands knew me, and his voice scratched an itch in the back of my memory. "Jason?"

"Yeah. You're not Sunny." He sounded bored.

Yup, it was Jason. I had met him through my moody friend C.C. ten years earlier, when my hair had been dyed black, I smoked clove cigarettes, and dark, flowing clothes were my signature. Thank God for evolution.

Back then, C.C. and I were both awed freshman trying to act like we weren't scared by the vastness of the U of M and its forty-thousand-plus students. We had ended up as dorm mates through the luck of the draw, two small-town girls, and hit it off from the word go. She had brought me to her hometown of Battle Lake on Thanksgiving break of our first year. A couple months later, I introduced her to the guy who gave her genital warts, so I suppose looking back we're even.

During that first introduction to Battle Lake, I met Sunny, one of C.C.'s close friends. I also met Jason, a high school classmate of theirs. I knew him from the parties C.C. and I would road-trip to during college breaks, but he and I never really connected. He was the guy always trying to get in everyone's pants, the one who tried to marry anyone not dumb enough to sleep with him.

He was tall, over six feet, with dark hair and dark eyes, cute in a way that would be hot if he were an actor but was just average since he was a perpetually horny fiber-optic cable layer. In small-town tradition, Sunny and Jason had slept together in high school, as had most of their friends. Musical beds. I suppose the process evolved out of long winters and bad TV reception.

I hadn't seen Jason in over five years. Word was he had to move to Texas to find a woman to marry him since every woman in Minnesota had turned him down. Apparently he hadn't gotten the news that Sunny had moved to Alaska for the summer, and he was making his area horn call.

"What're you doing back in Battle Lake?" I asked. I felt lightheaded and ill. It occurred to me that Otter Tail County had some sort of magnetic pull on people who entered. That's the only way to explain why I was still here, running the library and writing for the local newspaper, after the last month I had lived through. I had just started falling for a guy when I found him shot through the head in the library a week later.

When I had first met Jeff, I was impressed with his maturity and character. After he was shot and left for me to find, the lesson that how I feel about someone doesn't affect whether they get to live or die was reinforced. I thought I had learned that one well enough when my dad died in a car accident the summer of my junior year in high school, but in my experience, life keeps bringing you back to the same table until you pick the right food. Anyhow, the whole Jeff ordeal taught me the mental benefits of tying up loose ends. I also turned twenty-nine last month, but that got lost in the shuffle.

Jason sat up and rubbed a red scrape on his shoulder, his back to me. He had put on about forty pounds since I last saw him, and I couldn't help but notice that he had stripped down to his faded black boxers. Confident guy. "I'm in town to visit the 'rents. Got anything to eat?"

My mouth opened in a yell, but he was up and in the kitchen before I could answer. If he wasn't getting laid, he was getting fed. I squelched the urge to hand him a mirror. I had seen a show on monkeys on the Nature Channel and was pretty sure the shiny glass would keep him busy for hours. No, better to get rid of him. I hissed at the part of me that was thinking like a schoolgirl, worried that he would get mad at me if I was rude to him when I knew I should be kicking the trespassing bastard out on his ass. Media conditioning is a bitch.

I threw on some shorts and a T-shirt and followed him to the kitchen, mulling the best way to get him to leave without a fight.

"So, I bet your parents are happy to see you."

"Haven't been there yet." He flicked on the kitchen light, grabbed a pot from the particleboard cupboards, and stuck his hand in the food cabinet all in one smooth move. "You're gonna need more Potato Buds."

I sucked in a deep mouth of air in a trapped sort of way and sat on the island in the kitchen, prepping myself for a confrontation. I knew from experience that it would be easier to get rid of him full than kick him out hungry, so I promised myself I would make him go as soon as he was done eating. This was my house, and I wasn't going to let him intimidate me in it. At least not for longer than half an hour.

Now that I was over the fear of an intruder in my bed, I could no longer ignore a buried-alive memory that was squirming itself out of my distant subconscious. I didn't want to be overwhelmed by the remembering, but I couldn't sit on it any longer, not now that we were in the light and I was watching him make himself comfortable in my kitchen. The summer before C.C. and I would graduate from college, Jason hit on me at a bonfire party. I was flattered by the male attention but not drunk enough to latch on to the token male slut so early in the evening. When I walked into the woods to pee, he followed me quietly. He waited until my pants were down to push me back on the ground and cover my mouth with his fist. His hand smelled musty, like composting leaves.

I heard Sunny call my name at the same moment the zip of Jason's pants cut through his fumbled grunting. He jumped off me when Sunny appeared and then staggered back to the party. She was weaving and giggling like we were playing hide-and-go-seek and didn't stop him when he shoved past her. Though she helped to clean me off, she didn't have much sympathy for my situation. She wanted to keep the good times rolling and said he was just drunk and had misinterpreted my interest. She seemed mildly offended that I would even consider that a good friend of hers could be a potential rapist. I started to wonder if maybe I had overreacted.

I saw Sunny laughing with Jason later that night as I sat on the fringes of the party and tried to act normal, chain-smoking so I'd have an excuse to keep my hand in front of my swollen mouth. I still don't know what was more of a betrayal—Sunny's lack of support for me or Jason's aggression.

In the small-town tradition of German descendants, however, we never talked about that bad night again. Life went on, and when I saw Jason, he was distant and vaguely mean. Everyone else treated him like a loveable goofball, though I did notice that some people made a point to steer clear of him. Myself, I got to the place where I wondered whether I had imagined the whole thing, or maybe he had been too drunk to remember any of his attack on me.

Despite the passage of time and my own self-doubt, it was still impossible for me to get comfortable with him in my house, but I didn't want to work myself into a panic attack, either. There were plenty of people who liked Jason, and he did have a good sense of humor. I stopped just sort of making excuses for his past behavior, turned my back to him, and tried to relax.

The June night was unusually warm, following the precedent set by May, and soaked in the smell of fresh-cut grass and black dirt. If I listened below the boiling of water and clattering of pans, I could hear mosquitoes whining. Whiskey Lake's waves lapped against the rim of its sheltered arm six hundred yards from my front door, and the oaks and elms stood still as stone, their fresh leaves hanging straight and a little too green from the exhilaration of spring. I cocked my head. If there was no wind, there should be no waves. I stood up and walked to the open door and peered through the screen. Sure enough, I caught the low hum of a motorboat on the far side of this sheltered offshoot of the lake. I looked at the clock hung by the door. It was 2:34 a.m.

"What's a boat doing out at this time of night, and with no lights on?" I whispered, my fingertips on the cool screen.

I jumped as Jason answered from directly behind my left shoulder. "Probably looking for the diamond. This lake'll be crawling by tomorrow."

TWO

When Sunny's parents disappeared nearly twenty years before, all of their property had automatically gone to their only child. It came to a little over one hundred acres of the prettiest land in Minnesota, with a sky-blue farmhouse planted in the center of it. The house had burnt down a year ago and been replaced by a doublewide, but that only marginally affected the charm of the place. There were still rolling hills, wild prairie freckled with thick hardwood groves, and tillable farmland. And the jewel was the lakeshore. Sunny owned the whole side of Whiskey Lake from the public access boat landing to the little private beach a mile from it.

The only break in her empire was the jutting arm of land known as Shangri-La Island. Technically, it was a mini-peninsula and not an island, as it wasn't completely surrounded by water. It shared the driveway that went into and past Sunny's farm and twisted down onto the island. A good stretch of this isthmus of a driveway was waterlocked, Sunny's pond on one side and Whiskey Lake on the other.

The dwellings on Shangri-La—a beautiful main lodge and four cabins for the help—were built in 1924 by Philadelphia millionaire Randolph Addams and his wife, Beatrice Carnegie, granddaughter of Andrew Carnegie. Addams had fallen in love with the area on a fishing trip and hired local workers to build the main structure out of fieldstone and cedar. Local legend had it that one summer a wealthy guest of the couple's had gone swimming wearing a diamond necklace—a gold chain with a diamond dewdrop as big as a gumball dangling from it. She came out of the water without the necklace, and the other guests and staff searched frantically. The jewel was never found.

According to Jason, that was about to change. A travel magazine had published a story on the diamond in an article rating the resort that now occupied Shangri-La Island. Surprisingly, a few people read the article, and one of those people was an editor at the *Star Tribune* in Minneapolis. She had family in the Battle Lake area and thought the missing diamond necklace would be an appealing human-interest story.

The front-page headline of the Friday, June 1, "Source" section read, "Hope for a Diamond in Minnesota's Gorgeous Lake Country." The paper was going to plant a fake diamond in a weighted box in the lake on Monday the fourth, and they were offering five thousand dollars and a paid week at Shangri-La to whoever found it. They apparently did not have complete faith in the legend of the real diamond or, if they did, had decided it was beyond recovery. But the article made good copy and was a boon for the tourist industry that drives Minnesota summers.

Unfortunately, the paper had not seen fit to warn either local papers or residents. Here I was, Mira James, star reporter (well at least reporter) for the *Battle Lake Recall* and living on the very shores of Whiskey Lake, and I had to get the scoop from a guy who liked ketchup and Easy Cheese on his rehydrated mashed potatoes. Technically, it was Sunday morning, which meant the contest started tomorrow.

"So how'd *you* hear about it?" I asked peevishly.

Jason took a chug off the can of Dr. Pepper he had found in the back of the fridge and burped. I noticed he hadn't really looked directly at me since I had shrieked at him bedside. I felt a suddenly overpowering and asinine need to be validated by this man. I took a moment to blame that on my father, who was often too drunk to give me attention, and then I remembered I was a grown woman and let that go. Still, although I wasn't a wet dream, I wasn't fish bait either. I ran my fingers through my shoulder-length brown hair, feeling for cockleburs or lice, and surreptitiously wiped the inside of my eyes. Then, in a brilliant reclamation of my self-respect and womanhood, I picked my nose and hung a small booger on the tip of it. I was going to gross him right out of this house.

He turned to put his shirt on. He had folded it in a pile with his pants and shiny dock shoes outside my bedroom door, next to a flashlight and a six-pack of cheap beer. "Word gets around."

"Even to Texas?"

I could see his shoulder blades tense. Although he hadn't minded talking about the diamond between shovelfuls of Potato Buds, when it came to discussing his life, he wasn't very forthcoming. I watched him rub the scratch on his back again, this time with more intensity. It looked an angry and infected red in the light, and I could see two lighter scratches running parallel to it. I wondered if he was getting cat scratch fever. The kind you get from getting scratched by a really big cat. "I left Texas a while ago. I was working up on the East Coast."

"Doing what?"

"Working." He pulled his shirt sharply over his head and covered the scratch. Suddenly, he couldn't get out fast enough.

"Mmm-hmm," I said. I blinked at him, doubtless much like a pit bull does when it senses it should probably let go of the person in its mouth but can't remember how to unlock its jaw. "What kind of work?"

He stopped in mid-tuck and turned toward the door. "Construction."

"House or road?"

"Jesus, Mira, back off!"

I felt my neck twitch in response to his tone of voice. He had more than blue balls on his mind. If I was reading this situation correctly, Sunny's house had been Jason's first stop. If he were really in town to see his parents, then he would have already been there at least once. Horny or not, he was still a born-and-bred small-town Lutheran boy, and he knew his mom would never stop the nagging if she heard he had come to this house first.

No, there would have had to be more to pull him over Sunny's way than the promise of tuna surprise and Potato Buds. The diamond was the obvious reason, but how had he found out about it? He didn't have a reputation as much of a reader, so it was unlikely he had heard about the missing jewel all the way over on the East Coast by perusing the travel magazine or an online version of the *Star Tribune* article. And since no one in the Battle Lake area knew about the diamond search, because if they had it would have gotten back to the *Recall* given the momentum theory of small-town words, it was even less likely that someone from here had contacted him. He was almost out the door, but I suddenly wanted him to stay and tell me how he had found out about the lost necklace contest and find out why he was so reluctant to tell me what he had been up to.

He brushed past me quickly, flashlight and beer in hand. His elbow connected with mine in a sharp crack, and I couldn't tell if it was intentional. At the door, he turned and glanced once into my eyes, his dark brown staring down my gray. And then the screen door slapped closed and I was left alone with a crusty potato-making pan, a counter full of open condiments, and a feeling that Jason and I would be seeing each other again really soon.

I wiped my nose and began cleaning up, not relaxing until I heard the roar of his car starting and could follow his headlights as they ran perpendicular with the house up the mile-long driveway. My hands were still shaky, and I felt displaced and edgy. I knew one thing that would calm me down for sure, but I didn't like to give in to the bad habit. I paced the kitchen Jason had brought his chaos into and listed all the reasons it would be a bad idea to rip into my old standby: although it made me feel good for the moment, coming down was always hard, empty calories at night go straight to the designated ass pockets, and I'd have to brush my teeth again. *Screw it.* I walked to the freezer and pulled out a red and green Nut Goodie package quickly, before I could talk some sense into myself.

Frozen Nut Goodies are the only way to go in the summer. The cool chocolate slides around on your tongue, and the maple center gets hard and chewy all at once, like iced-up honey. I peeled the wrapper from a corner and bit off the chocolate lip, letting the sweet darkness and nuts merge in my mouth. When I got to the light brown maple center, I had to leverage the bar in the back of my mouth between the molars to get a piece. I braced a chunk and sucked it slowly, letting the crystallized, nutty sugar dissolve into my veins. I felt a warmth around me as I settled into my Nut Goodie high, the world and all its creatures right for one perfect moment. I was even able to stop myself from eating all of it by turning my now-composed mind on the mess in my house.

It was 3:23 Sunday morning by the time I had the kitchen cleaned up, and I had a focused to-do list buzzing in my head. I needed to get an article in Monday's *Recall* ASAP so we didn't look like dorks, I needed to ask around about Jason to satisfy my curiosity, and I needed to get online and find out what I could about Whiskey Lake and the real diamond necklace. Oh, and I needed to rent some diving equipment while there was still some to be had.

After the kitchen was picked up, I forced myself to lie down and concentrated on the inside of my eyelids for two full hours. I considered it a major achievement that I only spent seventy-five percent of that time thinking that Jason Blunt was bringing nothing but bad luck with him and that maybe I wouldn't be lucky enough to get away this time.

ABOUT THE AUTHOR

Jess Lourey teaches English and sociology full time. When she isn't gardening, reading, or navigating the niceties of small-town life, she spends time with her kids, Zoë and Xander, and their black cat, named Zoso.